LOVE VERSES

By

HUNTER TALEN

ACKNOWLEDGEMENTS

This book is dedicated to my one and only son and my parents. Son, thank you for being resilient and patient with my busy schedule and long hours, between my working a full time and a part time job, and working on my book. Mom and Dad, thank you for your love and support throughout my journey in creating this piece. Your love story is inspirational, and a testament that true love still exists.

Special thanks to my best friend C. Crank for being a constant in my life for over two decades. You stuck by me through everything, even when you had tough issues of your own with which to deal. You are truly one of the strongest people I know. Your strength motivated me to push through hard times whenever I felt like throwing in the towel.

Another special thanks to M. Clark for not only teaching me, but living by example how to put God first in everything I do, and how to work within my God given talents to achieve the success and happiness He intends for me to have.

Thanks to B. Tillman for being enthusiastic every step of the way, for letting me bounce ideas off of you, and for inspiring me for the cover of the book.

Last, but not least thanks to my friends and my readers for your support. Being an author is my destiny, and this book is my first big step towards it. Your support is a big part of that. Thank you for taking this journey with me. I hope all of you will be there every step of the way. I encourage everyone to use your gifts and seek your calling. I believe only then can true fulfillment and happiness be found. When on the brink of your destiny, your perspective of your world changes for the better.

ABOUT THE AUTHOR

Hunter Talen was born in the concrete jungle of Baltimore, Maryland on August 22, 1977. From an early age she knew that she wanted to leave a positive mark on the world and was driven by big hopes and dreams. Somewhere along the way, she fell off course, and her life wasn't going as she had planned. Faced by the disappointments of her life, incomplete college studies, a failed marriage, and the added challenge of single motherhood, she had to find a way rediscover hope, revamp her dreams, and reinvent herself. What it would take to accomplish that wasn't always clear. The path to figure it out was filled with even more disappointments, mistakes, challenges and doldrums. One day while working at a dead end job, she had a conversation with a coworker who was realizing her dreams and on her way to unimaginable success with her baking business. She revealed that her secret was keeping her faith strong working in her natural gifts, and putting God first. This concept wasn't new to Hunter, but had long been overshadowed by her will. As the saying goes the light bulb went off, and she realized that she should have been seeking His will all along. With that she handed Him the wheel, and is now enjoying the ride excited to see where it will take her.

"Every great story, love or otherwise, has its own path, and none are without some level of pain, mistakes, trial and tribulation, whether it's storybook or real life. Without them, you'll never know if your love has resilience and substance. It's easy to love when things are good, but how will your love fair when things are not? There is no good without bad, just as there is no day without night. The test of true love or yourself is how you triumph over it all. Nothing worth having comes easy all of the time. It takes hard work, strength, passion, perseverance, forgiveness, patience, understanding, love and trust. But the reward is even grander than the sum of its parts. It will be better and stronger than ever, and last forever. If it is worth having, then do whatever it takes to fight for it."

--HUNTER TALEN--

TABLE OF CONTENTS

PROLOGUE

AIKO PIERRE

She is of a caramel complexion with tinges of butter cream in places where the sun's fingers cannot reach. Her skin is beautifully imperfect, tattooed with signs of her battle scars, and endearing clumsiness. She is plump, but shapely with breasts like ripened, peeled cantaloupe. French surname, but her round, high cheek bones suggest a Native American heritage. Her full face, long lashes, and puckered lips give way to a child-like innocence, while her deep, almond shaped eyes tell of another tale. They betray her facade of strength and an impenetrable fortress. They reveal the hurt and pain of her past. With each tear drop, they leak the vulnerability she tries to hide. She is surviving, but not living. A part of her is missing. She knew true love once over a decade ago. No man since then has been able to replace it. At this point, what else can she do? What little strength she has left from her battles to find true love again, she pours into her love child hoping it gives him an advantage to avoid the same mistakes she's made. In the meantime, she reinforces her fortress, moving forward, denying her hope of finding true love again, and succumbing to her new found disbelief.

It's Friday night. Another long, hard work week has come to an end. The summer Baltimore air is filled with signs that the weekend has begun. One whiff teases the senses with hints of pizza, cheese steaks, and Chinese food. For the ears, loud base filled music that rattle the windows of the cars blasting it as they drive by, and kids' playful laughter as they enjoy being outside past their normal bedtime. As usual, she has no plans, no suitors at her door to take her out for a good time. Her so called boyfriend Randall is a no call, no show again. Predictably, he'll have another lame ass excuse. Her cell phone is quiet, except for the buzz of the occasional email or Facebook alert, most likely one of her friends bragging about an engagement, an 'in a relationship' status, pregnancy, or how they have the most wonderful husband in the world, all of which made her eyes roll until they hurt. Whenever it buzzes her heart jumps as if she expects by some miracle a man would call. She laughs at her wishful thinking, dims the lights in the living room, pours another cranberry and vodka, lights a joint, and presses play and repeat on the stereo. John Legend's "So High" fills the room. From the first piano note, her heart swells and aches. To her, this song puts into words her fantasies about how being in love should feel. She closes her eyes and soars to the top on a cloud with the rhythm, letting the lyrics touch her soul. The alcohol begins to warm her veins. With each drag of the joint, she hopes to achieve a meditative, near out of body experience to escape her dismal reality. She attempts to suck back the emotions overwhelming her without success. Her throat is sore from choking back tears, but the tears break free, dragging pain and mascara down her cheeks. What went wrong in her life still remains a mystery because she did the best she could with the hand she was dealt until she was forced to fold. Clearly, her best wasn't good enough. She's always imagined that at this point in her life, she would be happily married with at least two kids, and a bright future ahead. Instead, she's divorced, paying bills and raising a son on her own, with no sight of a happy future because she can't see past the smoke in her eyes. For the most part, her life as it is now is good. Most people would be satisfied with it, but not her. She has a great family, a wonderful child, and she travels the world. Sure, she also has a successful career, but she doesn't want money in her California king bed, she wants a man. All the money, success, and material possessions in the world cannot fill the void of a lonely heart. Nights like these with idle time on her hands reminds her of what's missing. It doesn't make sense. She was raised with two loving parents who set the example of a strong, lasting marriage. That gave her hope that she could have the same. She admires them for beating the odds, and wants so much to share the love and commitment with someone that they share with each other. It always seems beyond her reach. She wipes the tears from her cheeks, puts out the roach, and lights a Newport. The rumble of an approaching thunderstorm growls from a distance, while the CD player gears up to repeat the song for a third time. She leans back into the couch limply, sinking into the plush cushions and taking a long, exaggerated drag of the cigarette, and exhaling the same. She begins to think about her first crush, Andrew Lantry.

CHAPTER 1—Track 1—Back in the Day

She remembers the year was 1987 when they first met. She was the tender age of nine. She and her brother Dante were playing catch in the backyard of their new house. She accidentally overthrew the ball over the fence into the yard facing theirs. A blue-eyed freckled face brunette white boy came from behind the fig tree that hung over the fence from his yard into theirs. He handed the ball over to her. She apologized. He smiled with slightly yellow teeth, still cute, and said "That's okay. Hi, my name is Andrew." She replied, "Hello, I'm Aiko, but you can call me Koko. That's K.o.k.o. no dash. This is my little brother Dante." He introduced his little brother David, who was a blue eyed blonde with less of a baby face, but still adorable. He was two years younger than Dante. They all decided to play doubles tossing the ball over the fence. Whoever dropped the ball first loss that round, unless the ball hit the big tree in her yard, then they got a do over. The light, breezy, sunny spring day was filled with laughter and shrieks of joy from little black kids and little white kids playing harmoniously, until a deep, loud and scratchy voice from the distance yelled, "Go back where you came from niggers!" The ball seemed to drop from her hands in slow motion and hit the ground with an echo. She looked over to Dante and the tears started to well in his eyes. She felt tears of her own coming to the edge, but it was more important to her to stay strong and shelter her brother. He was too young to fully understand what just happened, but he knew it was wrong. She was already aware that they were the first black family on that entire street, but she never expected this, especially since they were just children. She held Dante to her chest while he cried. Andrew jumped over the fence and wrapped his arms around the both of them, while David stood in his yard, both hands gripping the top of the fence, mouth wide open, and looking around as if he were trying to figure out where the insult had come from. Andrew couldn't find the right words to say, so he remained silent. Aiko could feel his compassion in his gesture. That wasn't the last time they were victims of bigotry. A few weeks later someone wrote 'Nigger' on the side of their house by the water hose in pencil. The culprit obviously was too much of a coward to vandalize properly. Spray paint would've shown some commitment to the crime. It made no permanent damage to the house, but it caused irreparable damage to their youth. Their innocent views of the world were shattered, and they were forced to face the ugly realities of it. They learned to be on guard. In some respects, it fine tuned their intuitions at an early age, which would prove to be useful later in life.

After a while the incidents ceased. They became even closer to their new neighborhood friends, including Jim, Helga, and Sarah to whom Andrew had introduced them. For the cherry on top, their favorite cousin Tony moved in with them. He was three years older than Aiko, and he was like a big brother to her. That summer was a blast. The whole gang hung out every day playing dodge ball, freeze tag, backyard baseball and football, Simon says, ring toss, badminton, bike riding, and collecting lightning bugs and caterpillars in glass jars. They went everywhere together from the local park, 7 Eleven, the library, and the corner store, which was their favorite. After long day of play they hung out on one of their porches eating Boston baked beans, Lemonheads, Pop rocks, popsicles, fudge pops, orange sickles, gummy bears, now and laters, sunflower seeds, chips, onion pickles, and duplex cookies. The ice cream truck never got their business because the corner store had all of the goodies they loved for less than one dollar.

One day it was Andy and David's turn for the streetlight porch hang out, and their parents surfaced for the first time. Aiko made some quick observations about them. Their Pekingese dog Honey came out of the door first. Aiko loved dogs, but her parents wouldn't let her have one yet, so she adopted Honey as her own. Honey made her rounds getting adored by all of them while the mom stepped out next. She was a short brunette with blue eyes, and a female version of Andy, though he took the more attractive genes. After her was the grandmother, who also lived there. She was slightly taller than the mom, and looked like an old, silver haired, hunched back crone with a big nose with oversized, oily pores, and a mole on it. She was the witch in every child's nightmares, but she wasn't the worst. Out comes the dad. He was over six feet tall and three hundred pounds with salt-and-pepper hair and beady, ice blue eyes that chilled and pierced Aiko's soul. She could tell right away that he was prejudiced. In her mind he was definitely a Klan member with a laminated membership card in his wallet, a Confederate flag keychain, and a stark white, dry cleaned Klan suit hanging in his closet. Worst of all, his attempts to hide it were fake and poor at best. His only saving grace was his fatherly love for his sons. They had nigger friends that they loved, so he tolerated it for them. After that, there was a quick introduction of the three ink spots on the porch to the parents then everyone was sent home for the night.

The months that followed were full of fun. The seasons changed and school was in session, but the gang remained close. Some of the activities had to be adjusted due to weather and school schedules, but they found ways to keep the fun going. They had super Nintendo Mario tournaments over a Aiko's house, and Sega Genesis Sonic the Hedgehog marathons over Andy's house. Both Aiko and Andy's families were strong Christians. They took turns visiting each other's churches. He introduced them to white Christian artists such as Amy Grant. "Father's Eyes" was her favorite of Amy's songs. She introduced Andy to black Christian artists like Take Six, Commissioned, and the Winans, BeBe and CeCe Winans included. Andy and David would come over for prayer and Bible study every Wednesday at seven PM. Aiko, Andy, Dante, David and Tony even formed a Christian band. Aiko played the keyboard, Andy played the trombone, Tony played the drums by banging on the dining room table, and Dante was the official preacher. They recorded their powwows on cassette tape. This connection grew the five of them even closer to each other than they were to the rest of the gang. Meanwhile, there was still the hovering, dark cloud of resistance and feeble tolerance from Andy's father. It grew more dark and resistant the closer they got to each other. It didn't slip by him the delighted looks that Andy gave Aiko when he saw her in nice church clothes, heels, and lip gloss.

A couple of years had passed and the gang was still going strong. Aiko and Andy were pre-teens, and they were both developing, though her development was in more obvious ways. Andy started visiting without David and only came to see her. During the summer she loved getting up early and opening her bedroom window to let in the fresh, morning summer air. She would voluntarily do extra chores to take the load off of her mom when she got home from work, and to impress her dad. She would blast Debbie Gibson's "Electric Youth" when doing chores. Upbeat songs always made doing chores more fun. Afterwards, she would fix breakfast for Dante and Tony. By mid day she was done, and she sat in her bedroom window sewing a hole in her slouch socks listening to her dad's contemporary jazz collection on CD. Her favorite group was Spyro Gyra. The soothing tunes seemed to be the official soundtrack for lazy summer days. Music was therapeutic for her, not that she really needed therapy, but she could find a song to suit her every mood. It felt good to let the songs carry her through her moods, which were ever-changing since she was at the brink of puberty. Her small bedroom was her solace. Posters of kittens and puppies, and her collection of Garbage Pail Kids cards took up almost every inch of her walls. Her daybed was covered with stuffed animals, all of which she had given names. Her biggest and favorite one was a white teddy bear with a red bow tie and bright blue eyes. She felt protected by them and imagined they were enjoying the music too. The tight walls of her room made her feel encompassed by the music. The window connected her to nature outside, while still being in her sanctuary.

One particular day when she got up to go to the bathroom, she heard a familiar voice calling her from her bedroom. She finished up and went towards the voice. It was Andy. He had pulled the ladder from underneath the deck in her yard and used it to climb to her window. She thought it was a little dangerous, but very sweet. She sat in her usual spot and they talked for a couple of hours. They covered subjects like music, God, and the future. By the end of the two hours, she knew for sure she was falling in love. He risked injury getting to her in a fairytale manner. He was easy to talk to and an even better listener. He devoted precious time to her. His visits became more frequent, and eventually were daily. Andy's witchy grandmother tried to interrupt as much as she could. It was in vain. Andy would come right back. His room faced the backyard as well. At night they both would go to their windows and blow kisses good night to each other. She renamed her big white teddy bear Andy and held it as she slept. Aiko's parents thought their puppy love was adorable. They teased calling her "Rapunzel" and "Mrs. Lantry". Needless to say, she was bashful and less than amused by their humor.

The season changed once again. It was getting darker earlier and much too cold for long window talks. Aiko's house had a closed in front porch, so they communed there, but for shorter times. She felt it was time to make it official. She devised the plan and enlisted Dante and Tony to help. There was a song by the Winans called "Love Has No Color". Since she was black and he was white it was perfect. It was Dante and Tony's job to get Andy over their house to the living room. Once there, Aiko would queue the song, kiss Andy, and tell him that she loves him. Everything went according to plan. Andy was there in the living room taking in the lyrics to the song. When it was done she kissed him on the lips for three seconds then told him that she loved him. His face turned so red that the brown freckles looked almost purple. He stood there in shock and said nothing. She was waiting for him to say he loved her back, but he didn't. He was frozen. Her heart sank to her feet. Bursting into tears, she ran to her room, locked the door, and hugged Andy bear. She listened to Debbie Gibson's "Lost in Your Eyes" repeatedly. Time seemed to stand still. She didn't know how much of it had passed before Dante and Tony came knocking on her door. She screamed at them to go away. They told her that Andy had sent Helga and Sarah over with a message for her. She didn't believe them at first, until she heard their voices. She slowly opened the door, pulled them in, and shut and locked it again. The message was that he was sorry. He did love her too and wanted to know if she would be his girlfriend. Aiko was shocked. *Why couldn't he just say that himself?* She realized then that she had caught him by surprise. She probably would have reacted the same way. She sent Helga and Sarah over a message of her own, "Yes". With that, it was official. They were a couple. The first few days were a little awkward because they were both shy and embarrassed about the surprise kiss incident. Before, long they were back to normal. She was blissfully happy and so was he. They had no expectations. They just lived in the moment. And the dark cloud still hovered, growing darker.

One spring, Saturday morning, Aiko received a call from Helga. She had asked to come over. She heard the panic in her voice and agreed for her to come. It only took five minutes for Helga to get there because she lived one street over on Andy's street. What Helga told her should have surprised her, but it didn't. What it did accomplish was hurt her to the core. As Helga spilled the words from her lips, she choked on them as if disgusted by the taste of them on her tongue. David accidentally mentioned Aiko and Andy's relationship while their dad was within earshot. The dark cloud rumbled, swelled, and exploded into a storm. Their dad went into an uproar and demanded that Andy break it off immediately because he didn't want a nappy headed daughter-in-law, or half nigger babies for grandchildren. When Andy told his father that he loved Aiko, he grounded him for two months in an attempt to drive a wedge between them. Andy was instructed to call Helga to send the message to Aiko that the relationship was over.

She was devastated. She could only imagine what Andy must have been going through and wished she could be there for him. That night she kept checking to see if he would come to the window to say goodnight like he had done so many nights before. He never showed. She was heartbroken. It was the first of many heart breaks. She counted down the days until Andy's punishment was lifted with hopes of seeing him again. She also hoped that they would be allowed to be friends. His dad still wanted them to keep their distance. Andy used his friendship with Dante and Tony as a way of convincing his father to let him hang out so that he could sneak and see her. His father agreed, but enforced strict time restraints. They never tried to have a relationship again, but they didn't want to lose their friendship. Even still, Aiko, Dante, and Tony felt uncomfortable. They stopped going over Andy's house altogether. They only spent time on his block over Helga's or Sarah's houses.

That summer Aiko was to turn thirteen. She was planning a big backyard party. She figured Andy's dad would let him and David attend since he could watch Andy closely from the kitchen window. Meanwhile, Andy and David got a pool. Andy told her that she, Dante, and Tony were not allowed in the pool per his father. He didn't want their black to come off in it. Baltimore has hot and humid summers, and that year was no exception. To have a pool one fence away and can't enjoy it was cruel. What was worse was watching and hearing them splash around having fun every day. To add salt to the wound Helga, Jim and Sarah were allowed to swim. Their playful sounds were almost exaggerated as if all five of them were trying to make the little black kids jealous. Aiko would blast her The Boys cassette tape to drown out the noise. Karma took vengeance for them. By the end of July, the pool got busted on the side and Andy's parents tore it down. She was more than pleased to see it go.

The second week of August rolled around quickly. It was ten days before her birthday party. She noticed a lot of movement and boxes coming out of Andy's house. She watched from her bedroom window. She saw Andy come out carrying a small box. She hollered for him to meet her at the fence. That's when she heard the worst news of her life thus far. It was confirmed that Andy's family was moving. He didn't know the new address yet, but he promised to keep in touch. Now she knew why the pool really got torn down. A busted pool depreciates the value of a home and can drive down the sale price. She remained strong in front of him as they said their goodbyes. Not only was he moving, but he was going to miss her thirteenth birthday party. When she got back to her room, she put on The Boys' song "Happy". It is a song about a sad little girl whose boyfriend moved away. It spoke to her soul. She lay in fetal position gripping Andy bear crying until she cried herself to sleep. As time went on, Andy never called, he never wrote, she never ran into him anywhere. He had broken his promise. She tried to convince herself that it was his dad's fault.

It had been eight months since Andy moved away. Aiko still missed him, but it was easy for her to get over him since she had a couple of cuties in her eighth grade class to distract her, even though she was nowhere near on their radar. Plus, she had the eighth grade class trip, graduation, summer, and her attending high school to look forward to that year. So, she had more reasons to be happy than sad. Andy obviously moved on with his life, and she was determined to do the same. Tony moved on too. He found a new best friend named Bobby. They were juniors at the same high school. Aiko was paid ten dollars a week to walk Bobby's little sister Shelly to and from Maplewood elementary school. She spent most of it on goodies and wooden airplanes for Dante at the corner store. Like Andy and David, Bobby would come to seven PM prayer and Bible study. She thought he was cute in a goofy sort of way. He had blonde curly hair and blue eyes and blushed at the drop of a hat. She enjoyed making him blush to see how fast his face would turn red. Admittedly, she had a crush on him too, though it didn't compare to the feelings she had for Andy. He was always nice to her and greeted her with a smile. She never thought of it as nothing more than him being friendly, until the day she was proven wrong.

She always made it home from school before Tony did because her school was only five blocks away and Tony and Bobby had to catch the bus. This particular day everything went normally, so it seemed, until the doorbell rang. Tony had forgotten his keys. Bobby was with him. She opened the screen door to the closed in front porch and led the way into the house. She heard the front door slam unusually hard. She turned around only to find just Bobby standing behind her. Tony had locked the door and was holding it shut on the other side. Bobby grabbed her face with both hands and aggressively forced his tongue into her mouth. His kisses were sloppy and uncoordinated and left her cheeks, nose, and chin feeling damp and disgusting. He pushed her down onto the loveseat and whipped out his penis. It was the first white one she had ever seen. She had seen black penises before. Unfortunately, they were attached to a couple of her male cousins when they were coming out of the bathroom with no towel from showering. Either that was done on purpose or they were just plain uncouth. Nevertheless, those experiences gave her a gauge. Bobby's penis wasn't small, but in comparison to her cousins', the stereotype of black men being well endowed remained intact. It was hard and red, almost ruby in color, looking straight at her like a Cyclops ready to spontaneously combust. Bobby put his weight against her and pulled her left hand towards the Cyclops, begging her to touch it. She refused emphatically, and kept yanking back her hand. He tried at least four times to get his way, and she refused each time. Nothing about his approach or his penis made her willing. In addition, she was a virgin and simply just wasn't ready, especially in this way. Tony had set her up. He wanted to get his best friend some coochie at the expense of her innocence and virginity. She managed to get through to him to stop. Undeservingly, she apologized to him. She felt sorry for him because he seemed embarrassed. They both pulled at the door and hollered through for Tony to open it. Bobby went home with his tail between his legs. Tony gave her the third degree about what happened. She gave him a quick, cold synopsis of the event, then went to her room and slammed the door. She was angrier at him than at Bobby. As her big cousin and brother figure, he was supposed protect her innocence, not serve it up on a silver platter. By today's standards, that would have been considered sexual assault, but back in the day it would've been dismissed as part of growing up. It was normal for hormone filled kids to explore with games like seven minutes of heaven, spin the bottle, and dry rubbing through pants to satisfy curiosities. She eventually forgave Tony. After all, he was family. After six months, just like Andy, Bobby moved away. Years later she ran into Bobby. He revealed that he was engaged and studying to become a pastor. She would have never predicted that for him, but she was happy for him. She had no doubt that her family's Bible study sessions contributed to it. One by one, the rest of her crew all moved away that year. She took the loss of her friends hard, but she was resilient. Making new friends wasn't hard. Her internal battle was whether making new friends was what she wanted and whether she was going to make the effort.

CHAPTER 2—TRACK 2--Now It Gets Good

A year had passed. Aiko was fourteen going on fifteen. She was hanging tight with her friend Chelsea. She had known her since the fifth grade, but had just begun to get closer to her after eighth grade graduation. She had finally decided it was time to make more meaningful friendships. Chelsea was dark brown skinned, and about four inches taller than her. She wasn't as pretty as Aiko, but still attractive. She had a head full of thick, beautiful hair. There was so much more she could have done with her hair, but it was wasted on a ponytail most of the time. She was a bit of a plain Jane, and not really into makeup, hair, and fashion for herself like Aiko. She hoped that her sense of style would eventually rub off on her. Her best feature was her large, full breasts and she knew it. She used it to her advantage whenever possible. Chelsea lived one block away from the bus stop, so she spent a lot of time at her house after school, and she would sleep over occasionally. Chelsea had an older sister named Diane, who was six years older than them and already in college. Her life was kept very quiet. Any advice or experience she had was never shared, at least not with Aiko. Chelsea was possibly in the dark too. Either there was really not much to tell, or her closet of secrets was like Pandora's Box.

Music was still a big part of her life. She was still infatuated with The Boys, but her music choices began to mature. She was into artists like Keith Sweat, Bell Biv Devoe, Tony! Toni! Tone!, En Vogue, and Johnny Gill to name a few. Attending concerts of her favorite artists was quickly becoming one of her favorite pastimes. She still loved her Christian music and she sometimes felt guilty simply listening to secular music because some of the lyrics and messages were not Christian, and were feeding her spirit improper values. All music was so important to her, and she strongly felt that it shouldn't matter what genre as long as she liked it. So, she decided to listen to it all indiscriminately.

Like every Saturday she listened to the radio while she washed her hair over the tub. It was down to her shoulder blades. She hoped that she could get it to grow to the middle of her back. Chelsea came to visit and kept her company. Tony came rushing to tell Aiko that he had a friend named Derek whom he wanted her to meet out front. She wanted to let the conditioner sit in her hair a few more minutes, but she washed it out anyway. She figured it would take too long to blow dry, so she wrapped a towel around her head. It was warm outside, so catching cold wasn't a concern. When she looked up, Chelsea had disappeared. Aiko went outside only to find Tony sitting on the steps alone. He looked up at her then pointed up the street to the left. Chelsea and Derek were taking a stroll together engrossed in conversation and clearly into each other. She had stolen the guy her cousin brought home for her to meet. *Such a sneaky bitch!* With thoughts like that, maybe the secular music had begun to affect her.

After the Derek incident she still remained close to Chelsea, but she knew better than to trust her, particularly when it came to the opposite sex. She now knew the hand that Chelsea was playing and just how low she will go to get what she wants. She tolerated her braggadocios stories of how things were going with Derek. She was almost certain that she had slept with him, though Chelsea never mentioned it. She rolled her eyes behind her back. She had to fake being interested and happy for her. Fake wasn't something she was accustomed to, but she did it in order to keep the friendship alive. After all, boys come and go.

One night, like many nights before, she and Chelsea hung out on the steps of a vacant house on the busy street around the corner from Aiko's block. They talked and danced to the music cars were blasting passing by. A dark, burgundy car with tinted windows pulled up in front of them. The window on the passenger side rolled down. There were two guys at least in their twenties in the front seats. They summoned them over to the car. It crossed Aiko's mind that they must have thought that she and Chelsea were hookers. She didn't see how because they weren't scantily dressed or had on any makeup. The guys asked them if they wanted to go for a ride. Aiko stepped back. Chelsea tugged on her arm and begged her to go because she didn't want to go alone. She agreed only because she would hate herself if something happened to Chelsea. The guys drove them to a park about two miles away. Since parks close at dusk, Aiko began to feel even more uneasy. There was no telling what could happen. The possibilities neared infinity. She began to play out some possible scenarios in her head. Before she knew it the words, "Take us back!" exploded from her mouth. The guy in the passenger seat replied, "Relax. We are just going to have a little fun." That didn't make her feel any better. The driver put the car in park. She knew her way home from there. The moment anything went wrong she was going to run. She was on the track team, so she could put some distance between them quickly. The guy in the passenger seat got out first. Aiko was sitting in the seat behind him. He opened the door to let her out. Chelsea slid across the seat, got out, then got into the front seat holding a Capri Sun she was nursing. Aiko and her guy sat at a table that was about fifty feet away from the car. It was on a patch of dirt surrounded by grass, and under a dimly lit lamp. The lamp gave her some peace. It wasn't very bright, but at least it wasn't pitch black either. They talked under the stars twinkling through the dark, navy blue sky while the crickets sang. She was still on edge, but she wasn't as scared because he seemed nice. He kept looking over his left shoulder at the car. She was curious as to what was distracting him. She was a little worried about Chelsea, so she peeked around him to see. It was dark, so all she could see was the silhouette of the guy in the driver seat, which was reclined. His head was cocked back, and the rim of his cap was facing north. She saw movement next to him, but she couldn't make out what it was. She squinted. That's when she realized that it was Chelsea's head bobbing up and down. She knew then that she was sucking him off. She instantly became uncomfortable again. It was clear that was kind of fun the guy sitting next to her expected as well. She became antsy. He got up from the table, stood in front of her, grabbed her hands, and pulled her to her feet. She didn't know what to expect next. He wrapped his arms around her shoulders and jammed his tongue into her mouth. When she tried to pull away, he locked her into his arms around her waist with her arms at her sides. She kept squirming and grunting to give herself strength. It wasn't working. Then, she did what she felt was necessary. She bit him really hard on his chest, which was where her face came to since he was almost a foot taller than her. That was enough to loosen his grip so that she could get away. Aiko was a big fan of karate movies and watched kung fu theater on channel fifty four on Saturdays after cartoons and Soul Train. The first thing that came to her mind was the opening scene of Enter the Dragon when the young woman was chased through Shang Hai by a group of men trying to rape her. When she was about eight years old, she used to reenact the scene in her parents' townhouse living room. The young woman in the movie killed herself with a large, sharp, shard of glass to avoid being gang raped. She wasn't willing to go that far, but she was going to fight back hard like she did. Needless to say, her mind goes to strange places when under duress, but she used whatever resources she needed to survive in the moment, strange or not. She kept running as fast as she could just as she had planned. Branches slapped her in the face or snapped into two across her body. All she could hear was her panting and the rustling of leaves. She was getting away! She looked back to see how far she was from him. That was a big mistake. She had watched so many horror films where she yelled at the television screen at the dumb broad who tripped over nothing and fell in just enough time for the bad guy to catch up with her. Here she was doing the exact same thing. She tripped and fell flat on her stomach with a thud. She scrambled to get to her feet. Just as she was almost to her feet, he grabbed her around her hips, flipped her onto her back, and put his weight on top of her. She knew she could run fast, but she hadn't considered his weight and strength over hers. She knew she had to fight dirty. She kicked, screamed, and squirmed until she could think of something. He kept slapping her and tried to cover her mouth. Every time he did, she bit his hand. Every time she bit him, he slapped her again. He grabbed both of her wrists and pinned them to the ground above her head. He pulled off his belt and tied her wrists together with it. The belt was tied so tightly that it was cutting off her circulation. He unzipped his fly and started to slide her jean shorts down without unbuttoning or unzipping them. She wiggled trying to get him to stop, but that made her shorts slide down more. It was time to make her move. She gave herself a push backwards with her legs to give herself some room to flip over to her stomach. Hands still tied, she grabbed a handful of dirt and grass. He snatched her ankles, dragged her back, and flipped her over onto her back again. She tossed the contents of her hands into his eyes. He fell back onto his butt and rubbed his eyes with his hands growling in agony. She kicked him in the balls and ran in the direction of the car. When she got there, she threw her body against the window where Chelsea was sitting. By that time, she was out of breath and crying. The salt in her tears were stinging the cuts on her face. Before she could even see Chelsea's reaction, she felt her body being yanked backwards. He caught up to her, flung her to the ground, and removed his belt from her wrists. She thought she must've either just missed his jewels with her foot, or he had balls of steel because she thought for sure he was going to be down for a while. He opened the passenger door, yanked Chelsea down to the ground and replaced her in the seat. The driver asked him, "Hey man, what happened?" He replied, "Man, that bitch wasn't trying to give me no play! Let's go!" They pulled off posthaste leaving two young girls alone in a dark park. Chelsea helped her to her feet, and assisted her in dusting off and adjusting her clothes. As they walked back home, Aiko filled her in on everything. Chelsea appeared to be sympathetic, though the sentiment didn't last long. The moment Aiko seemed to have calmed down, Chelsea filled her in on her part of the excursion. She listen to her with very little reaction, just an occasional 'oh my gosh' or 'wow' to reassure Chelsea she had her attention, but she was in a daze. One part of Chelsea's story did snap her out of it for a few minutes. Chelsea confirmed that she did suck the guy off, and that she used the Capri Sun on his dick for added grape flavor. Interestingly enough, Aiko didn't respond with 'ew'or 'gross'. Instead, she asked, "Didn't that make it sticky?" Their eyes met, and they burst into laughter. The echoes of their laughter seemed to fill the air infinitely. Aiko's ribs were sore, so the laughter was bittersweet, but worth it. They finally got control of themselves. Chelsea asked a question of her own, but there was nothing funny about it. "How are you going to explain your injuries to your parents?" She hadn't thought that far ahead yet. They had about a half of a mile left to walk, plenty of time to think of an excuse. She had to make sure it was feasible and left no consequences for her. At first she thought that maybe she could say that she got hurt playing football with the guys. *No, that wouldn't work. It has too many holes*. She would have to tell the guys what really happened, then include them in on the lie. On top of that, her parents wouldn't allow her to play football anymore. Next, she thought she could say she was in a fight. *Nope, that wouldn't work either*. She looked like she had lost. Any make-believe fight she would be in, she would be certain her body would look like it was an easy win for her. Plus, her parents would interrogate her. She would have to fabricate details like what the people look like, and on what street the brawl took place. She finally decided that she would say that she fell off of her ten speed bike into some thick bushes. It explained the bruises and cuts, and it was believable because she was clumsy, and there was a wooded creek a few blocks away from the house. The rest of their journey was spent in silence. They got back just in time for Chelsea's mom to pick her up five minutes later.

She rushed into the house, took a long shower, treated her wounds, and did a load of laundry that included the clothes she had worn. There was only one entry in her diary that night "Capri Sun." She only wanted a phrase that reminded her of the events of that night. She wasn't sure if her mother snoops in her diary, so she couldn't leave any evidence. She took a couple of Tylenol for her pain, got into bed, and put on her favorite song by Nirvana "Smells Like Teen Spirit", followed by some Pantera and Nine Inch Nails. Any type of slow jam or love groove was not conducive to what she was feeling. She was angry and rock music seemed more appropriate. To mellow out before she fell asleep, she listened to Led Zeppelin's "Stairway to Heaven" and Jimi Hendrix's "Wind Cries Mary". She liked old-school rock n roll as well, partly because she grew up with her parents listening to it, and partly because she's always felt that she had an old soul. Surprisingly, she wasn't angry at the guy. She was angry with herself, and for number of reasons, the most obvious being getting into the car against her better judgment in the first place. Both of their lives could have been lost prematurely. She debated with herself whether running was a bad decision. Maybe he wouldn't have reacted so aggressively if she hadn't. Certainly, she wouldn't have had the cuts and bruises. *What about Chelsea? Suppose her guy did something to her like that, or worse?* She would've been too far away to do something to help. She didn't even think to get the tag numbers on the car. *What if they do this to another pair of girls? Stupid,*

stupid, stupid! She had to find a way to forgive herself and come to terms with the situation in order to move forward. The last thing she wanted was to be stifled. The choices that they made that night may have been foolish, but the bottom line was that they both survived. It was best that she considered it a learning experience. She prayed hard that night thanking God for protecting them. So many girls would have not walked away with a few scratches and bruises, if at all. She had seen it many times on the news. It was in that moment that she realized that she had a guardian angel assigned to her.

A few weeks had passed and she had gotten over the "Capri Sun" night very well. She and Chelsea stayed away from that house for a while to avoid running into those men. It crossed her mind to go there anyway in case they drove by so that she could recover the tag numbers, but she decided not to take the risk. Out of everything in that situation, that was the only good decision she had made. Truth be told, the men were probably more fearful of running into them. Eventually, they did start to hang at the vacant house stairs again once they felt enough time had passed. They did it gradually, one day a week, then two, and so on. The fear and intensity subsided. They never saw that car again or just didn't notice. What she did notice was a dude that was always walking with his friend from the side street across the road. He was about five foot seven with a smooth, brown complexion, and always wearing a cap. She nicknamed him "Capboy". They would always stare at her and Chelsea, but would never cross the street. Whenever she stayed long enough, she would see the boys coming back with bags from either the convenience store, the Chinese joint, or the family restaurant just a couple of blocks down the road. She finally decided to point them out to Chelsea in case she hadn't already noticed them. She told Chelsea that from what she could see from there, Capboy was cute. Chelsea stood up, walked to the edge of the curb, and yelled over to them, "Hey, boy in the cap! My friend here thinks you're cute!" She immediately regretted saying anything Chelsea. She should've known better. There was nothing she could do but gather her composure. Capboy and his friend didn't hesitate to cross the street that time. In what seemed like two seconds, they were face-to-face. The four of them made general introductions and engaged in some small talk. Naturally, Chelsea gravitated towards Capboy's friend, who turned out to be his 18-year-old cousin Aaron. Capboy was sixteen, and his real name was Neil Deats, but everyone just called him Deats. He was bare-chest with his T-shirt hanging from his back pocket. He had a gap between his two front teeth, but it didn't take away from his looks. Close-up, he was even cuter than she thought. He was naturally well-defined and muscular. His skin was flawless. It took all of the composure she possessed not to gently run her fingers along his bicep. When he talked, his six pack tightened, deepening the creases around each bulge. She pictured herself running her tongue along those creases like a maze down to his perfect and clean inny bellybutton and beyond. She could only imagine how soft, plump and smooth his bare ass would feel in her hands. What she was feeling the good Book describes as lust. It never seemed real until she experienced it firsthand.

From that point on the four of them met there just about every day. Sometimes they would walk down to the store together and bring the food back to the steps to eat and talk. The weather always seemed to cooperate, warm with lots of sun, and perfect for their gatherings. She dreaded the day when rain would come. The day that it did rain, she wondered if she and Chelsea should bother to go to the spot. Chelsea wasn't about to let the rain stop the show. From the basket by the door, she grabbed a colorful tote umbrella for herself and gave Aiko the large, black umbrella big enough to dub as a cane. *It figures she would give herself the better, more convenient one.* They arrived at the spot and waited on the porch. Within ten minutes, Deats and Aaron appeared at the top of their street. This time Aiko and Chelsea crossed over. They all agreed on Chinese food. It was too wet to eat on the steps, so Deats suggested that they eat at his house. The girls saw no harm, so they agreed. His house was decent, but the decor could have used a woman's touch. Since Deats was a year older than her, she knew that there was an adult that lived there, but she was almost certain that it was a father figure only. The four of them headed to the basement. It had a large TV and two long couches. Chelsea and Aaron sat together on one, and Aiko and Deats on the other. They ate and watched a movie. After eating, Chelsea and Aaron wasted no time locking lips. Deats, feeling challenged to make a move, slid closer to her, put his left arm around her shoulder, and stuck his tongue in her ear. She didn't like it one bit. To her, it felt like getting a wet willy. She hunched her right shoulder up and eased herself to the left. That didn't discourage Deats. He leaned in, grabbed her face, and started to kiss her. He was a good kisser. He wasn't practicing, he was skilled. Clearly he had done this before. Although nervous, Aiko wanted to practice herself. Up until then she'd only kissed Andy and Bobby, but she considered those amateur times. The only other practice she had since then was on her hand and on the bathroom mirror. Kissing Deats was better than she had imagined so many times. His kisses were soft and made a light smacking sound. He had full lips, but he never overpowered her small set. He treated her lips like they were sweet candy, or an ice cream cone, tracing them with his tongue, and gently sucking and nibbling on her bottom lip. She felt her body leaning back into the couch. Deats guided her deeper into it by slowly pushing her body with his. He lay between her legs. His shirt was off, but her clothes were still on, so she wasn't worried. She ran both her hands up and down his back. It felt like silk. Her hands glided across his skin. Before she knew it, her hands were sliding underneath the top of his boxers. This was her chance to feel that sweet ass of his. He loosened his belt and unbuttoned so that she could get her hands down further. She wasn't disappointed. It was as smooth, plump, and tight as she had pictured it. She squeezed it over and over almost uncontrollably. His cheeks bounced back like a rubber ball. "Damn", she whispered up at him. She gave a devilish glance then smacked it. She laughed because it resembled the sound of snap it firecrackers. He stared at her with an intense look then kissed her lips and neck. He worked his shorts all the way off, leaving on his boxers. She felt him tug at the top of her capris. She put her hands over his to stop him. He put his lips really close to her ears and whispered, "I just want to touch it." Naturally, she was reluctant. She had never been touched there by anyone before bare skinned. She was curious enough to let him proceed. She whimpered in shock. Her clitoris was swelled and sensitive. They continued to kiss. Deats' fingers massaged between her legs slowly and skillfully. She was in so much pleasure that she forgot that there were two other people in the room. Knowing Chelsea, she was doing the same as she was if not more. Suddenly, Deats' stopped. His hand was still down below, but hewasn't touching her anymore. She started to lift up to investigate the where and why. Deats eased her back down with his upper body kissing her along the way with his right hand still out of sight. The next thing she felt was pushing against her vulva in the wrong place. "What are you doing?" she said terrified of the answer to come. "Just relax." he replied in a calm, almost coaxing tone. She felt an even harder, more forceful pressure, this time closer to the mark, but still no bulls-eye. The light bulb went off in her head, and not a moment too soon. Deats was trying to steal her coochie. She yelled, "No! Get off of me!" She tried to push him off of her, but he didn't budge. That's when she spotted her umbrella on the floor next the couch only a foot away. She grabbed it with her left hand and whacked it across his beautiful back. Stunned by her attack, he budged that time. She jumped to her feet and fixed her capris. She started whipping Deats with the umbrella again across his back, head, and arms. "Nigga, you tried to sneak it! And you tried to sneak it with no condom! I'm a virgin, you jackass!"

Just hearing herself saying it out loud made her even angrier. She began to hit him even harder. She was determined that she was going to break something that day, whether she cracked his skull, or snapped the umbrella into two pieces on his back. She wanted him to have a beautiful back no more. It was going to look like Kunta Kinte's back when she was done. That's when Chelsea grabbed her from behind and Aaron grabbed the umbrella. He asked Deats, "What happened man?" Aiko didn't let him respond. "He tried to take it without asking! That's what happened!" Aaron turned to him. "You tried to just take the jailbait? Man, you're stupid!" He smacked Deats on the back of his head knocking his cap into his lap. "You need to apologize to that girl right now!" "I'm sorry." Deats mumbled under his breath. "Say it loud enough so she can hear you before I hit you myself with this umbrella!" Aaron barked at him. "I'm sorry!" he said loud enough to appease Aaron. Aaron handed Aiko the umbrella then turned to Chelsea. He instructed her to take Aiko home and promised that he would talk some sense into Deats. The girls exited out of the basement door. No sooner than the door shut, they could hear Aaron yelling at Deats. They could still hear him once they were four houses away. Deats had made a big mistake, but at least he had a cousin that was going to make sure he would never make that mistake again. On the way home, Aiko didn't say much, though she did tell Chelsea the details that led up to Deats' beat down. Chelsea was so excited about how Aiko handled it. She treated her as if she were a heavyweight champion, reenacting the scene with a twinkle of admiration in her eyes. Leave it to good old, selfish Chelsea to use this unfortunate incident for personal amusement. "Ko, can I just say one thing?" "Sure." "You really need to stop being a tease. If you ain't going to go all the way, don't do anything at all." Aiko was slightly offended. "Wait a minute. Hold up. Let's get something straight. I am not a tease. A tease promises things and then doesn't deliver. I never promised him anything. As a matter of fact, he never even asked me. So there it is." "But, your body said yes." "And my mouth said no. End of discussion." As irritated as she was, she hated to admit it, but if it weren't for Chelsea's selfishness, she might not have been able to defend herself. Because of it, she had the big, ugly umbrella to use as a weapon. She decided to let Chelsea have her fun and accepted her championship belt. *Why not?* She was proud of herself too. She felt empowered and strong. She also felt guilty because she took out on Deats all of the anger she had harbored from the "Capri Sun" night. She made peace with her guilt. If her actions kept Deats from turning out like those guys, it was worth it. She never did find out what went on between Chelsea and Aaron that day, nor did she bother to ask. Whatever happened, she was sure it was nothing Chelsea did not give him permission to do. He made that clear.

The entry in her diary that night was "umbrella". That ugly, oversized umbrella that she resented Chelsea for giving to her had protected her purity. Ideally, she wanted to wait until she was married before she had sex. Fornication is a sin, and she wanted to avoid it for as long as she could. However, her raging teenage hormones were becoming harder to keep at bay. If she decided to have sex before marriage, it was going to be with someone she deemed worthy of it, not someone who tries to take it against her will. She leaned over the edge of her bed and popped Boyz II Men's "Uh Ah" into her boom box. She couldn't stop thinking about how good it felt when Deats was touching her. She lifted her nightgown and slid her hand down her panties. She began to touch herself, trying to mimic every move Deats had made. It wasn't as good as when he did it, but it was still very pleasurable. She grinded up against her hand pretending it was her future lover making love to her. She moaned quietly so that no one in the next room could hear. Her clitoris swelled and hardened, and the rhythm of her hips became faster as she reached her climax. She gasped as she exploded with an orgasm. It was forceful yet sweet, and her body jerked at its release. Instantly, she felt the sensation of water trickling down her head, face, and neck, followed by guilt that passed within seconds. She curled up into a blissful slumber.

CHAPTER 3—TRACK 2—REFRAIN

The summer was coming to an end. Aiko was treated to a Bobby Brown concert by Chelsea and her mom for her fifteenth birthday. The day before, she had her hair done special for the occasion. She had a blue black rinse for color, bangs fingered waved up into rod curls cascading down the right side of her face, a French roll in the back, and blue glitter. She had to sleep cute that night so that she wouldn't flatten her style. Aiko had a knack for flair, though she rarely used it. She needed a reason to, and a birthday was just that. Otherwise, she didn't like to draw too much attention to herself. She kept her flare just enough to be unique, though her hairstyle might have crossed the line that time. Her mom spent one hundred dollars for it, so she was going to rock it proudly until it was time to get a new hairdo for the new school year. She had a good time at the concert except for a couple of issues. She was short, so she had to stand on her chair to see and take pictures. Then, Bobby Brown told all of the girls with their real hair to scream. Chelsea pointed at her and laughed hysterically. She was embarrassed and pissed. The only things fake about her hair was the color and the stuffing in the French roll to make it fuller. Chelsea was lucky her mother was there because Aiko had a few choice words of which she was spared. If Bobby Brown would have told all of the girls who weren't hoes to scream, the table would've been turned. To think of all of the secrets she had kept for Chelsea, and the first chance she had, she publicly ridiculed her. It was not that many people noticed. They were at a concert with loud music and fan cheers. It was the fact that she did it. Chelsea had plucked her last nerve. She decided that after the concert, she was going to cut back on hanging with her for a while. She needed a friend that was more her speed.

A couple of days after the concert, Aiko, Dante, and Tony were sitting out front on the steps enjoying the peaceful night air. The crickets were chirping louder announcing the end of summer. She still had on her blue sunshades from earlier when the sun was out. They matched her hair and she just didn't feel like removing them. She was reflecting on the past few months. So much had happened that summer and there were so many secrets she had to keep. If the eyes are the windows to the soul, then her sunshades were her curtains. She spotted three figures walking up the street towards them. As they approached closer, she could see that they were three girls. Their clothes weren't the most fashionable, but they were neat and clean. Before long, the girls were right in front of them. Aiko was in the diva mode and wasn't inclined to speak first. She didn't have to. The girl with the glasses spoke first. "Hi." she said with a bit of a country drawl. Aiko, Dante, and Tony said "Hi" back to her collectively. "I'm Karla, and these are my cousins Kammie and Trisha." Aiko made her introductions. Karla and her family had just moved into the house three doors down. She was two years younger than her, about five foot six, medium framed, and cute as a button. She had such an innocent face. Aiko could feel the good spirit in her. In comparison to Chelsea, Karla was a breath of fresh air. After the introductions and small talk ceased, the girls continued on with their stroll around the neighborhood, but not before Karla turned back towards them and said, “See y’all around.” “Bye.” they replied in unison.

The school year was off to a smooth start. Aiko’s plan to cut back on hanging out with Chelsea fell into place. Naturally, hanging out on school nights wasn’t an option. Aiko attended Westlake high school, and Chelsea went to Burton high school. That eliminated hanging out during school hours like they had done in middle school. So, that left the weekends. She could easily make an excuse whenever she saw fit to dodge a Saturday get together. She didn’t want Chelsea to get hip to it, so she still talked to her on the phone. The friendship wasn’t over, just on hiatus. Meanwhile, she and Karla became close. Every day after homework was finished, they spent a few hours talking and watching videos until dinner. Karla had four older, very cute brothers, and a younger sister named Ramona. Aiko described her as a tagalong or bad seed. She was nothing like Karla. Aiko sensed Karla’s tension whenever Ramona was around. For that reason alone, Aiko disliked her. Anyone that made such a sweet person like Karla uncomfortable had to be evil. She purposely antagonized her. She was determined to be the bane of Karla’s existence. She followed her everywhere, stripping her of peace and privacy. She attempted to push her into the shadows whenever possible. It was also evident that she was jealous over their friendship. Something needed to be done about this girl, but there was only so much she could do. She had no right to interfere in family affairs. The best thing for her to do was to support Karla and be her friend. Eventually, the rest would take care of itself.

It was a day like any other day. Aiko sat in the window seat on the bus to school across town. She had placed her book bag on the aisle seat hoping it would deter anyone from sitting next to her. That was highly unlikely because she had caught one of the earlier buses. She had computer lab that morning, and wanted to get to class earlier so that she could grab her favorite computer. Add to that the heavy rain, it almost guaranteed the first bus would fill up quickly with people escaping the downpour. The bus came to a stop. Five students got on passing her one by one. She avoided eye contact sending a signal that she didn't want a seat buddy. She was in the clear, so she thought. The last student doubled back her way. The back of the bus was the hangout spot for high school cliques. If you weren't in it, you weren't welcomed. Rosa Parks made huge sacrifices for people of color to sit anywhere they pleased on the bus. Thirty plus years later it became a popular place to sit in the back. It was hard for her to decide whether it was a slap in the face to Rosa Parks or a compliment to her efforts because now sitting in the back was a choice not a rule, yet young black kids still gravitated back there as if still enslaved to that mentality. The fifth student asked to sit next to her. She looked up and recognized him right away. His name was Glenn. He attended Westbrook, the once all boys high school turned co-ed that was situated right next door to her school. Westlake was still all girls. Glenn was the boyfriend of Tasha, who attended her school. She had seen them together many times, and for that reason, she kept their conversation to a minimum. She didn't want to give him the wrong idea, not that she was really attracted to him anyway. He was tall and thick, which she liked, but that was as far as it went physically. He was funny and easy to talk to, which she was sure won girls over more so than his looks. He made the rainy bus ride to school more pleasant. Once they arrived, they said their goodbyes.

After school, she decided to get on the third bus that takes her route. Since all three of the buses left within minutes of each other, it didn't get her home much later. The third bus usually had less people, which made for a quieter ride home. The sun had peeked through the clouds by then. She stared out of the tinted window squinting to the sun in her eyes. She spotted Glenn getting on and off the first bus within a minute. He did the same with the second bus. She thought that was strange. When he got on her bus, he looked around scanning faces until he spotted hers. His face lit up and a big smile spread across his face. He made his way straight to the seat beside her. This time he didn't ask to sit there. He plopped down like it was waiting just for him. *Oookay? Was he looking for me? There goes my quiet ride home.* They picked up the conversation where they had left off that morning. She was relieved when his stop came. For one, she could get some wiggle room because his large frame crushed her up against the window. For two, she could finally go back inside her head. His jibber jabber majorly cut into her thinking time. She decided she needed to avoid him as much as possible. The best way was to play musical buses. She had to switch up the buses she took daily, at least in the morning. She couldn't do as much for the afternoon because just like that day, he'd look for her. She set her plan into motion the next day. For weeks it was hit or miss. She might not have been enthusiastic to talk to him all the time, but he kept conversations interesting. She gave him props for that. He always had a jolly demeanor, until the day he revealed that Tasha had broken up with him. She felt sorry for him, but she really didn't want him to cry on her shoulder. He didn't give her much choice. She was on his radar. He would find her and spill his guts. He had put her in an awkward situation. Tasha's friends took the same bus route. They were her spies. Aiko always made sure her body language sent out a 'not interested' vibe to him and Tasha's friends. What she wasn't sure of was whether her friends reported the same message to her.

Two weeks later, Glenn called her on Friday night. He explained he was still feeling down and needed some company. She was disgusted by his antics. *He's really milking this breakup.* She told him that she would come over only if she could bring a friend, and he had a friend for her. He agreed. Immediately, she called Chelsea, who was more than willing to accompany her. She was her safety net. This was not a situation in which she wanted to have Karla involved because she was still in middle school. When they got there, everyone was introduced and they made their way to the living room. His parents weren't home, so they were free to cut up and get loud. They played spades and Uno while Michael Jackson's "Remember The Time" blasted on the stereo. They all bopped their heads to the beat. Glenn showed no signs of suffering from a broken heart because he got up from the couch and did his best Michael Jackson dance impersonation. It was the worst she had ever seen. He pulled her to her feet urging her to dance. It took a minute for her to shake off her shyness. She danced, but she didn't dare to try to do Michael Jackson. The other two joined them. They danced themselves to exhaustion. She and Glenn flopped on the couch and gulped down cans of soda. Glenn's friend James popped in a Johnny Gill CD. He queued it to the song "My, My, My," dimmed the lights, grabbed Chelsea, and started to slow dance. The last thing she wanted was to be stuck in a romantic setting with Glenn. In silence, they watched the other two dance together. Glenn must have given James some sort of signal behind her back because James responded with thumbs up and whispered in Chelsea's ear. She gave a quick head nod, and they went upstairs. Aiko's body got stiff as a board. She didn't have an umbrella this time. She searched the room with her eyes with what little light she had looking for any blunt object within her reach. She was preparing for the worse just in case. He scooted closer. To her surprise, he grabbed her hands and held them in his. "I really like you." he said trying to catch her eyes with his. "Yeah, I like you too. You're a good friend." she responded in the most neutral voice she could give. "Can I have a kiss?" "On the cheek." she replied still in neutral. He gave her a few soft kisses on her left cheek. He leaned back, grabbed his crotch, and said "See what you do to me?" She looked down then back up to his face and said "You did that to yourself." "Come on. Touch it for me, please?" he begged. "Um, I don't think so." She snapped at him. "Why you gotta be like that, girl? You're gonna give me blue balls. Come on. He doesn't bite." he said trying to lighten the mood. He unzipped his jeans and pulled out his dick through the slit of his boxers. It was slightly darker than the rest of his complexion and fully erect. He was average in size, but still the smallest she had seen thus far. *Guess that black man stereotype of being well endowed is officially busted.* Nothing about it aroused her. It didn't have a lot of width, it was curved like the letter 'C', and it was leaning far to the left. Glenn was left-handed, so that made sense. Apparently, he masturbated *a lot* and neglected to switch hands occasionally. He grabbed her right hand and placed it around it. It fit perfectly, which wasn't saying much because her hands were small. She began to stroke it up and down. He threw his head back moaning and sighing. Glenn was the only one enjoying himself. Aiko was utterly bored. She wished that she had a piece of gum to pop, smack, and blow bubbles. At least that would have brought her some amusement. After twenty minutes, she'd had enough of tracing the 'C' with her hand. She made an excuse that it was almost her curfew and that she had to go. Glenn went to get the other two. After washing her hands, the girls left. Thankfully, this time it was without drama.

The next week she hadn't seen Glenn on the bus morning or afternoon. She figured he would feel awkward seeing her afterwards, but she was indifferent about his feelings and the whole situation. She enjoyed having a row to herself again. It was just about time for the bus to leave. Tasha, Glenn's supposed ex-girlfriend rushed onto the bus. Aiko knew that she lived on a different side of town. She had never caught that bus before unless she was going home with Glenn or one of her friends. *Perhaps today is one of those days.* She headed straight to the back where she knew her friends usually sat. As she passed her row she casted Aiko an evil eye. She knew about her and Glenn, and she wasn't trying to hide her anger. How much she knew was the only thing in question, though there really wasn't much to tell in Aiko's opinion. Her only interest in him was a friend, and that was flimsy at best. She braced herself for what was sure to be a very uncomfortable ride home. She could feel Tasha's hateful glare from behind her burning at the back of her skull. Tasha and her friends began having a very heated discussion about someone. Aiko was sitting in her usual window seat in the last row before the back exit door, so she was within earshot. She didn't hear her name, but she knew this person was a female because of the excessive use of 'hoe' and 'bitch.' There was no doubt that they were unjustly referring to her. For thirty minutes, they verbally attacked her without calling her name. The more they talked, the more rowdy they became resembling an angry mob. All they needed were torches and pitchforks. Instantly the mob went silent. A few seconds later Aiko felt a hard and hostile tap on her left shoulder followed by, "Excuse me bitch!" Aiko continued to look straight ahead, nor did she bother to respond. Tasha may have been looking for confrontation, but Aiko wasn't. *Maybe if I ignore her she will go away.* Another hostile tap assaulted her shoulder confirming that she wasn't going away. "Excuse me bitch! I'm talking to you!" Tasha spewed rolling her neck so hard that her head should have popped off of her shoulders. Aiko still said nothing. This time she turned her head towards her and slowly ran her eyes from Tasha's feet, stopping at her face, and giving her an indignant stare straight into her eyes. She never broke the stare. She wasn't even sure if she blinked. Tasha's friends were drooling from bloodlust like a pack of wolves. She could see confusion on Tasha's face. She didn't know what to make of Aiko's reaction, or lack thereof, but she had an audience to entertain, so she continued to put on a show. "I heard you was messing with my man." "Who is your man?"Aiko replied keeping her voice calm and monotone. "Bitch, you know who my man is! Glenn!" "That's not what he said, but we're just friends. I don't like him like that and I don't want him," Aiko replied with a matter-of-fact tone. "That's not what I heard," Tasha said cutting her eyes at her wolf pack. "Well maybe you should find better sources for facts instead of believing lies from your minions back there." "Oh, so you think you're funny now bitch? Get up!" Aiko turned her head to face the front again and said, "I'm not fighting you Tasha." "Oh no bitch, we fighting!" Tasha punched Aiko square on the left cheek and grabbed her up by her hair pulling her to her feet. She could hear her ears ringing. The wolf pack broke into frenzy. Aiko felt her entire body climb to boiling fury. She started punching Tasha all over her upper body trying to avoid her face. She didn't want to take it there. By this time, the whole bus had a front row seat. The bus driver kept going as if nothing was happening, sneaking peaks in his rearview mirror. It was just another day on MTA with a bus full of high school students. The wheels hit a bump and Aiko lost her balance falling backwards into her seat. Tasha didn't let the opportunity to gain an advantage slip by her. She jumped on top of her and started throwing punches of her own, purposely aiming to destroy Aiko's face, but not for long. Aiko kicked her in the stomach knocking her onto her backside. She mounted Tasha, this time striking her face blow after blow like a mad woman. Since Tasha decided to open the door to facial mutilation, Aiko walked through it. She picked her up by the back of her head and slammed her face directly into the metal pole connected to her seat. She heard "Damns" and "Oh shits" come from every direction. She caught a couple of breaths before she said, "You can keep that hook dick nigga, bitch!" She rang the bell for the next stop and grabbed her book bag. The wolf pack was now a litter of puppies. Neither of them dared to walk past Aiko to help Tasha for fear that she would go ape shit on them too. Instead, they left Tasha in the bus aisle, bleeding from her nose until Aiko exited out of the back door. When she stepped down, she noticed that her new, white, high top, bubble gum sole Reebok sneakers were scuffed. "Damn!" It was nothing that shoe polish couldn't fix, but it still annoyed her. She got off about fifteen minutes away from her usual stop. She didn't mind the walk because she needed that time to cool off her temper. On the hike home she began to replay everything in her head. She scared herself at how angry she had gotten. She thought that maybe she had swelled with green muscles and purple cut off shorts or something because not even Tasha's friends jumped in to help. She was easily outnumbered. She didn't think that she had a bad temper, by any means, but her level of rage when provoked was off the charts. She didn't feel sorry for Tasha. She asked for that ass whipping. Nor, did she regret issuing said ass whipping in self defense. She just wished it hadn't had to go that far because it was unnecessary and over something so stupid. *Oh well, survival of the fittest, and apparently the craziest.*

When she got home she cleaned herself up and treated her scratches. Her face was swollen. Thank God she didn't have a black eye. Her mother would have flipped. Just when she was about to get her homework done and out of the way for the weekend, the doorbell rang. It was Karla, glistening with perspiration and breathing heavily. Her eyes were red and watery. She was angry and fueled on adrenaline. Aiko could almost see the steam coming out of her ears. "What's wrong?" Karla was too heated to even notice Aiko's puffy face. "I just got into a fight with Ramona." "Oh my God! Girl, come on in so you can tell me what happened."

Karla revealed the real story behind Ramona. They weren't really sisters. Ramona was actually her third cousin. She couldn't keep out of trouble, so Karla's parents decided to take her into their home to help her. She resented Karla for being 'the good one.' She was envious of her for having a close, loving family. Karla represented everything Ramona was not. She possessed everything Ramona did not. For these reasons she hated Karla. Karla tried to keep the peace, which is why she tolerated so much from her, but she couldn't take it any longer. Ramona had crossed the line. She told Karla that she intended to replace her in the family. She was going to make her life a living hell until she drove her to insanity so that they would put her away leaving her nothing but time to take over. That's when Karla snapped. She beat Ramona to a pulp right on the front lawn. Her brothers sat on the porch laughing and instigating the fight. Every guy enjoys a good chick fight whether it's in mud, water, a ring, or in this case a frozen front lawn. Karla said, "Girl, I was surprised my brothers didn't break out the popcorn." They both belted out laughter until their guts hurt. Aiko said, "Well, well you whipped out your kahunas, and you've got a set of big ones, huh? I'm proud of you. Is there any of her left for me?" They broke into laughter again before Karla replied, "Nope. But, looks like you've already been fighting girl. What happened to you?" Aiko filled her in on the details of her scuffle. An hour had passed. Karla wasn't ready to leave and Aiko wasn't ready for her to go. They were both sure to be grounded for the weekend, so it was best to have their fun while they could. She threw a frozen pizza in the oven and turned on videos on The Box channel. They ordered Jodeci's video "Stay" and Mary J Blige's "Real Love." It had cost three dollars and ninety-nine cents per video on the phone bill, so Aiko limited the orders to two. After that, they just watched the videos everyone else ordered who subscribed to United Artist cable. Most of them were the videos they liked anyway. After Karla left, Aiko called Chelsea to get her up to speed. Chelsea had some information to share with her as well. James had told her that Glenn used her to make Tasha jealous as revenge for breaking up with him. Aiko wasn't surprised. She sensed she was a pawn in his game, but she was the one who proclaimed 'checkmate.'

When she turned in for the night, she selected "Hold Me" from Commissioned's "Number 7" album. After the day's events, she needed to feel closer to God. She wanted to feel his love to replace the anger. The entry in her diary that night was "The Incredible Hulks." She made it plural because she wanted to log the memory of Karla's day too. It was a day that they both discovered their inner beasts.

CHAPTER 4—TRACK 3— VAUGHN CHAMBERLAIN

Christmas was approaching. Aiko never had any more trouble from Tasha and her friends. Glenn avoided her and caught only the buses on which she was not sitting. Aiko had experienced a rough year. She felt herself slowly falling into withdrawal. The stakes for dating were too high. Thus far, her safety and purity had been jeopardized. She had become disillusioned about the true nature of human beings. She wasn't sure whether it was intrinsically good or evil. She searched the Bible for the answer. The Bible states that we are all sinners and must repent. Even then people are still not without flaw, some less bearable than others. She was convinced that people gravitate towards evil more so than good. Withdrawal was the only way she could ensure that she could protect herself. No one could hurt her if she didn't let them into her inner circle. She socialized at school, though her options were limited since Tasha and her friends had forged her a label of "Loco Lady." If it meant that people would leave her alone, she didn't much care what label she was given. Still, the burden of loneliness was sometimes overwhelming. Having just one close friend at school could at least keep her grounded preventing her from being completely sucked in by the black hole of her withdrawal.

During Christmas break, she decided to spend more time with Chelsea. She could still see Karla every day too since she lived three doors down from her. Chelsea had her ways, but she genuinely liked Aiko. She sensed that Aiko was in a dark place and she wanted to help. Her older sister Diane had a boyfriend named Ethan who had a younger brother named Ian. Diane wanted to introduce him to Chelsea. Chelsea suggested that Ian bring a friend for Aiko. She didn't much like the idea, but Chelsea wouldn't take no for an answer. The date was set before she even asked her. She just asked as a formality. It was to be a date over Chelsea's house. She had a beautiful, fully furnished club basement with a big floor model television they could watch.

In the days leading up to the date, Aiko found herself giving too much thought to the outfit, shoes, makeup, jewelry, and perfume she was going to wear for the blind date. She didn't want to get too excited about it. To her that would mean that she was leaving her comfort zone, exposing herself to potential harm. She finalized her decisions and made a point not to give them another thought. The day of the date, Chelsea had Diane picked up Aiko one hour early to prevent her from chickening out. Granted, she was apprehensive, but a coward she was not. Nothing proved that more than how she had faced the clamorous situations of her year. She had no intention of bailing out of the blind date completely.

When she arrived, she and Chelsea headed straight to the basement. Diane had set up a tasty spread of pretzels, chips and dip, popcorn, cheese curls, and Kool-Aid. The pizza and wings were going to be ordered in thirty minutes. The veggie platter was chilling in the refrigerator, and the scent of steamed shrimp filled the air. She had gone all out for the occasion, though Aiko was positive it was mostly to impress Ethan. Aiko grabbed a handful of chips, flopped into the armchair and said, “What if I don’t like him? Do I really have to go through with it the whole night?” Chelsea frowned with annoyance at Aiko’s pessimism and replied, “Oh yeah, you’re going through with it! But, I tell you what, if you don’t like him, we’ll create a code word for you to say to let me know. Just at least give an hour before you use it.” “Okay, like what?” “Hmm, well you don’t like orange Kool-Aid right?” “Right.” “So, when the pitcher is empty, I’ll grab it to go make some more. I’ll ask everyone if there’s a particular flavor they want me to make. If you don’t like him, just say orange. Okay?” “Okay, then what?” “Then I’ll know that you don’t like him.” “And?” “And, you’ll go through with the night as planned. Then, you’ll go home. He’ll go home. That’s it. You’ll never have to see him again. Okay?” “Yeah, I guess, whatever,” Aiko mumbled under her breath.

The pizza and wings arrived within minutes before the young men did. Diane and Ethan grabbed some food and snacks then headed upstairs to the kitchen to give the younger couples some privacy, as well as their own. There was an instant connection between Chelsea and Ian. For Aiko, it was not so much, at least not on her part. His name was Vaughn Chamberlain. Luckily for him, his looks weren't hideous like his name. He was cute, about five foot nine, and brown skinned with a medium build. His hair was cut into a curly fade. He wore a Coogi sweater and black corduroy jeans. She couldn't help but notice he walked with a slight limp, which could easily be confused as a bop in his walk. He was from the country of Jamaica. Aiko found his accent to be his most attractive feature. Chelsea and Ian took the couch while Aiko stayed anchored in the armchair, and Vaughn sat in the recliner. Chelsea had chosen a line of scary thriller movies so that she could duck into Ian's chest as a way of flirting. The movies included "Pet Cemetery," "Cape Fear," "Candy Man," and "Faces of Death." "Faces of Death" was watched first. It wasn't as scary as it was gory. A couple of times Aiko turned her head at the gross parts because she was eating. The real blood, autopsies, dismembered body parts, and grueling animal attacks were enough to make anyone lose their appetite. She caught Vaughn staring at her each time. By the fifth time, it was apparent he was watching her more than the movie. She twitched in her seat but couldn't get comfortable anymore. She knew every move she made was being watched. She stood up and said, "I've got to go to the bathroom." "Well, what are you announcing it for? Just go!" Chelsea said annoyed by the disruption. Aiko sucked her teeth at her. The bathroom was in the rear of the back room of the basement. There was a long, spooky hallway leading to it. She had always had a hard time finding the light switch to the hallway. The bathroom light was already on, which was enough for her to see her way there. She wished she could stay in the bathroom until the group left, but that would be too obvious that she was hiding. She needed some extra time to shake off the feeling of Vaughn's eyeballs on her, but staying too long would make everyone think she had to do number two. That would be too embarrassing. Ten minutes was a reasonable amount of time, five minutes for doing her business, and five minutes for primping. She checked herself one last time in the mirror. She looked beautiful. *No wonder Vaughn stared.* This was what she wanted to avoid, but she was too vain to present herself any other way. It was because of her vanity that she had caught the eye of Vaughn. She could only hope that it didn't mean more trouble for her. She had endured enough that year. She crept back into the den area hoping he had enough time to get into the movie and ignore her. She had no such luck. Even Ian and Chelsea were looking at her. The whole atmosphere had changed as if they had talked about her in her absence. She shrugged it off as paranoia. She took her seat. Chelsea hadn't bothered to pause the movie. Vaughn's stares became more intense. Her left leg began to nervously shake. She put her hand on it trying to stop it, but that just made her feel silly. So, she crossed her legs instead. The knee-high skirt she was wearing rose up to mid thigh, exposing more of her smooth, caramel flesh. Vaughn's eyes traced every curve of her thighs as if trying to memorize them. Now, he was the one twitching in his seat, and tugging on his jeans and sweater trying to hide his arousal. She enjoyed the fact that now he was uncomfortable. She had gained the upper hand with one cross of her leg, and she was going to use it to her advantage. Her discomfort disappeared as she embraced the power of her sexuality. From then on, her moves were calculated, deliberate, and tantalizing. She made note of his every reaction paying close attention to what turned him on the most. She was in control and she loved it. Chelsea was intrigued. She had never seen that side of Aiko before. She smiled at her with pride. She had always hoped Aiko would find her power. With it, she didn't have to be a victim any longer. The movie ended. Chelsea flicked on the light long enough to put on "Candyman." While she was changing the DVD, Aiko decided to go in for the kill. She kicked over her glass hoping Vaughn would assist. "Oops, I'm sorry," she said forcing sincerity where there was none. Within two seconds Vaughn was on his knees by her left side swabbing up the mess with a napkin. "I got it." He had a close up view of her thick, shapely legs. His nose caught a hint of the perfume she had dabbed behind her knees. He closed his eyes savoring the scent. She thanked him. "My pleasure darling," he replied as he rose to his feet. He replenished her drink and handed it to her. "Be careful dis time." "I will. Thank you," she replied bashfully. She couldn't help herself. That voice and accent of his turned her on, but, she was determined not to relinquish her power, so she regained her composure. Chelsea killed the lights and started the movie. Unlike "Faces of Death", "Candyman" was scary. When Candyman appeared in the mirror, Aiko jumped to her feet and ran over by the snack table next to Vaughn. He chuckled at her and said, “Come gyal, sit down here,” tapping his lap. She glanced at Chelsea who said, “Go ahead scaredy cat.” “No, I don’t think so. I’ll just go back to my chair.” “Come on gyal, sit down pon mi lap. I don’t bite. I’ll protect yuh.” With hesitation, she eased herself onto his lap conscious of her weight trying not to put the full bounty on him. “Yuh sit down light as a feather. Give me all of you.” “No, I may be too heavy. I don’t want to hurt you.” “I can handle it. Come on. Give it to me.” “No!” She insisted. Vaughn pulled the handle on the recliner sending them both leaning back forcing her whole body onto his. “See now gyal, it’s okay.” She could see that there was no arguing with him. If she tried to get up she could possibly break the recliner or hurt them both. She was trapped. It wasn’t a bad place to be trapped either. He smelled so good, wearing Giorgio’s “Red” for men. It worked very well with his body chemistry. His hands never moved below her waist, nor did he try to grope her anywhere else. He was a gentleman. She began to relax her body into his, and he absorbed it all without complaint. Not since her father held her when she was a little girl had she felt that safe in a man’s arms. Candyman showed up again issuing a gruesome death to another victim. Aiko buried her head into his shoulder covering her eyes and cringing in fear. He rubbed her back, gently lifted her chin until her eyes met his and said, “It’s okay. It’s over.” She gave him a lingering, soft kiss on his cheek. “Thank you.” As much of a gentleman he tried to be, another part of him acted independently of his intentions. Her kiss got his blood boiling and his nature began to rise. Aiko felt the crotch of his pants grow into a large, hard, bulge against the back of her thigh. “Wow,” escaped her lips. It was meant to remain an inner thought. He chuckled in a deep and confident tone. "Yuh woke him up." "Yeah, I see. I'm sorry." "He's not complaining. Neither am I." She covered her face with both hands trying to hide her embarrassment. He moved her hands away and looked directly into her eyes. "Don't cover your face like that. Don't worry. It's okay." "Okay," she sighed. She gave him a smile and leaned her head on his shoulder again. *Is he really that sweet, or like the others, just smooth with his game?* Either way, she liked his style.

Chelsea flicked on the lights unexpectedly, causing everyone to shield their eyes. "I'm going to make some more Kool-Aid. Aiko, what flavor do you want?" Aiko dreaded hearing endless "I told you so's" later, so she responded "Orange please." Chelsea narrowed her eyes at her in full contempt of her response. "Orange? Really? You're serious right now?" she said clenching her teeth. "Yes, orange. And make it snappy please. I'm parched." Chelsea flicked her middle finger at her and marched upstairs to the kitchen. She returned with a full picture of fruit punch, put it on the table, and rolled her eyes at Aiko. She dismissed Chelsea's hissy fit with the flick of her hand.

They watched "Cape Fear" for the last feature. When the night ended, the girls escorted the guys outside to the front porch. They separated into three groups of two saying their personal goodbyes. Vaughn took Aiko into his arms and held her closely. Her head came to his chest. She could smell his cologne on his sweater. She inhaled deeply with her nose trying to sniff his scent into her brain. She wanted to remember every detail of that night. He gently kissed the back of her left hand. "Until next time darling." "Bye. Good night." Her goodbye wasn't nearly as elegant as his was. She felt as though she should have curtsied afterwards, although she was the one who felt like royalty that night.

After the fellows left, Diane retired to her room. Chelsea waited with Aiko on the porch until her mother came to take her home. “So, do you like him?” “No. I asked for orange Kool-Aid didn’t I?” “Stop lying Aiko! I saw y’all over there all lovey-dovey and whatnot.” “I was just being nice.” “Whatever. He’s going to call you, so be prepared.” “How’s he going to do that? I didn’t give him my number.” “Nope, I did.” “When? I didn’t see you.” “When you went to the bathroom. Ha! How do you like that smart ass?" "I knew something was up when I came back." "Anyway, he likes you. He told me so." "Yeah, well, that doesn't mean anything." "Not yet." "Maybe not ever." "Well, we'll see." "I doubt it." "See. That right there. That's your problem. Why do you have to be so difficult?" "Because I can."

Chelsea was done arguing with her. She stared off in silence into the direction her mom was sure to come from since it was a one-way street. Her mom arrived soon after. She was not in the mood to talk, but her mom shot off like a machine gun with questions. She answered them using the last bit of patience she had left. She was anxious to get to her sanctuary. She ran through her mind choices of music that she wanted listen to in her room. She decided on Jodeci’s “Forever My Lady.” As she lay in her bed, she began to wonder if Chelsea had a point. *Am I too difficult? Is my difficulty the root of some of my recent problems?* Certainly, she was not willing to cast her morals aside to give men her most precious possession. Nor, does she want to be considered as easy. Difficulty was her shield. Her gift must be worked hard for, earned, and appreciated. She was a good girl and proud of it. Anyone who had a problem with that could go to hell as far as she was concerned. The entry in her diary that night was "Orange or Fruit Punch?" She wasn't sure whether she liked Vaughn or not. The only thing she was sure of was that she liked the way he treated her. She didn't know him well enough yet honestly say she liked him. A part of her was afraid to even find out. Either way, she may have something to lose. If she decided to give him a chance, she would have to be cautious.

For weeks she dodged Vaughn and Chelsea's phone calls. She deleted their messages on the answer machine, and threw away the sticky notes with messages on her bedroom door that Tony or Dante had left. She needed more time to think. Chelsea would argue that over thinking was another one of her problems. That was a conversation she did not want to have. Winter break was over. Aiko was looking forward to a fresh start in the new year. She had plenty that she desired to leave behind from last year. Vaughn and Chelsea's calls had come to a halt almost simultaneously. She was relieved that they had given up because it took the pressure off of her to make a decision that she wasn't ready to make. Her brain hurt just thinking about it. She stared at the clock on the wall above the black board counting down the minutes until the final bell rang. Mentally, she had already checked out thirty minutes prior. Latin class bored her to the point that she thought her skin was going to molt and her head was going to explode. Martin Luther King day was that coming Monday, so she had a three-day weekend of peace planned. The first thing she was going to do after she got home work done was get her weekend soundtrack together. Hanging with her home girl Karla was a definite must too.

She entered the third bus as usual. She expected to see familiar faces of those who caught the third bus daily as she did. She expected that they were going to sit in their favorite seats just like she intended to do. What she didn't expect was to see Vaughn sitting in her row on the aisle seat saving her window seat with his book bag. He studied her face trying to read her reaction, but there was none. Her face was blank. Although on the inside she was shocked, she couldn't seem to bring that feeling to the surface. "Um Vaughn, what you doing here?" "I came to see you. I saved your seat." He stood up to make room for her to sit down "Thanks. Let me guess, Chelsea told you what bus I take and where I like to sit right?" "Yes." "So, y'all cooked this up together." She said it in more of the form of a statement rather than a question because she already knew the answer. "Why didn't you return my calls? Did I offend you?" "No, it's nothing like that. I just... I don't know, just needed some time. Last year was rough for me." "I know. She told me." "How much did she tell you?" "Enough to know that you need a good man in your life." "Damn, she has a big mouth." she mumbled under her breath. "Don't believe everything you hear unless it comes from me." The bus started to move. "So then, you tell me now." She turned her head towards the window watching everything disappear behind them. She couldn't find the words to say, even if she were willing to disclose her past. Vaughn really didn't need her to tell him. He could see the pain and fear in her eyes. In his opinion, getting it off her chest was for her benefit not his. He sensed that it was a heavy burden for her to carry. He merely wanted her to release it.

"KoKo, when you're ready, I'll be here to listen. Okay?" "Okay." She kept her head towards the window. He put on his headphones. He had them up so loud that she could hear every word. She wished she hadn't forgotten to put batteries in her portable CD player, or she'd be doing the same. Vaughn started to sing slightly off key but he still had a nice voice. Still facing the window, she tried to hide her laughter at him when he tried to hit high notes and his voice cracked. From her peripheral, she saw people around them rolling their eyes and turning around to cast mean mugs expressing their aversion to his singing. Whether he noticed or not didn't matter. He was enjoying himself. Aiko tapped him on his knee. He lifted up his right ear muff just enough to let in her voice. "What are you listening to?" "Huh?" She leaned in closer to his ear. "What are you listening to?" "Buju Banton." "Can I listen?" "Sure." He placed the headphones on her. She turned the volume down some. She bopped her head. He waited until she listened to a few songs. "Well, do you like it?" "Actually, I do. What else you got?" He opened his book bag and pulled out a half dozen of CDs. She had a choice from Bob Marley, Super Cat, Bounty Killer, Shabba Ranks, Beenie Man, and Lady Saw. She picked Shabba Ranks. It was a little watered down with a touch of rhythm and blues, but his beats were bumping. For the duration of the ride home, she sampled songs from all of his CDs. They were about four stops from her house. He reached over her and rang the bell. "This isn't my stop." "I know. Come on. I have a surprise for you." "Where are we going?" "You'll see." He stood up and took her hand into his. She yanked her hands back out of instinct. She was wary, and rightfully so. This could be another bad decision or at least more strife. He touched her face, leaned down close to her, and looked into her eyes without saying a word for what seemed like minutes instead of seconds.

He wanted her to search his soul and find his sincerity. “Trust me.” He held his hand out again for hers. She took a deep breath and gave him her hand. He helped her to her feet. As they walked, she tried to figure out where he was taking her. There were nothing but retail stores, restaurants, and hair salons on that stretch of road. It didn’t take long for her to figure out that he was taking her to her favorite Chinese restaurant. Sure enough, he stopped there and opened the door for her. Before she entered, she looked at him and said, “Chelsea?” “Yup, Chelsea.” She shook her head and walked inside the restaurant. Chelsea had given him all of the tools he needed to work on her. What annoyed her the most was that she had no tools of her own. She knew nothing about him. Her work had to be done completely from scratch, which afforded her a handicap. He had all the advantage, which agitated her trust issues.

The hostess greeted them and escorted them to a small two-person table in the corner. It was dimly lit and cozy. The lunch crowd had gone. They were the only two there except for the patrons that occasionally stopped in for carry-out. She never got tired of looking at the beautifully delicate and intricate Chinese artwork on the walls. She spotted a few new portraits. Hypnotized by the shiny red and gold details, she studied each one, interpreting the stories they were telling. Each detail, every tiny line and paint stroke was perfectly and carefully placed, important individually, but more important as a group. She tried to get ideas about the techniques used to add to her artistic abilities. “KoKo, your eyes are dancing.” She snapped out of her trance. “Oh, I’m sorry. I was just checking out the art.” “Yeah, Chelsea told me that you are artsy fartsy.” She took a deep and annoyed sigh. “Can we not mention Chelsea anymore today? Let this be just about you and me please?" "You're right. Ready to order?" "Yes." She ordered beef yat gaw mein and he ordered pepper steak. She had never tried pepper steak. He let her stick her fork onto his plate to sample it. It was delicious. She didn't care for the large chunks of pepper and onion, or how they squeaked against her teeth. She would have preferred them to be diced. That was her only critique on the dish. They continued to discuss music and art. She learned a lot about Jamaica and its culture. Much to her surprise, he was very candid about himself too. His limp was from the amputation of his right baby toe due to acute frostbite and gangrene when he was about five years old. His family had just moved to the states and had never seen snow. He had played in the cold too long because of his excitement. She also learned that they had a few things in common as well. Besides their love of music, they both aspired to work in the music industry. Before she knew it, she was having fun. Once again, he had managed to get her guard down. His patience with her made the transition easier. They had long finished their meals and spent the majority of the time talking. They never ran out of things to talk about. Vaughn waited for a pause in the conversation, however brief. There was one particular subject he was anxious to broach. "So, I hear that you have a Valentine's dance at your school next month." "Yes, but I'm not going." "Why?" "Because I don't have a Valentine or a date, separate or one in the same." "Take me. I'll go with you." "That's sweet, but I believe that couples should be in love for that sort of thing. Don't you think?" "You'll be in love by then." "Oh really? How do you figure that?" "Because I'm working on it now." Aiko couldn't help but laugh at his zeal. It was immensely bold and assumptive. "Well, we'll see about that." "Yes, we will." The hostess came over and asked if they wanted dessert. They both said no and she handed Vaughn the check.

Aiko reached into her purse to get some money to contribute to the bill. “What are you doing girl?” “I’m paying for my food that’s what.” “Put your money away. I’ve got it.” “No, really, I can…” “I said I’ve got it girl. You don’t owe me anything.” “Okay, if you insist. Thank you.” He put a twenty dollar bill on the table, stood up, and held his hand out for hers again. She placed her hand in his without hesitation that time. She didn’t want to give him any more flak for the day. On the way out, she grabbed a few Chinese calendars. It was after five PM and getting dark outside. Vaughn insisted on walking her home. She showed him a shortcut to her house. When they arrived, she noticed the front porch light was lit. Her mom never left that light on unless she was expecting someone. Clearly, Chelsea had covered all bases. She had called Aiko’s mom and filled her in on she and Vaughn’s surprise date. She already knew to expect her a little later. In this instance, Aiko was glad that she did, otherwise, she might’ve gotten in trouble for not calling herself. She turned to Vaughn. “Thank you. I really had a nice time.” “You’re welcome. So did I. Don’t forget to let me know what colors we’re wearing to the dance, okay?” “Vaughn, I…” Before she could finish her protest, he leaned in and kissed her gently on the cheek, purposely not on her lips, but just next to them on the corner. He then lifted her hand which was still in his, and kissed the back of it. “Until we meet again Aiko. I’ll call you when I get home safely.” He turned and walked away. He didn’t want to wait for her response. He wanted her to marinate in the moment. She watched him until he disappeared from her sight. As soon as she got in the house, her mom told her to call Chelsea because she had been ringing the phone off of the hook. Aiko wasn’t in any hurry to call her back. She wanted to let Chelsea wait it out for a day. Although the date turned out to be a pleasant surprise, Chelsea shouldn’t have meddled. Aiko knocked out her homework then retired to her room. She was conflicted about how she felt about the day's events. On one hand, she didn't much care for surprises because, good or bad, they meant that for that moment she wasn't in control. Then there was Vaughn. She didn't appreciate that he learned things about her behind her back. He embarrassed her on the bus with the singing, and he refused to let her pay for her own food. On the other hand, in this case her disturbance may have been an overreaction. He treated her kindly and respectfully. The singing wasn't horrible, just loud. She had been embarrassed by worse things than that on the bus. As far as him paying for her meal, that simply was her pride. That's what a good man is supposed to do. She was a stubborn ox when she wanted to be. She hadn't even considered the fact that she may have offended him or hurt his pride. Not that a man's pride is more important, but it's more fragile. Her mom had always taught her that a man's pride is not just an emotion, but it's almost part of his genetic makeup. A man's pride should never be tampered with except to help build his confidence. She went through her CDs and cassette tapes and couldn't figure out what she wanted to hear. It had never been that hard for her before. Nothing she had seemed to fit her mood exactly. That made sense because she was straddling on the fence about everything. That's when her bedroom phone rang. Normally, she would answer, but since she was ducking Chelsea, she would let someone else answer in the kitchen. The rings stopped after three times, and within seconds, a light tap drummed her door before it creaked open to a crack. It was her mom. "KoKo, it's that boy Vaughn on the phone for you." "Okay, thanks Ma." She grabbed the cordless phone from her mom and closed the door instead of just picking up the phone in her room. She needed to prevent her mother's maternal urge to eavesdrop. She listened for her footsteps to gain distance from her room before she spoke. “Hi Vaughn.” “Hey KoKo. I’m home. What are you doing?” “I’m in my room going through my CDs and stuff. I can’t decide on what to listen to.” “Oh yeah? Well, maybe I can help. Where is your book bag?” “It’s right here. Why?” “Look in the front zipper.” “Okay, give me a second.” She opened it only to find his Shabba Ranks and Buju Banton CDs. “Oh my gosh Vaughn! When did you do this?” “When you were looking at the paintings.” “You didn’t have to do that.” “I know.” “Well, how long can I keep them?” “As long as you want. If or when I want them back, I’ll let you know. Don’t forget that I know where you live now.” He started laughing “What’s so funny? Am I supposed to be scared or something? Was that a threat?” “No, not at all. It’s a promise that you’ll be seeing more of me. That’s a good thing.” “Well, thank you for the CDs.” “You’re welcome. Enjoy.” “I’m going to get to it right now.” “Okay. Good night darling.” “Bye Vaughn.” She popped in Buju Banton first. She closed her eyes and tried to picture herself in Jamaica amongst all of its beauty and culture just like Vaughn had described. He promised that one day he would take her there. That’s something she wouldn’t hold her breath for, but it was nice to imagine. She rolled over onto her stomach and started writing in her diary using no phrases this time. All of the events of that day made it from her head to the page. There was nothing to hide. She planned to tell her mother anyway. Chelsea was going to be ecstatic for sure. It was the best day she’d had experienced in a while, and she didn’t want to forget any details. She could only hope that with him it would only get better.

Just about every day since that day for almost three weeks, Vaughn showed up on her bus after school. Chelsea had nothing to do with it those times, though she got the gossip later. Aiko was careful not to tell her too much. A part of her still struggled with trusting her. She had already stolen a man from her once before. Vaughn had potential. She didn't want him to get snatched because she painted a desirable picture of him. Her mother schooled her on that subject a long time ago. Vaughn had taken her to all of her favorite spots around the neighborhood and paid for it all. If nothing else, he was generous. She came to look forward to his daily visits. She enjoyed his company. He had brought her out of her shell. She felt happy, secure, and beautiful when around him. Each Friday, she got on the bus extra excited because it was time for her to swap out CDs to borrow. Her eyes automatically focused on their seats, but for the first time he wasn't there. She quickly glanced around the whole bus thinking maybe he had picked new seats for them. There was still no Vaughn. She sat down and put her book bag on the aisle seat to save it for him in case he was running late. She kept peeking out of the window searching the crowd of faces for him. Fifteen minutes had passed and the bus took off en route. Her heart sank. There had to be some explanation. *Maybe he had missed his bus to get here on time. Maybe he is sick. It is in the dead of winter and we have spent a lot of time outside together. Maybe he isn't interested anymore. With my luck, that's possible*. She had come so far from that dark, lonely place in which she had hidden herself for so long. She didn't want to go back, not now. Her thoughts were askew. She put on her earphones and blasted the Lady Saw CD that Vaughn had loaned her. She needed to drown out the sound of her thoughts clashing.

Her stop was approaching, so she put her CD player way. The clamor of her jumbled thoughts returned. Anxious to get to her room to play one of her own CDs befitting of her mood, she sprinted down the block to the side door of her house. It was the closest entry to get to her room faster. The frozen blades of grass crunched beneath her feet. Fighting back the tears welling, she struggled to see and find the right keys. She lost her grip and the keys hit the ground. "Damn it!" A voice came from the back porch. "KoKo?" For a moment she thought she was delusional from the cold. "Vaughn?" "Yes, it's me." "Oh my God! What are you doing here?" "Waiting for you." "How long have you been out here?" About an hour give or take." "Oh my God, you must be freezing! Come in the house and warm-up. We don't want you to lose another toe." She casted him a playful eye. "Ha, ha very funny." "Yeah, I thought so too." She put her books down and filled a kettle with water. "I'm going to make us some hot chocolate. Okay?" She put the kettle on the stove. When she turned around, Vaughn was right on her heels and standing within inches of her wearing a big smile. "What's with you?" From behind his back, he pulled out a huge, colorful, bouquet of flowers. "For you." "Wow, they are beautiful! Thank you. What are they for?" "Beautiful flowers for beautiful woman." She thought that was cheesy and clichéd, but the blush on her face said otherwise. She put them in a vase on the dining room table. He approached her from behind, wrapped his arms around her, and whispered in her ear. "Now will you take me to the dance?" "Vaughn, I told you I…" "Please?" He kissed her earlobe. "Please?" He kissed her neck. "Pretty please?" He kissed her shoulder. If she wasn't warm enough before, she was completely defrosted from his kisses. She could let him coax her with kisses forever, but she needed to shut the debate down. She turned around to face him. He didn't budge from her not even an inch away. She took a deep breath. “Look Vaughn, I appreciate how you’ve treated me and everything you’ve done for me the past few weeks, but are you telling me you did all of that just to go to that stupid dance?” “No, I did it because I really like you.” “Well, I like you too, but like I said, that dance is for people who love each other.” He moved even closer to her, not that there was much from left between them. “Look me in my eyes and tell me that you don’t love me not even a little bit.” She turned her face away, or at least she tried. He matched her moves from one side to the other and back keeping their eye contact unbroken. “Come on Vaughn stop it.” “Tell me and I’ll leave it alone.” She paused. “I don’t.” “You lie.” “And how would you know? You can’t tell me how I feel.” “I know because it’s in your eyes. I know because I feel the same way about you.” For a moment she thought she had stopped breathing, but it was the passionate kiss he had laid on her that was stealing her breath away. His lips were soft, full and tasted of coconut lip balm. He had slipped her just enough tongue to tease. His kisses were different from Deats’ in that they were not choppy or rushed, but more naturally slow, smooth, and rhythmic. Behind them were no heavy expectations to go further afterwards. They had no goal to reach except to become one with her lips and to deliver the physical expression of his new love for her. She felt every drop of it coursing through her veins. Her body warmed to a slow boil, awakened by desire. The temptation to let him have her was undeniable, but she couldn’t yield to it. Her body was ready, but her mind was still trapped by the shackles of her traumas. She reached her arms around his neck, leaned into his body, and moaned. Although she knew she wouldn’t go any further than the kiss, she wanted to get all that she could out of the moment. He gently removed her arms and unlocked his lips from hers. “You’re getting too excited. Not now. It will happen. Have patience darling." "Okay." She gathered her composure as best she could, but a boil takes time to cool. "I'm hungry." "Good because I have something for you to try." He pulled out a carry out bag from his book bag and opened the goods inside. "What is it?" "Curry goat and rice." "Goat? Ew!" "Just try it for me." "All right, I guess I can try." She took a tiny forkful so as to not waste much if she had to spit it out of her mouth if it wasn't tasty. To her surprise, it was delicious. "Oh my gosh, this is really good." "See, I told you." She took a second and a third much bigger forkfuls. "Now wash it down with this." He handed her a bottle of ginger beer. "Is this alcoholic?" "No, it's like root beer." She took a swig. "It kind of tastes like ginger ale. It's good." "Glad you like everything. Enjoy the rest darling. I've got to go." "No, don't leave yet. Please?" "I have to before my desire for you gets the best of me too soon." She brushed her body up against his, biting her bottom lip to fight her urge to tell him to go for it. He took a step back. "You're a bad gyal. Calm down. Think about what colors we're wearing to the dance. I'll call you when I get home." "Okay, I'll walk you to the front door. Oh, I almost forgot. Got any new CDs for me?" He handed her Bob Marley and Beenie Man. "Thank you for everything." "No problem." Before he descended down the front stairs, he turned to her and gave her an abbreviated version of the kiss they shared moments earlier. It was shorter, but still powerful. They stared at each other speaking only with their eyes, exchanging "I love you's" until he broke the silence. "Goodbye darling." "Bye Vaughn. Be careful." "I will." She watched him walk up street until the bitter cold forced her back inside the house.

Once inside, she headed straight for the food. That poor goat had to die twice because she devoured it, except for a corner that she saved for Karla to try. Normally on Fridays she would get her homework done early and lock herself in her room. But, that day, she was bursting at the seams with excitement. She needed to spill some of it onto her bestie Karla. As soon as Karla was passing her house, she scooped her up inside to dish. It was a good thing she had only saved her a corner of the food because she didn't like it. She did however enjoy the reggae music and even showed Aiko a few dance moves. Karla and Aiko discussed color and outfit choices for the dance. Red was not an option. Everyone wears red for Valentine's Day. Aiko was one to always go against the grain. She wanted to stand out. There was no reason not to. Loco Lady had nothing to lose. The final decision was black and gold, sleek and royal. Vaughn had no complaints about her choice.

On the day the dance, Aiko was a bundle of nerves. Karla and Chelsea showed up while she was getting ready for moral support, and to be a little nosy, but they both were very happy for her. They knew of the progress she had made to escape her shell. She had her hair up in a pinned curl bun and spiral curls cascading around her face. She added a gold butterfly hair clip to accent her gold dangling earrings and butterfly pendant necklace. Her dress was a floor-length, mermaid style, V-necked, black and gold chiffon capped sleeved gown with beaded pleats. It was formfitting and hugged all of her curves and accentuated her full breasts. Her outfit was finished with black four inch heel pumps and a black purse with gold beads on the front and strap. She did her own makeup which was simple and flawless. She looked and felt like a Disney Princess.

Vaughn had arrived on time. His older cousin Sean had loaned him his car to escort Aiko to the dance. Vaughn only had a provisional driver's license, but Sean trusted him. Aiko, on the other hand had reservations. She worried about being pulled over by the cops and them both getting into trouble. Regardless of her worries, she was excited about her big night with Vaughn. Nothing within her control was going to ruin it for her. As for the transportation issue, there really was no need to worry unless something negative actually happened. She covered them both with a quick prayer of protection.

He waited patiently in the living room. He was decked out in a full tuxedo with a gold necktie, cumber bun, and cufflinks. When Aiko turned the corner, his eyes lit up and his mouth dropped open. "You look beautiful." "Thank you. You look handsome yourself." "Thanks. Are you ready to go?" "Yup, let's go." Her mom stopped them in their tracks. "Let me get a few pictures first." "Aw Ma, please don't take a ton of pictures. I don't want to be late." "Oh shut up girl and come on." She snapped five pictures of Aiko and Vaughn in different poses, five of Aiko alone, three more of Aiko with Karla and Chelsea, and of course she had to get a few more with Aiko and herself. Aiko sucked her teeth annoyed by her mom's obsession with photography. Every event from backyard cookouts to weddings, she squeezed in her amateur photo shoots. On the bright side, at least this gave them a chance to practice some poses beforehand. The three of them walked Aiko and Vaughn to the door. Vaughn was perfectly chivalrous opening the doors for her and helping her into the car, being careful not to snag the tail of her dress. On the way to the dance he played her favorite reggae music from the CDs she borrowed. She kept a watchful eye out for cops, although she really didn't have to. Vaughn was an excellent driver, obeying the speed limits and maneuvering defensively. In addition, Sean had installed a radar detector on the dashboard. That combination was enough to put her at ease.

When they arrived, the professional photographer station wasn't far from the entrance, but it was far enough away to elude the crisp, cold air bullying its way through the door. Aiko decided to use one of the poses she and Vaughn did for her mom's photos. She couldn't wait to get them back to show her. Her mom was sure to feel honored by her gesture. They headed towards the main hall. Bell Biv Devoe's song "Poison" assaulted the walls with heavy bass echoing through the building. There were foil and papier-mâché hearts, arrows, and Cupid shaped decorations adorning the walls and hanging from the ceiling. They walked through the doors to the main hall. She saw Tasha and her gang standing to their left. Much to her surprise, Glenn wasn't by her side. As for the rest, some had dates and some did not. They gawked and pointed at her whispering behind cupped hands. One of them had the guts to speak loud enough for her to hear. "Would you look at that, Loco Lady has a date. Watch out for her man! She's crazy!" Instantly, Aiko came out of her shoes and charged after her. She was seeing red like a bull, and Miss Bigmouth was her target. Apparently, that girl hadn't learned from Tasha's beat down. Aiko had no problem issuing seconds. She had moved so swiftly, that the girl didn't have time to react before Aiko was right in her face. Before she had a chance to reconstruct her face, Vaughn swooped in, grabbed her from behind, and held her back. The girl's eyes were bugged out in shock of how close she came to getting punched dead in her mouth. Still, she had more to say. "You're lucky your man is here bitch!" At that point, Vaughn was just as pissed as Aiko. "Keep talking, and I'll let her go!" Afraid of eminent defeat, she finally shut her mouth. Vaughn turned her towards him to make eye contact with her. He needed to snap her out of her rage. "Calm down baby. I've got you. You are too beautiful tonight to fight. It's not worth it. Okay?" Jaws still locked in a grip and chest heaving from anger, she nodded yes. He grabbed her shoes and walked her over to an empty table. He pulled a chair close to hers. He lifted her feet to his knees and put back on her shoes. "Are you hungry baby?" "Yes I am." "Okay, I'll go fix you a plate."

There was a buffet set up with mostly finger food. Vaughn brought them both back some punch and a plateful of almost everything on the menu, including shrimp, buffalo wings, meatballs, stuffed mushrooms, and vegetables with ranch dip. As they ate, Vaughn kept the conversation going to distract her from the incident and the dirty looks that Tasha and her friends casted their way. Despite that, she was still enjoying herself, especially the music. The DJ had a musical arsenal of which she dreamed to have. If she had enough gall, she would rob him blind of it. Instead, she took mental notes of the music that she wished to add to her collection legally. He played everything from Etta James "At Last," Isley Brothers "Living for the Love of You," Luther Vandross "Here and Now," and Ralph Tresvant "Sensitivity." Vaughn decided it was time to refill their punch. For some reason, it took him longer than it did for him to fix their plates. She suspected that may be there was a long line, so she waited patiently for him to return.

He finally returned with punch in both hands and wearing a sneaky grin that he was failing miserably at trying to hide. She pointed and swirled her finger in small circles at his mouth. "What's that all about?" "What?" "That stupid grin on your face?" "Oh, nothing. Here's your punch." "Mmm hmm, I don't buy that for a minute. Anyway, thanks." "You're welcome." He began to anxiously tap his right foot. He was waiting for something. Whatever that something was, she knew it was related to that stupid grin.

"Around the Way Girl" by LL Cool J had just ended. The DJ approached the microphone. "All right everybody, this next song is dedicated to Aiko from Vaughn. He wants you to know that he loves you very much baby." Her mouth flew open so wide that her bottom lip should've hit the floor. She looked at Vaughn who was standing up again with that stupid grin on his face. "Always and Forever" by Heatwave began to play. He extended his hand out as an invitation. "May I have this dance?" To make it worse, the spotlight swung their direction and highlighted her dumbfounded, deer in headlights expression to the entire room. She accepted his invitation. The spotlight followed them to the middle of the dance floor. He wrapped his arms around her waist. She hung her arms around his neck and nestled her head onto his shoulder as they swayed to the groove of the music. Other couples joined them on the dance floor, but the spotlight remained on them, adhering to Vaughn's specific instructions. Towards the last verse of the song, he lifted her chin to meet eyes with her. He gently laid a sweet kiss on her lips. She closed her eyes to avoid seeing the reactions of her peers, but there was no way to close her ears. They funneled in the "aws," "woos," and "all right nows" from every direction of the room. The song ended, followed by cheers and an ovation from the crowd. The spotlight left as quickly as it came. The DJ kept the mood going playing Freddie Jackson "You Are My Lady." Aiko and Vaughn continued to dance. She felt so special. There was no doubt it was because of how Vaughn treated and protected her. In that moment, she admitted to herself that she was in love with him. She wouldn't dare reveal that to him yet. He already had the upper hand on the situation from the beginning. Reserving even the smallest iota of power was relevant to preserving her pride and keeping her grounded. She didn't believe in losing herself completely in a man.

When the dance was over, they headed towards the exit with their arms locked together. Once again, they passed Tasha and her gang in the doorway. They seemed to have deliberately placed themselves in a spot where they could get a good look at the happy couple. They sent jealous glances, hateful mumbles, and rolling eyes their direction. Aiko and Vaughn paid no attention to their angst. It wasn't her battle anymore, at least not alone. Vaughn had her back. Even when he is not around, she'll have her confidence with which to fight, not just her fists.

They arrived back to Aiko's house. Her mom usually would have been waiting on the porch for her, but this time she knew she would want some privacy. He walked her to the door and they sat on the enclosed front porch. It was still chilly, but warmer than outside. Her mom thought ahead enough to put a space heater out there for them. "Thank you." "For what?" "For having my back, protecting me, and sort of making me the belle of the ball tonight." "You don't have to thank me. "Well, I feel that I do." "I only did what a man is supposed to do for a woman that he cares about." "Yeah, I guess so. You must think that I'm crazy though right? You've never seen my temper until tonight" "No, I think you're brave, and your temper doesn't scare me. It means that you're passionate." "I can't scare you away can I?" "Are you trying to?" "No, I just figured that by now, you would have been, given how I am and all." "And how is that?" "Weird." He burst into laughter. "That is not true. Don't be so hard on yourself. You did what you felt you had to do. I admire that. Case closed. Okay?" "Okay." "I've got something for you." "What is it?" "Close your eyes." She closed them enough to appear to be closed, but she could still see. He was hip to it. "All the way, Aiko!" Vaughn draped a one inch thick fourteen karat gold herringbone necklace around her neck. "Oh my God Vaughn, it's beautiful! But, I can't accept this. It's too expensive." "Not for you." "I don't know what else to say." "Say you'll be my girlfriend." "Are you sure that you really want that? I'm a handful you know." He chuckled at her comment dismissively. "You think that I don't already know that? I can handle it. I've proven it already. I wouldn't ask if I didn't really want you." Aiko couldn't argue with his reasoning. Still, she had reservations. She had convinced herself that she had too much baggage to have a real, successful relationship. It would be bound to be destroyed somehow. The only way to find out was to take a chance and see what happens. "Okay. Yes Vaughn, I will be your girl." "Now that's what I wanted to hear. Come here girl." He grabbed her face with both hands and kissed her deeply, defrosting the chill on her heart and her body. Before they got overheated, he pulled away, kissed her hand, and exited. She watched him drive away through love struck eyes.

That night, the entry in her diary was "Heatwave" to commemorate the heated altercation and the fiery love that sparked her new relationship with Vaughn. She couldn't wait to tell Karla and Chelsea about the details of the night in the morning. She listened to "Always and Forever" as she replayed the night in her head. Finally, she belonged to someone who really loved and accepted her for who she is. He was everything she could ask for in a man. He was kind, loving, understanding, patient, protective, and generous. He was everything that she saw in her father that made her mother so happy and fulfilled. She never thought that she could be so lucky, which only made her wonder when the other shoe would drop.

CHAPTER 5—TRACK 4—LILY BLOSSOM

The rest of Aiko's sophomore year went relatively smoothly. Tasha and her gang had given up on targeting her. They failed miserably against Aiko's shield of confidence. True to the nature of a pack of wolves, when a prey is lost or conquered, a new victim is targeted. Aiko didn't much care as long she had peace in her world. Selfish, maybe, but high school is an environment of survival of the fittest, and their new quarry had a battle of her own to either win or lose.

It was summer again and June was passing by quickly. Besides working at the movie theater in Silver Circle mall, much of her time was spent with Vaughn. With school being out, she was still able to spend equal amounts of time with Chelsea and Karla. There were occasions where all of them, including Tony and Dante hung out together. Since Vaughn was a major part of her life, she felt that blending time with all of the people close to her was important as well. In those instances, she kept a watchful eye on Chelsea. There was no telling what she would do since Aiko actually had a boyfriend to steal.

Chelsea's birthday was on the fourth of July, and she was planning a huge house party birthday bash. Aiko helped her plan every detail. Since Chelsea's parents were wealthy, money was not an issue, so they were free to be creative. Between Chelsea's friends and cousins who were all welcomed to bring a guest, the party was sure to burst at the seams. On the day of the party, Aiko showed up early to help prepare some of the food, decorate, and gather the music. She brought some of her music collection since Chelsea's selection wasn't as large or diverse as hers. Afterwards, she went home to grab a two hour nap, leaving her ninety minutes to get ready, which was just enough time. Vaughn and Karla met her over her house. Her mom drove the three of them to Chelsea's house. Tony and Dante had no interest in going, which was fine by her. She had planned to let loose, and she didn't want them in her business. Plus, she loved Dante dearly, but he was a holier than thou, stick in the mud, snitch. He would just cramp her style anyway.

When they arrived, there were already at least twenty guests in the basement mingling and working on the two bushels of crabs. Chelsea had Luther Vandross "Power of Love" playing. Great song for background music for an adult party, but this was Chelsea's Sweet Sixteen. It was time to get the party started. It was a good thing that Aiko was the DJ. *Lawd have mercy, Chelsea is clueless.* Aiko rolled her eyes and looked at Vaughn and Karla. "I've got to fix this music y'all. Be right back." She turned on the strobe light and popped in her mixed tape of Baltimore club music into the tape deck. The Baltimore club mix "It's Time for the Percolator" was the first track. "Aw shit, that's my jam!" emerged from the crowd. Instantly, people started doing the percolator dance. Even the people anchored down eating crabs started bopping in their seats while popping Maryland crabmeat into their mouths. That was just the beginning. As thirty plus more guests arrived, Aiko kept the music flowing, changing tapes or CDs to keep the party jumping. Music from 2 Hyped Brothers & A Dog "Doo Doo Brown," Frank Ski's "There's Some Whores in this House", "Kwame's "Only You," Kriss Kross "Jump," Montell Jordan "This Is How We do It," Wreckx N' Effects " Rump Shaker," Duice "Dazzey Dukes," and Miss Tony's "How You Wanna Carry It" and " Pull Your Gunz Out", along with many others pounded the four, full sized speakers with excessive treble and base. Aiko got her groove on between sets. DJ or no DJ, she was there to have fun. Karla, being the usual wall flower, had let her guard down. She hooked up with a fourteen year old boy to dance and mingle with all night. Aiko had a connection to the crowd, instinctively sensing their mood, and playing music to suit them. She threw in some Shabba Ranks and other mainstream, cross over reggae artists that she knew they would like. She took the music old school too, playing Afrika Bombaataa "Planet Rock" and Run DMC's "It's Like That" to satisfy the nostalgic vibe from the audience. It was nostalgic for her too, reminding her of fun and humid summer days playing with her cousins on her mother's side of the family on north Lakewood Avenue.

As the 'just came to eaters' began to leave, there were mostly couples left. The atmosphere became more intimate. It made sense for her to throw in some slow jams in between. Janet Jackson "That's the Way Loves Goes," H-Town "Knockin Da Boots," and LL Cool J "I Need Love" started off the slow jam portion. All of the punch she had drank finally got to her bladder, so she put on another song long enough for her to make the trip to the bathroom and come back in time to put on another song. When she returned, she discovered that her timing was off and Chelsea was at the helm of the music station. She had queued up a list of R. Kelly songs that she knew were Aiko's current favorites to set a mood solely for her and Vaughn, though the other couples could benefit too. She wasn't sure if Vaughn was part of the plan, but her mind was made to question him about it later. R. Kelly's "Slow Dance" started to play. Just then, he came up behind her and grabbed her by the waist. Being startled, she yelped like a puppy. He chuckled at her reaction. "It's just me baby." He turned her towards him and pulled her close, pressing her hips against his and guiding her hips to the beat of the music. The other couples followed their lead. She wrapped her arms around his neck and let him pilot their groove. He leaned down putting his lips close to her ear and sang the lyrics to her. His bottom lip grazed her earlobe on some words, sending tingles down her spine. Each time, she sucked in air trying to fight her arousal. He ignored her feeble protests, and continued to send counteracting blows. She only had seconds to gather her composure before R. Kelly's "Honey Love" chimed in next, followed by "Your Body's Callin'." Vaughn, having complete control, sustained his attack on her determination to resist. His efforts in conjunction with R Kelly's "Seems Like You're Ready" delivered the proverbial knockout. Whether she wanted to admit it or not, she was ready, and he was the one.

About two hours later, the party finally came to an end. Vaughn, Aiko, Karla, and a few others stuck around to help clean up and put what was left of the food away after they packed their doggy bags. Vaughn declined a ride home from Aiko's mother because Sean was going to come get him. She had some concerns about Vaughn being at Chelsea's house without her, but she trusted him. If Chelsea made any attempt to seduce him, he would decline her offers. She was too exhausted to write an entry in her diary that night. She decided to do it in the morning after good night's rest. There was enough music stuck on repeat in her head from the party that she let her stereo have a break for the night. Music wasn't the only thing stuck in her head. As she drifted off to sleep, she replayed thoughts of her R. Kelly dance with Vaughn. It was up in air whether he had chosen her or she had chosen him. After much inconclusive deliberation with herself, the fact remained that she wanted to give him the gift of her flower. Although saving herself for her wedding night was a top priority, she rationalized her decision with the premature notion that they were so in love that they were going to get married anyway. In fact, they've had many discussions on the subject. She wasn't sure of the day or the hour, but she was sure that it was going to happen. About an hour after she fell asleep, a light tapping on her window jolted her out of her slumber. Since she was a light sleeper, it didn't take much to awaken her. She popped up like a Jack-in-the-Box, jumped out of bed, and went to the window to investigate. Fearful of what was on the other side, she carefully parted the curtain just enough to see but not be seen. She was pleasantly surprised that it was Vaughn. She sighed in relief that she wasn't in any danger, at least not the violent or deadly kind. "Vaughn what are you doing here? I thought Sean was picking you up." "He did. He came five minutes after you left. He drove me a block away from your house. We waited in the car until we thought everybody would be asleep then he dropped me off here." "Okay, but I don't understand. Why come all the way over here just to drive you ten minutes away? You could've walked." "Well, one it's late. I didn't want your mom taking me home because I would have had to wait longer to come see you, and I didn't want to hang over Chelsea's house extra time because I know that you wouldn't have been comfortable with that. So, he came to make sure I was safe and to give me a lift home just in case you didn't come to the window. As a matter fact, hold on. I've got to tell him that he can leave." He descended down the ladder and jumped the fence. She rushed to the bathroom to brush her teeth, get the crust from her eyes and fix her hair. He had already seen her in her knee length nightgown, so there was no need to change. In less than five minutes, he was back at the top of the ladder again. "Well, are you going to invite me in or not?" "Okay, but be quiet." He climbed in and sat on the edge of her bed crushing Andy bear. "Hey! Watch it! He's my favorite," she scorned in as much of a whisper as she could manage. "Sorry. So, this must be Andy bear, huh?" Which one of these other ones is named after me?" "None of them." "None? Wow, I'm hurt. I'm just going to have to fix that then." "How so?" "You'll see." "Whatever. Anyway, why didn't Sean just let you drive his car over here for the party in the first place? Wouldn't that have made your plan easier?" "Yeah, but he needs his car early in the morning." "In the morning? How long were you planning to stay?" "All night." He pulled her between his legs with his arms around her waist. He kissed her slowly and vehemently as his hands slid down to her ass, where they squeezed and massaged her cheeks coaxingly. She responded to his kisses with just as much intensity. Her mind couldn't fight it any longer because her heart and body had already conceded. She loved him and it was beyond the point of denial.

He gently guided her body onto the bed. He lay on top of her and continued kissing her, traveling to her ears and neck. She could feel the heat in his breath ripple across her skin setting her desires for him aflame. His fingertips grazed her thighs, hips, and waist as he slid her nightgown up until it was over her head and off of her completely. Her hands rested above her head where they parted with her nightgown. His fingers ran down her arms as he kissed his way down to her breasts. She moaned as his hot, wet tongue swirled and flicked on her nipples. She had never been kissed there before. The sensation hardened her nipples and sent shooting twinges of pleasure through her body, awakening all of her parts. Parts of her body that she wouldn't even have thought could react began to scream for attention. Even her skin seemed more alive, reacting to the very slightest brush of air around her. Her pussy began to throb, begging to be touched. In tuned to her body's needs, he moved his tongue to her navel, giving it only seconds of attention before he buried his face into her beseeching pussy. She choked on air as titillation flowed through her body. Arching her back and grabbing the headboard, she managed to keep her moans at a controlled pitch so as to avoid giving them away. She could hear him moaning too, indulging in the taste of her. As she reached the brink of an orgasm, her body tensed. Her breathing became more rapid and sporadic causing her to hyperventilate. Squirming about, she tried to break free. She suspected that it was going to be grander than the tiny orgasms she'd had masturbating. She wasn't sure if she could handle it. Determined to get her to finish, he pinned her legs down so that she couldn't move, holding her prisoner to her surmised explosion, but conjecture it was not. It was everything she suspected and more. She squeezed her eyes shut as a tidal wave of pleasure zipped through her body from her head crashing down into her pussy, propelling a forceful eruption of her nectar. She opened her eyes to see dots of red, blue, yellow, and green speckled across the dark room. Vaughn emerged from her center, wiping her juices from his cheek onto her inner thigh. He lay between her legs. He gave her a sweet and gentle kiss. “Are you okay?” Still recovering, she was unable to speak, but nodded yes. He was patient, allowing her as much time as she needed. When she finally spoke, it was simply “Wow!” “Are you ready for the rest?” Her breathing then under control, she whispered, “Yes, I think so.”

He looked her directly into her eyes searching for any doubt. “Are you sure?” “Yes, I’m sure. Is it going to hurt?” “Maybe just a little, but, I’ll be gentle. I promise.” “Okay.” He undressed then placed himself on his knees between her legs. He paused, remaining still and statuesque. She figured he needed a moment to prepare. That gave her time to inspect his body. He was naturally muscular. It wouldn’t take much effort for him to chisel it to absolute refinement. The moonlight peeking through the curtains cascaded over him like a shear, luminescent cloth, highlighting his bulging veins and silky cocoa skin. His dick was thick, long, and fully erect. It was as smooth, brown, and flawless as the rest of his skin, with a perfectly bulbous shaped head. She couldn’t have imagined or painted a more beautiful dick than what was about to be inside of her and stealing her innocence like a thief in the night. “We’re going to take this slow. Okay?” “Okay.” He eased his way in inch by inch, pausing in between to check on her comfort level. She felt a sharp pinch. “Ow, Ow, Ow!” “I’m sorry baby. This is the painful part. Do you want me to stop?” “Just for a minute, please.” “Okay.” He gently kissed her for head then looked into her eyes. He knew that she was nervous, but in her eyes he could see her determination to go through with it. He kissed her eyes, nose, cheeks, and lips. At her lips is where he stayed, kissing her fervently to put her anxiety to rest. When she seemed relaxed, he gave one more, slow, forceful push. She shrieked at the shock and pain that passed quickly. There was residual stinging at first. As he slowly stroked, the pain subsided, being replaced by pleasure. He wrapped his arms behind her knees and lifted her legs higher, giving him straight path to her G spot. He hit the bull's-eye repeatedly. She put her hands in the small of his back guiding him to go deeper. Her hips grinded back matching his strokes blow for blow. The passion between them heated the room like a wet sauna. The moonlight accentuated the beads of sweat on their bodies giving them the appearance of tiny crystals. He released her legs, grabbed her hands and kissed her, as he continued to stroke in a circular motion, inducing a flood of more of her nectar onto his dick. As he reached his climax, his pace quickened. He withdrew with only a second to spare, avoiding making a deposit, and spilling life onto her sheets. For minutes they lay still, catching their breath. Vaughn broke the silence. "Are you okay?" "Yeah, I'm fine. I'm more than fine. A little sore though." "I'm sorry baby." "There's nothing to apologize for. It comes with the territory." "I know. It doesn't mean that I won't feel somewhat bad about it." "That's because you're so sweet." She gave him a peck on his right cheek. "I'm thirsty. Are you thirsty?" "Very." "Okay, I'll get us some water." "And a warm rag please so that I can clean up?" "Sure, okay." She crept out of her room and tiptoed to the kitchen. She knew where every creaky floorboard was and avoided them skillfully. She fixed a huge cup of ice water, enough for them to share and still quench their thirsts. Two cups would have been too obvious. If anyone ran into her holding two cups heading to her bedroom, she would have been busted for sure. She stopped by the bathroom to prepare a warm washcloth and to grab a dry towel for the wet spot on her bed. She made it back to her room undetected. Vaughn cleaned up himself and her sheets, giving her time to quench her thirst first. He placed the dry towel over the wet spot and motioned for her to lie down first. He gulped down some water then lay next to her. He handed her the cup. “Here, you can have the rest. I’m good now.” “Thank you.” His consideration made her smile. She swallowed down the rest the water then crunched on an ice cube. She put the cup down then snuggled in his arms, lying on his chest. They remained silent until they fell asleep.

Vaughn snuck out of her window around six thirty AM after he gave her a long goodbye kiss. He didn’t want to leave just as much a she wanted him to stay, but he had to go before everyone awakened. She watched him descend down the ladder, tucked it under the deck, and jumped the fence once again. She left the window open letting the bird songs be her soundtrack for the morning. She was too tired to do anything that day. Not to mention, she had just fornicated a few hours prior and her guilt was growing into a nagging pang. She was not yet ready to face God about her transgression. She decided to fake a tummy ache so that her family would give her some space. They had plans to go out that day anyway. Given all that had happened in the last twenty-four hours, being alone with her thoughts would be ideal, and an empty house was just what she needed. She grabbed her diary to get caught up on everything. She had trouble deciding what code word she wanted to use honor that night. There was no way she could log any detail about her midnight rendezvous with Vaughn. She chewed on the top of her Bic pen mindlessly as she forced her drowsy brain to think. Now that she was no longer a virgin, she was on step two of her journey of blossoming into a woman. The first step was getting her period. “Hmm, blossom,” she said aloud to herself. She began to create a trail that linked to that word. *Flowers blossom. Lilies are my favorite flowers. I’m blossoming into a woman. That’s it! Lily blossom.* She jotted the title down at the top of the page. She filled the rest of the page with doodles and drawings of lilies, musical notes, fireworks, and other objects using them as coded pictographs about the entire night. She tilted her head and smiled to herself proudly at her work. She tucked her diary away and grabbed a quick shower.

As she was getting dressed, she noticed a fresh, quarter sized bloodstain on her throwback Strawberry Shortcake bed sheets. There was no question where it came from. She ripped them off, pretreated the stain, and tossed them into the washing machine. Although she could easily explain it is a period stain, she still didn’t want to leave any evidence. Her mom wasn’t just an amateur photographer, she was also a super sleuth. Add to that maternal instinct and it equaled being busted for certain. She wouldn’t put it past her mom to check the wastebasket for used sanitary napkins. Aiko was decent at lying, but not so much with keeping her lie and her face on the same page. Her mom would see through it like a pane of glass. Whether her mom would call her out on a lie or not was a tool that she used at her discretion. It depended on whether she wanted to catch her then, or catch her later. After the sheets were done, she remade the bed, popped eight hundred milligrams of Tylenol for her aches, and took a nap. Chelsea and Karla would not be told just yet. She wanted to keep it to herself for a while. *Besides, they don't have to know everything.*

CHAPTER 6—TRACK 4—THE CHORUS

About three weeks had passed. Aiko and Vaughn had gotten in a few more sessions. At the rate they were going, they were bound to beat her training wheels off in record time. She had managed to get up enough courage to tell her mom that she was sexually active. Her mom immediately took her to gynecologist and put her on birth control pills. Much to her surprise, her mom handled it rather well, keeping her cool and being nothing but supportive and understanding. They both agreed that the secret should be kept from her father.

Her sixteenth birthday was approaching in another three weeks. She didn't care to have a big birthday bash. Chelsea's party was enough for her. Instead, she wanted to go out to breakfast with her family. That would leave her free to spend the rest of her special day any way that she chose. She would most likely spend some time with Karla and Chelsea, then the rest of her day with Vaughn.

The morning of her birthday, she awoke to an overwhelming sense of excitement. She was finally sixteen, an age that she had looked forward to since she was thirteen. She felt more like an adult. She had a great family, great friends, and a loving boyfriend. Her life at that point couldn't be better. The shell that she kept herself in seven months ago was becoming a distant memory. Going back there was something she never wanted to do, if she could help it. The way things were going, she may never have to, but she took comfort in knowing that it is there if she ever needed it.

After a long, full body stretch, and a quick chat with God thanking him for another year, she got out of bed and opened her drapes. The day greeted her with bright, glimmering, golden rays of sunshine, light, warm breezes, and uplifting bird song. If this was an indication of how her day was going to be, then she had a perfect day ahead. She could only hope that the moment was not the pinnacle, leaving the rest of the day to go downhill. The only way to find out was to get the day started. She selected her birthday ensemble and placed it on her bed. She took an exceptionally long shower. The water felt too good to rush. Plus, she needed time to think about the hairstyle and makeup that will complement her outfit. She was the first to arise that morning, so there would be ample time for the hot water to rebuild before anyone else took their turn. It was a perfect day to listen to her Spyro Gyra CD again while she waited for everyone to get ready. Before long, her mom tapped on her door. "Ko, are you ready to go?" Instead of replying, she just opened the door with a big smile. "Happy birthday!" Her mom planted a big kiss on her right cheek and squeezed her until she was about to pop. "Thanks Ma." Her dad was standing in line for his turn. After Tony and Dante issued her birthday licks, her parents directed everyone to leave out the front door instead of the side basement door they usually used. Aiko thought that was strange, but didn't read into it too much. When she got outside, there was a shiny, black 1990 Volkswagen Jetta with a big red bow on the hood parked in front of the house. Her father yelled, "Catch!" and tossed a set of keys at her almost hitting her eyes. "What's this?" "Car keys dummy." Tony said playfully. "That's right. Your car keys." her dad added. "Oh my God! Are you for real?" Her mom chimed in, "Yes! Now, are you going to drive or what?" "Oh my gosh! Thanks mom and dad! I love it!" They all squeezed in for a group hug. "We love you." "I love y'all too. Come on, let's go!" They jumped into the car. She made sure that everyone put on their seatbelts. She adjusted her seat and mirrors and started the engine. The engine came to life with a smooth hum. It was a sound just to soothing as music to her ears. She put the radio on 95.5 because that station played an even mix of contemporary and classic rhythm and blues. That way all of her passengers would be appeased as far as music selections for the ride. They arrived around brunch time at their destination of Denny's. It was shortly after the restaurant chain had been accused of being racist. Aiko wasn't very comfortable eating there for that reason. She wanted to say something before they went inside. "Daddy, you know this restaurant is racist, right? Should we just go to the IHOP across the street?" "That's all the more reason to eat here. They're scared. We'll get the royal treatment." *More like get our asses kissed royally.* "So we're eating here to get our butts kissed and loogie seasoned omelets, compliments of the chef? Great." Her mom was irritated. "Ew Koko. Nobody wants to hear that before they eat!" "Well, at least the heat from the grill will kill the germs." Her dad laughed at his comment, only amusing himself with his dry humor. Aiko could see where the conversation was headed. It had to be put to rest. “Let’s go inside. We’ll just pray over our food extra hard, okay.”

As they suspected, they were greeted in a phony, overly saccharine manner. It was borderline offensive. Actually, it was offensive. It was the equivalent of being served a pile of feces on a plate sprinkle d with a ton of powdered sugar and a cherry on top. It made her think of the civil rights sit-ins at Woolworths in the 1960s. She could only imagine the excitement, fear, and hesitation those brave African-Americans felt, and under more dangerous and risky circumstances. Surely, they could manage to handle this, especially under a less volatile environment. Despite her reservations, she decided that they should stick this one out in honor of those who made history for the freedoms of posterity.

She ordered a steak, medium rare with over easy eggs, and a side of hash browns. While they were eating, her dad announced that he had one more birthday present for her, but she had to wait until after their meal. *What could possibly be better than the car?* After the meal was paid for, her mom, Tony and Dante excused themselves from the table and headed outside. “I’ve asked everyone to leave so that we could be alone for a few minutes.” “Okay.” “You are my firstborn, my love child. Today you turned sixteen. You’re becoming a woman. Although it’s very hard for me to accept that you’re growing up, I’m very proud of you and who you’ve become. You have made every sacrifice worth it. I have no doubt that you will be an exceptional, successful woman one day.” He reached into his pocket and pulled out a diamond embossed gold watch in a black, velvet lined case. On the back was an engraving that read “To the most beautiful, intelligent and talented daughter a father could ask for. My love for you will stand the test of time and beyond. Love, Dad." "It's beautiful! Oh Daddy, thank you. I love you so much!" She jumped out of her seat, wrapped her arms around his neck, and kissed him on the cheek. "You're welcome. I love you too. Come on. We've got people waiting for us." He left a generous tip for the waitress and escorted her outside, but they didn't walk straight to the car, nor were her mom and her brother and cousin anywhere to be seen. He headed towards the Skateland behind the Denny's. "Why are we here?" "You'll see." They went inside to a group of about eighty people made up of cousins, aunts, uncles, friends and their parents, and a couple of plus ones. Of course Karla, Chelsea and Vaughn were there. Amongst them all she found her mom, Tony and Dante. Her parents rented the entire rink for a four hour private party. The owner shared a birthday with Aiko, so she was willing to make a special exception for her.

Everyone had gotten their skates except for Aiko and her dad. Once they did, the party began. The first song was "Humpty Dance" by Digital Underground. Mostly the teenagers jumped in the rink for that song. The adults mingled on the side. Back then, adults knew how to let a kid party be and stay a kid party. Next was Sir Mix-A-Lot "Baby Got Back" followed by Naughty By Nature "Hip Hop Hooray." Aiko, Vaughn, Chelsea, and Karla skated non-stop through them. The songs were just too good, and they were having too much fun. Aiko figured that her parents had clued the DJ in on her wide array of musical tastes. All they had to do was look through her CDs and cassette tapes. A Tribe Called Quest's "Bonita Applebum" started. They decided that it was time to take a break and refuel with some pizza slices while the music took a mellow turn. In the eatery was a table full of presents and cards. The cards and CD shaped gifts excited her the most. All she wanted was CD's, and if the cards had money in them, she would save half and buy CD's and beauty items with the rest. She could put her next paycheck in the bank too since she wouldn't need to use it to get caught up on her music collection. After they ate, they talked for a while to let the food settle before hitting the rink again. Aiko filled them in on her experience at Denny's with the staff, and showed off her new watch. She also promised to give them a ride in her new car. Vaughn excused himself to go to the bathroom. Chelsea used his absence as an opportunity to get the scoop on Aiko's relationship. "So, how's it going?" "It's going good." "It's been six months since you guys made it official right?" "Yeah." "There's something I've been dying to ask you." "What?" "Have you given it up to him yet?" Aiko met eyes with Karla. She had changed her mind and decided to disclose the loss of her virginity to her the week before, but wanted to leave Chelsea in the dark of it for as long as she could. She looked at Chelsea again. "I don't want to talk about that right now. Not here." "Aw, come on!" "No." "Fine. Okay. I already know that you did anyway." For a split second, it crossed her mind that Karla may have dished the dirt. "What makes you say that?" "Because no man is going to stick around for six months and ain't hit it yet. That's why. Plus, there's been something different about you. I couldn't put my finger on it at first then I figured it out." Aiko was annoyed, but she kept her voice calm and her words sharp. "Since you think you know already, then why the fuck did you bother to ask?" Before Chelsea could respond, Karla spotted Vaughn returning and cleared her throat to signal them to cut the conversation short. "Did ya'll have fun talking about me?" "Your name didn't even come up baby." Technically, that was the truth.

Chelsea added her two cents. “Yeah, we’ve got more interesting things to talk about other than you.” “Yeah right. Are you ladies ready to skate again?” “Yup! Let’s go babe.” She grabbed Vaughn’s hand, then licked her tongue at Chelsea, who responded with an ‘oh please’ expression. Salt-N-Pepa’s “Shoop” was playing when they hit the rink. About three dozen voices were rapping the lyrics, including Aiko, Karla and Chelsea. Another dozen or so voices joined them when Onyx’s “Slam” played. The DJ spoke into the microphone. “Alright everybody, the next skate is for couples only. This song is dedicated to Aiko from Vaughn. He says happy birthday and he loves you.” *Oh Lord, I should have known he would do that again*. Skate breaks skid across the floor as singles exited the rink and couples of all ages joined them. He grabbed her hand, and she smiled at him thanking him for the embarrassing, but sweet dedication. Tony Terry’s “When I’m With You” set the mood. That was one of her favorite songs. It was clear that Vaughn paid attention when she talked. He swung behind her and wrapped his arms around her waist. They skated in unison, swaying side to side to the groove. Some couples skated holding hands. Others skated facing each other with one skating backwards. She watched her parents skate hand in hand smiling at each other with so much love in their eyes. Her heart swelled. She couldn’t help but feel happy and smile too. Their love was definitely one of a kind and everlasting. Sade’s “No Ordinary Love” played next, and it was the perfect song for her parents because it was one of their favorites.

After Mary J. Blige “Sweet Thing,” the DJ came to the microphone again. “Okay folks this song is dedicated to the birthday girl from Mom and Dad. They say happy birthday Koko and they love you." *Oh my goodness, he's got my parents doing it now.* Vaughn let go of her, kissed her on the cheek, and moved off of the floor as her parents each grabbed a hand. "You're a Big Girl Now" by The Stylistics delivered her parents' message to her. As she skated with them, she saw Vaughn smiling at them from the side of the rink. She could see in his eyes that he wanted with her what her parents had with each other. The DJ spoke in his best great and powerful voice. "Enough of the sap, it's time to jam! Are ya'll ready?" The crowd replied, "Yeah!" "I can't hear you!" "Yeah!" "It's time for all skate. I need all the old heads and old souls on the floor! Let's go!" Michael Jackson's "Don't Stop" belted through the speakers. The mirror ball flickered as if it were made to work for that song. The DJ created a disco atmosphere with the colorful strobe lights. The adults, including her parents, showed off their fancy skating skills busting moves they used to do back in the day. Her parents had told her many stories of how they used to get down at Shake N' Bake skate rink. Finally, she could see them in action. They were amazing and so were the other adults. They popped and locked, spun around, dipped, kicked, jumped and split all while keeping to the beat. Parliament "Flashlight" and Funkadelic "One Nation Under A Groove" played back to back. Last up for the disco all skate was Earth Wind & Fire "September." It was a beautiful sight to behold of generations closing the gap through music.

After the ladies only skate, everyone took a break to sing happy birthday and eat some cake. There were too many gifts to open there, so she thanked everyone for the gifts and cards and announced that she would be opening them at home. There was only an hour left. The DJ called an all skate again, and started the last hour with Zhane "Hey Mr. DJ." Next was Tag Team's

"Whoomp There It Is" followed by Digable Planets "Rebirth of Slick." After about six more songs that included Vaughan Mason & Crew "Bounce, Rock, Skate, Roll" the DJ called for last skate and blasted "Summertime" by DJ Jazzy Jeff & The Fresh Prince. Everyone that wasn't too tired or injured jumped into the rink for the final skate. Aiko stopped skating before the song ended so that she didn't have to wait in a long line for skate returns, and to get a jump start on packing her gifts into her trunk. She couldn't fit everything into her trunk, so Vaughn put some in the trunk of his new 1993 Lexus 300 his cousin Sean had bought for him. Vaughn told her that Sean made good money running a store, but something told her that there was more to it. She had an idea, but never bothered to ask. It was none of her business. If it was what she suspected, she would rather remain in the dark about it.

As they were packing up the trunks, Kody, the youngest of Karla's four older brothers, ran up behind Aiko. He was the same age as Tony. He tapped her on her shoulder. Out of breath, he managed to huff out, "Hey Koko!" "Hey Kody. What's up?" "I have something for you." "Okay." "Here." He handed her two unlabeled CD's. "What's on these?" "They're CD's of the music from your party." "Wow, thanks Kody!" Karla added, "It was all his idea too." "Not really. We came up with the idea together, sort of. She mentioned that you love music." "He's just being modest. He bought the blank CD's and talked to the DJ and everything." He smiled big and bashfully. "Well yeah, but still, I wouldn't have come up with it if it weren't for your suggestion Karla."Aiko glanced over at Vaughn, who by that time, had jealous steam coming out of his ears. She cleared her throat. "Kody, have you met my boyfriend Vaughn?" "I can't say that I have. How are you doing man? Pleased to meet you." He extended his hand for a shake. Vaughn reciprocated. "Likewise." He squeezed his hand as a warning. Kody pulled back his hand shaking off the pain. "Nice grip." Aiko's mom walked up. "Hey Ko, the rest of us are going to catch a ride with your Aunt Pauline, so if you want to give Karla and Chelsea a ride home in your car you can." "Okay, cool. Thanks Ma." She turned to Vaughn. "Babe, I'm going to drop Chelsea off. Meet me back at my house?" " Sure thing baby." He leaned down to kiss her while his eyes were locked on Kody. If he didn't get the message from the squeeze, he wanted to make sure that Kody knew that Aiko was his. Kody glared back at him unintimidated. Chelsea, as usual, didn't miss anything. She picked up on what was going on and mumbled to Karla, "Awkward." Karla rolled her eyes. "Okay ladies, let's go in my new ride!" Vaughn waited until Kody walked away before he got into his car, then he watched Aiko pull off.

On the ride to Chelsea's house, Aiko popped in one of the CD's Kody had given her. Chelsea, staying true to form, wasn't going to let what she had just seen rest. "So, Aiko, Kody is fine. Don't you think?" Aiko and Karla met eyes in the front seat. They had a way of communicating with their eyes, knowing exactly what each other was thinking without saying a word. "Let it go Chelsea." "I'm just saying he's good looking, and I think he likes you too. Come on Karla, back me up here. He's your brother. You should know." "He's just a nice guy, Chelsea. That's it. You're reading into it too much. Like you said, he's my brother. I should know." "Oh, so the wallflower has a snippy side! Who would've thought? Make it the last time you direct it at me!" "Chelsea!" "It's okay Ko. I've got this." She turned around in her seat to face Chelsea. "Snippy does not begin to describe what I'm capable of. It's just the tip of the iceberg. Don't think for one minute that because I'm quiet most of the time, that I'm a pushover. I only tolerate you for my girl Aiko. If not for her, I would have been cut your ass up one side and down the other. Take that any way you want. I can back it up either way. If you want to find out for sure, come at me like that again and see what happens. Now that you know where I'm coming from, we can make this trio thing work for KoKo." Aiko had nothing to add. Karla had shut it down just fine by herself. She peeked in the rear view mirror at Chelsea, who was clearly shocked and embarrassed. She stared out the window mumbling to herself. She didn't feel sorry for her. She had it coming. She did feel bad for not warning her not to push Karla too far, not that it would have made a difference. Chelsea was always going to be Chelsea. Seeing for herself always had more of an impact with her. She turned up the music to drown out her mumbling and to lighten the mood. She and Karla sang along while Chelsea moped for the rest of the journey home. When they got to her house, she jumped out of the car as if her life depended on it. "Happy birthday Aiko. Bye. Bye Karla." "See ya around Chelz." Karla gave her a sinister smile in an attempt to make her feel uneasy. Aiko hollered out of the window, "Ima call you later. Okay." "Okay. Bye." They watched her go inside before they left. "I don't know why you put up with her Ko. She's selfish and a troublemaker." Aiko sighed. "I know, but I've known her for so long. I guess I'm just used to it. You lit into her good though, baby thug." They laughed out loud. "Yeah, well she took me there." "I know." "You mad?" "Nope, she needed that. She'll be a'ight. She's too self-absorbed to worry about it for long." "Ain't that the truth." "At the risk of getting my own tongue lashing, do you think that there's some truth to what she said about your brother?" "Maybe, but I don't see it. He's the kindest of all my brothers. He's thoughtful, and because you're my friend, he wanted to do something nice for you. That's all. Plus, he's seeing somebody. And, let me remind you, so are you." "Oh, no, no, no, it's not like that. I just asked because Vaughn was acting funny." "You mean jealous. Yeah, I saw that. That's normal. I wasn't worried about that. I would have been more concerned for you if he didn't. At least you know that he cares." "True, but I still want to apologize to Kody for the way Vaughn acted the next time I see him." "Okay."

When they arrived in Aiko's house, Vaughn was unloading the last of her gifts from his trunk. It didn't take long for the three of them to empty hers. Her parents wished her one more happy birthday, hugged her, then retired to their room. Tony and Dante played video games down the basement. Karla and Vaughn helped Aiko open her gifts. Amongst them were ten CDs and two hundred dollars. That only left her with five more CDs from her list to buy. Adding a few more CDs to her list was an option with the extra birthday money. After the gifts were opened and the pile of wrapping paper was cleared, Karla went home to leave the two love birds alone. They sat in the loveseat watching TV. "God, my feet hurt so bad." "Gimme your feet babe. I'll rub them for you." She put her feet onto his lap. "Thanks. That feels good. So, where's my gift?" "This is it." "What is?" "The foot rub." "What? Get serious." "I'm for real." Aiko poked her bottom lip out. "I'm sorry baby. I was broke." "Oh, see, now I know you're lying because you're never broke." He started laughing. "Okay okay, you've got me. It's on your bed." "Seriously?" "Yeah, go look." Aiko didn't let sore feet stop her from rushing off to her room. Vaughn was right behind her, but he took his time. She flipped the light switch. On the bed was a big, plush, chocolate bear holding a small black jewelry case and propped up right next to Andy bear. In comparison, Andy bear looked small, worn and raggedy. She grabbed the case. Inside was a pair of one carat diamond earrings in fourteen karat gold settings. Vaughn watched her excitement as the reflection of the diamonds flickered in her eyes. “They’re beautiful Vaughn! Thank you! Now I would believe you if you said you were broke.” “Nah, I’m good. It’s nothing to worry about. Like you said, I’m never broke. Press the bear’s right paw.” She did. Vaughn’s voice projected from the bear’s belly with “I love you Aiko.” “Aw, that’s so sweet baby! I love it, and I love you too!” She wrapped her arms around his neck and kissed him passionately. “You’re the best.” “No, you are. So, what is his name going to be?” “Hmm, I think I’ll call him Kody bear.” “What?” Hell naw! You’re not to name my gift after that nigga!” “Calm down, I was just kidding.” “Well it’s not funny to me. I don’t trust him around you.” “Yeah, I could tell. I’m sorry baby. I didn’t think that it would make you that upset. No more jokes about it, okay. Kissy? Please?” He kissed her, but she could tell he was still heated. “Come on, I want to finish my foot rub.” “Okay, just for little while because I’m getting hungry again. I want to take you to dinner.”

After a fifteen minute foot rub, they headed out to Phillips Seafood downtown. Vaughn drove his car. She was too tired to drive. She didn’t like driving downtown either. The congestion made her nervous, especially on busy summer Saturday nights. Downtown was infamous for jaywalkers, hitchhikers, hookers, crazies, and distracted tourists, all for which she didn’t want to catch an involuntary manslaughter charge. Vaughn was skillful and calm behind the wheel, and a perfect gentleman towards her. Because it was Saturday, the restaurant was packed, so they had a forty-five minute wait. They killed the time talking in the foyer. Her feet were pounding, and the pain was beginning to show on her face. Vaughn hated to see her suffer. He kindly asked a man who was sitting next to his girlfriend to give up his seat for her. The man had no problem obliging. He and Vaughn engaged in a friendly discussion about sports, while Aiko and his girlfriend gossiped about current events. Before long, they were seated. Aiko ordered surf and turf and Vaughn ordered a lobster platter. They sampled each other's food while she told him about Karla putting Chelsea in her place. He was more than amused by the story. Chelsea wasn't his cup of tea either. He felt that Karla was a much better friend for Aiko, and gained a new found respect her. They spent about ninety minutes at the restaurant before she was ready to go home. It had been a very exciting, but exhausting day.

He dropped her back home around eight thirty and kissed her goodnight. She wasn't too tired to sample her new CD's while she wrote in her diary. Her sixteenth birthday was a magnificent one, and she wanted to record every detail that night before anything had a chance to escape her memory. After an hour, she fell asleep with the lights on and the CD player still playing . A familiar light tap on her window awakened her from a deep sleep. Disoriented, she jumped up and reached for her alarm clock to put it on snooze. The tap repeated. Finally, she regained her senses and realized where the tap was coming from. There was no time to freshen up before he saw her. She opened the window, embarrassed of how she must have looked. "Vaughn, what are you doing back here?" "I wanted to spend the last moments of your birthday with you." "What time is it?" "Quarter past eleven." "I dozed off. You just woke me up. I must look a mess." "No, you look beautiful baby." "Um, I doubt it, but thanks. I'm going to freshen up. Be right back."

When she returned, he had dimmed the lights and put on 'Secret Garden" by Quincy Jones, Barry White, and three other male artists. He had made himself comfortable on her bed, lying on his back, holding the bear he had given her on his abdomen. She joined him. "Whatcha doin'?" "I'm playing with Vaughnie bear." "Vaughnie bear? I can't say that I'm surprised. I can change that I if I want to." "But you won't." "Yeah, you're right. I won't. But, for your information, I was going to name him that anyway." She stuck her tongue out at him teasingly. "You're so cute." "Thanks, I know. And you have a very jealous side mister." She poked his chest playfully. " It's only over you. The thought of someone else taking you from me makes me crazy." "You have nothing to worry about. I'm all yours." "Prove it." She moved Vaughnie bear to the side and straddled him. She leaned down to give him a hot, wet kiss. "Who's here with me in my bed right now?" "Me." "I wouldn't have it any other way. I promise." She kissed him again then removed her nightgown over her head. Underneath, she was bare naked. She had removed her under garments when she went to the bathroom hoping to make love. She unbuckled his belt and slowly and enticingly undressed him. He had never before seen this seductive side of her. He loved it because it meant that she was becoming comfortable with her sexuality. He also hated it because it could mean that one day he wouldn't be enough for her. But, the anticipation of making love to her consumed him, and any disconcerting fears dissipated as she disrobed him of his boxers, exposing his rock hard dick. She did not hesitate to engulf his shaft into her mouth.

Up until then, she had been much too nervous to perform oral sex on him, despite his generosity with her. But, he had challenged her to prove her loyalty. It was her chance to prove his importance to her by overcoming her apprehension about blow jobs. He guided her head with his hands. Contrary to what she had previously thought, she actually enjoyed it. He tasted sweet at first then salty as his pre-cum leaked. She was instantly addicted. He had a flavor that she could crave. He tapped her shoulder, motioning her to come up for air. She wiped his juices from her mouth and straddled him again. He grabbed her hips as she grinded on him. She put everything into pleasing her man. Any doubt that he had, she wanted to erase. He threw his head back and moaned, rolling his eyes in pleasure. She was in complete control and she loved it. The more he moaned, the more she winded her hips. If making love could kill, she wanted him to beg for his life. As he reached his climax, he tried to control the rhythm of her hips. She moved his hands away. She wasn't willing to let him take over. He inched his hands back to her hips. She grabbed his hands and pinned them down above his shoulders forcing him to take what she was giving. A wave of excitement rushed through them both. It was now a race to the finish line. She already knew that she would win. He always made sure that she finished first. She collapsed against his chest. She lay on him limply as she caught her breath. He kissed her forehead and stroked her hair. Out of the blue, he started singing the song he dedicated to her at the party. She couldn't help but laugh at him. That song was more of his 'C' list type of music, but he knew that she loved it. Apparently it was sticking to him as well. She looked up at him. "Where did that come from?" "Shh, hush now. I'm singing to you. Just enjoy it." She reached over to take a sip of ice water that she had sitting by the bed since before she fell asleep. She had emptied a whole ice tray into a huge cup, so it was still cold and the ice barely melted. She offered him some. He took a few gulps then continued to sing until they fell asleep.

CHAPTER 7 –TRACK 5— 209°F

Vaughn slipped out of the bedroom before dawn. That morning everyone had slept in late to recover from the party. Her parents especially rediscovered that roller skating, although fun, can be exercise in disguise. Over breakfast, they all griped about sore parts and bruises, and poked fun at who had the most embarrassing and comedic falls in the rink. After breakfast, she called Chelsea to check on her. Like she suspected, she had bounced back from her verbal beating from Karla, at least she made her voice seem so. She made plans to hang with her in a couple of days then made an excuse to get off of the phone. She wanted to avoid the conversation going anywhere near the subjects of Karla or Kody.

Later that day, she decided to go to the corner store for some snacks. She gathered a list from everyone then called Karla to accompany her. “Hey girl, what’s up?” “Hey Karls. Whatcha doin'?" "Nothing, just sitting here sore as hell. Why?" "I was going to the corner store. Wanna come?" "No, but can you bring me something? I would offer to pay you back, but I'm sure you can afford it Miss Money Bags." Aiko laughed. "Damn, you are just gonna hustle me out of my money like that? A'ight, what do you want gangsta?" "Some salt n vinegar potato chips, sunflower seeds, an onion pickle, and some lemonheads. Oh, and butter crunch cookies and a rocket popsicle." "Damn, are you going to eat all of that?" "No, the cookies and popsicle are for Kody." "Oh, well tell him that I ain't paying for shit for him." She was only kidding, but before she could say "psych", Karla had already told Kody in the background. She heard his voice get closer to the phone. "Gimme the phone. Hello?" "Hi Kody." "Hey. So, you ain't treating me?" "Nope." "Why?" "Cuz." "Cuz what?" "Just cuz." He sucked his teeth. "See, why you gotta be acting funny?" "Cuz I wanna be." "Aw, come on Koko, just this one time, please? I'll make it up to you." "A'ight, I've got you this time." "Cool, thanks. And don't bring my rocket back all melted either!" "Excuse me?" "Psych, I'm just playing girl." "Mmm hmm." "Okay, here's Karla." "Hello." "Girl, your brother is a trip." "I know. I heard his crazy ass." "Alright, I'm going to the store. See you in about fifteen minutes." "Are you going to hang down here for a while?" "Yup." "Okay cool, and thanks."

She asked Tony to wait on the porch for her so that she can drop off their snacks and head straight to Karla's house. She didn't want Kody's rocket to melt either, especially since she was spending her money on it, not to mention the mess it would make. On her way out of the store, there was a little girl trying to open the heavy door by herself. "Hi sweetie. Where's your mommy?" A voice from around the corner summoned the little girl. "Bria!" Aiko answered, "She's right here." The woman finally cut the corner. She was Aiko's complexion, and five foot ten with a perfect hour glass figure. She looked down to the little girl. "Hi Bria. That's a pretty name. I'm Aiko." "Hi Aiko." "How old are you?" "Four." She held up four pudgy little fingers. "Wow, you're smart." She turned to the woman accompanying Bria. "Your daughter is so cute." "Oh, she's not my daughter. I babysit her for my neighbor. I'm Cierra, by the way." "Nice to meet you. You must live around here, right?" "Yes, down the street in those apartments." "I live one street over from here." She leaned down to Bria. "It was nice meeting you too Bria. I hope to see you again." She pinched her chubby cheek. "Well, I do hair out of my apartment. Here's my card. Call me. I'll give you a discount." "Okay. I will. Thanks." Bria waved her tiny hand, and they exchanged quick goodbyes. Aiko sprinted home, handed Tony a bag, then headed down to Karla's house.

Karla was waiting on the front porch. Kody was standing behind the screen door. "It's about time, shorty doo wop." "Whatever, it didn't take that long." Karla chimed into the debate. "Well, how fast do you think a smurf can walk Kody?" "Oh, so ya'll got jokes. Okay. Well, how about I use my smurf legs to walk back home with ya'll snacks." "Or, we could jack you for all of the snacks right now and pluck your little ass home like a cigarette butt." "Go to hell with gasoline drawls on Kody!" Karla laughed herself to tears. Aiko reached to open the screen door, but Kody pulled on the knob to keep it shut. "Kody, stop playing and open the door!" Karla switched sides. "Yeah, it's hot out here." "I thought witches melted with water not heat." "Ha, ha, ha. Ima let you slide with that, but mommy won't. Ma!" Their mother hollered from a distance, "Kody, leave them girls alone and open the door!" He released the door knob. Aiko entered first, pushing past him with her left shoulder mumbling, "You get on my damn nerves." "Whatever, bet you got my snacks though." She rolled her eyes. Karla walked by and playfully bucked at him as if to hit him. He gave it right back to her. "Ma! Kody…" "Shh, shut up! Ma, ain't nobody doing nothing to her." Only their mother's voice came from the other room again. "Don't make me come in there!" "See what you did Karla!" "Whatever. That's what you get. Come on Ko, let's go down the basement." "Hold up. Let me get my snacks first." Aiko opened the bag and handed him his snacks. "Damn, my rocket is soft." Aiko and Karla looked at each other, reading each other's minds again. Aiko snidely remarked, "I bet it is." They burst into laughter at Kody's expense. "I have no problem in that department. I'll show you right now," He tugged on the elastic of his sweatpants. "Ew Kody! Koko, let's go downstairs please, before he does something gross." "Why? He ain't gonna really do nothing." "Wanna bet?" A crooked, devious smile spread across his face. "Koko, for real, he'll do it, and I don't want to see that." "So, go downstairs. I'll be there in a minute." She gave Kody an "I dare you" stare directly into his eyes. "Well, I'm waiting." He put his rocket into the freezer, walked over to her, leaned into her ear, and whispered, "You're not ready yet." To add shock factor, he swirled his tongue on the outer curves of her ear. The soft air and wet sensation sent tickly tinges down her right leg. His attempt to stun her was successful, but she couldn't let him know that. She jerked her head way. Fuck you, Kody!" " Ha, ha, you promise?" Karla's gross out meter cracked. "Ew! Come on Aiko, let's go!"

They set up camp for long afternoon of snacking and watching music videos and movies. An awkward silence loomed over them. They were both trying to avoid revisiting the discussion as to whether Chelsea had a point, especially after Kody's recent display. Finally, Aiko broke the silence. "So, Kody was showing off." "Yeah, he's trippin', but I don't know why he's trippin' that hard today." "Do you think that Chelsea was right?" "Hell no! And I don't want to talk about that anymore." "Okay, okay. I won't say anything else about it. Just chill out." After about an hour, Kody came down to join them with his refrozen popsicle. "Kody, get out! This is girl's night." "Oh, let him stay Karla. We can handle him. There's two of us and one of him." Karla was not pleased, and didn't bite her tongue about it. "Not a good idea." "It'll be fine. Stop worrying." "Okay, but don't say that I didn't warn you." "By the way Karls, mom wants you." "For what?" "I don't know. Go see." "Be right back Ko. And make sure that he doesn't eat my chips please." "Okay. I've got you."

As soon as she left, Kody tried to grab her chips. Aiko anticipated his move, and put them under her blouse. "Like that's going to stop me." "No, but my foot to your groin would. You know I would do it too." "Yeah, I heard about your crazy ass." He sat back down on the couch across from the recliner in which she was anchored with her left leg draped over the armrest. He peeled the wrapper from his rocket and began eating it slowly, making exaggerated slurping and sucking sounds to entice her. She scoffed at him. "Pervert." "Wanna find out how much?" "Hell no!" That wasn't the answer he wanted to hear. He stuck his hand down his sweatpants to grope himself. "I need some pussy." "I can't help you with that. I have a boyfriend." "Does your boyfriend have a tongue like this?" Not only was his tongue thick and wide, but he was able to extend it down until it touched his chin. Her eyes bugged out, but only for second until she caught herself. Any reaction of hers would be his signal to persist. She was at an absolute loss for words. As much as she loved Vaughn, there was no denying that she was also attracted to Kody. His blunt advances were the polar opposite of Vaughn's patient and romantic approach, yet she was intrigued and turned on by them. Clearly, he wanted her imagination to run wild with what he could do to her with his freakishly long tongue. "You like it?" "I can't say that I do." "You would if you felt it." "That cannot be proven considering that will never happen."

Kody polished off the rest of his popsicle with one slide along the length of the stick. He got on his knees and crawled towards her crotch face first like a lion on the prowl. Because her leg was already hanging over the armchair, it was almost as if she were a willing prey. Burying his face into her center, he began searching for her sweet spot through her capris with his tongue. Once he found it, he firmly pressed and flicked his tongue up against it. He had her pinned to the chair. She pushed his head away, but that didn't stop him. He just came back at her. There was not much else she could do; at least that's what she kept telling herself. She could have delivered harder blows to his head, but she didn't want to hurt him. She could have screamed bloody murder, but she would have to deal with Karla's "I told you so's." It wasn't that it didn't feel good, but she also felt awkward and guilty about it. Finally, she decided to say something. "Kody, that's enough. Please stop." He honored her request, but not before he gave her a long, sensuous tongue kiss. His tongue filled her mouth completely, but it wasn't invasive. Quite the opposite, he was controlled, gentle, and neat. She had imagined that kissing someone with a tongue that large would be like kissing a sloppy, slobbery dog. They both could hear Karla heading towards the basement, but he wanted to steal every second until the last to kiss her. He pulled away, looked into her eyes, smiled, and sat down on the couch just in the nick of time. Karla had no idea what had just happened. Aiko and Kody kept their composures at normal levels leaving their lustful encounter undetected. The three of them spent the rest of the afternoon having fun together snacking, watching movies, and cracking jokes. Some of the sexual tension between her and Kody had been relieved. She knew that this could be only the first time of many encounters between them, but that wasn't her main concern. Now, she knew what to expect. At the very least, she could avoid him as much as possible, but it was the times that she couldn't avoid that worried her. She wasn't afraid of what he would do. It was that she didn't trust herself to keep him from going too far.

The summer had gone just as quickly as it came. Aiko was enthusiastic about her junior year, if for nothing else, because it meant only one more year to go before graduating and getting the hell away from a school full of females. That's a recipe for drama. She was still kicking herself for jumping into the pot. Top school or not, if given a do over, she would have chosen Westbrook instead. Karla had a new venture of her own too. She was a freshman at Burton high school, the same as Chelsea. Chelsea showed her around and introduced her to upperclassman. She had some friends from middle school that were attending there as well. Aiko had no doubt that she would settle in comfortably in no time. Should any problems arise, she was confident that Karla could hold her own.

After about two weeks, Aiko and Vaughn picked up where they left off with their after school bus rides. The summer break allowed for last year's squabbles to settle, though the tension was still hovering. Aiko expected as much. On the days Vaughn had to work and wasn't on the bus with her, she felt it the most. In those instances, she would head straight to Cierra's house. Over the last few months, they had become well acquainted. Since she was older, it was comforting to have a nonrelated, mature woman's perspective on things. Aiko met her son Kenny, her mom Shirley, and her boyfriend Craig. Cierra kept Aiko's hair tight every two weeks like clockwork. She would do it free of charge since Aiko bought her own products, but Aiko insisted on paying. Cierra would only charge her twenty dollars. At times, Aiko's mother would come and get her hair done for the same price, though she would tip her another twenty dollars. Although Cierra's skills were worth it, she felt that her mom's gratuitous gesture was overkill. Plain and simple her mom was too nice, which would prove to be her Achilles' heel one day. It was also why she was very protective of her mother. Where her mom lacked thick skin, it was Aiko's job to be her mother's callous. Her mother was only ten years older than Cierra. Admittedly, she was jealous over a potential bond being forged between them that could overshadow the ones she had with the both of them. Nevertheless, she remained quiet about her concerns. Nothing was threatening relationships with either of them, so there was no need to stir the pot. What she needed to focus on was balancing her time more now that she added a new close friend to the mix. Cierra was cool, and she had known Chelsea since almost forever, but Karla was her best friend and road dog. It was important that she got the most attention, other than Vaughn. She could kill two birds with one stone by spending time with both Karla and Vaughn simultaneously. That was something she couldn't do with most of her female friends. She just didn't trust females like that. Cierra may have been comfortable flaunting her man around other attractive women, but Aiko was dead set against having her around Vaughn. Aiko was definitely prettier, but Cierra was good looking and had a body that could make even the gayest man look twice. She couldn't take a chance. She didn't consider herself insecure. In her mind, she was being smart and calculative about how she handled mixing the people in her life. The way she viewed it, she was the sun and her friends were the planets rotating around her in perfect harmony. It was her job to make sure none of them fell out of orbit and collided. Cierra never had to worry about her crossing the line with Craig. That would be a violation of one of her golden rules. Plus, he wasn't her type anyway, not that it would make a difference if he was. However, she had seen him look at her funny. She couldn't put her finger on it, but she sensed that he felt some kind of way about her. Determining whether it was a good or bad way was the challenge. He would always have a strange look on his face when she and Cierra were laughing together. He seemed uncomfortable whenever Cierra had to lean in front of her to shape up her hairline, or when her breasts grazed Aiko's back as she curled her hair, or even when Aiko played footsie with her to make fun of her light bulb shaped big toe. Light grazing of body parts is natural between stylists and client, and almost unavoidable. It was innocent as far as she was concerned, but Craig's curled up lip and flared nostrils expressed his jealousy and disgust over their close encounters. He tried to play it off with a smile and phony chuckles, and he treated her very nice outside of that, but dude seriously needed an enema to discard the stick from his ass. He also needed to get a life. There was no reason to be up in women's faces during beauty time. Most men make themselves scarce with their own friends, or at least find a sporting event on television to watch in another room. She was tempted to say something to Cierra, but some women take offense when you pull them up about their man. Her friendship with her was still fairly new. She didn't want to disturb the water, so she avoided broaching the subject.

In a blink of an eye, October came. It was a big month at school Aiko. First, there was junior week. Each day had a theme like pajama day and crazy hat day. Friday of that week was junior day. A big ceremony was held in the auditorium. All front rows were reserved for juniors who decorated the seats with a sea of purple and gold attire. The junior committee couldn't have picked better colors for their class. They chose the two most royal colors to represent the class of nineteen ninety-five. During the ceremony, it was announced that it was their turn to follow the tradition of picking a freshman to be there honorary little sister. There were no rules as to how many little sisters they could have as long as they had time to mentor them. Their class mascot was revealed as well. From the ceiling in front of the stage dropped a huge picture of Mickey Mouse decked out in the full purple and gold tuxedo. The cheers from the crowd, particularly the two hundred excited, screeching, female, pubescent voices of the guests of honor juniors rang through the auditorium like sirens triple their number. That ovation was matched with the principal announced that the juniors could leave school at noon to enjoy the rest of their day. The ceremony commenced with the juniors exiting first up the middle aisles towards the back doors while Crystal Waters "Gypsy Woman" blasted through the speakers. Aiko had lunch with her mom afterwards then she lounged on the back deck with shades on, basking in the warm Indian summer sun, while her CD player projected beautiful musical notes that surfed on the gentle waves of the breeze. No one disturbed her. Everyone knew not to bother her when she was in the zone.

Two weeks later was homecoming. Aiko wasn't impressed about it, but she participated because she wanted to get every drop of experience that she could from her junior year to avoid any regrets. Spirit week kicked off with a pep rally on the outdoor track and field. Cheerleaders dressed in the class colors of each class performed dance routines and the marching band played their rendition of the latest songs. She was seated next to two girls that she didn't know which was fine by her as long as Tasha and her gang were far away on the other side of the bleachers. The girl to the right of her was quiet and seemed very shy, though she kept cutting her eyes over at Aiko sneaking peaks at everything she did. That made her uncomfortable and annoyed to say the least. Aiko had passed her many times in the hallway, but never paid her any attention. It was very clear that she came from money. Her modest demeanor didn't quite seem to match her classy style of dress. She expected her to dress more homely. The girl took the liberty of introducing herself. She had a Jamaican accent like Vaughn. "Hi, I'm Sophia" "Hi Sophia. I'm Aiko." "Are you a junior?" "Yes. Why?" "Well, I know this may sound strange, but I'm a freshman and I haven't found a big sister yet. I was wondering if you could be mine?" "Well I have two little sisters already. I'm curious though. Why me? You don't know me." "I hope that this doesn't sound creepy, but I've been watching you, amongst others, and you stood out. I think we would be a perfect fit." "No, that doesn't sound creepy. That sounds *very* creepy! Stalk much? I hope *that* didn't sound like I'm put off." She made sure her voice delivered her words with sharp sarcasm, but it bounced off of Sophia's determination like a rubber ball. "See, that's what I admire about you. You're feisty, and no one ever sees it coming. Plus, you're very pretty, at the top of your class grade wise, and I must say that I love the way you dress." "Flattery? Yeah, that's original," she replied, spitting more sarcasm and rolling her eyes. "I tell you what. Give me one month, two months tops. If it's still not working for you, then you can walk away, and I'll continue my search. No harm, no foul. Is it a deal?" She extended her hand out, holding it steady, waiting for Aiko to seal the deal. Aiko hesitated to buy time to hash it out in her head. *It would only be for a month or two. The worst that could happen is that it goes sour and we part ways.* That would be of no significant consequence to her. She didn't plan to invest herself in it any way. Her inner circle was tight, leaving very little room for many new members. She had no problem permanently evicting anyone she saw fit. "Deal." She gave Sophia a firm, squeezing, admonishing handshake, staring her directly into her eyes looking for a glimpse of her soul. There was something sinister that instantly filled her with regret, but she had already shook hands on it. She could only hope that this could be the one time her instincts proved fallible.

CHAPTER 8—TRACK 6-- 210°F

The week after that was Halloween. Aiko already had her costume picked out, and it was top-secret. Not even Karla could get it out of her. She wouldn't even give her a hint. The concept, materials, and execution of it were original. Keeping her mouth shut was the only way to guarantee it stayed that way. Only her mom and dad knew she was going as Carrie from the movie of the same name. Her costume was from the prom scene. She had a white dress and a blonde wing drenched in fake blood. Suspended above her head would be a bucket with red metallic streamers hanging out of it to represent the pouring pig's blood. Her dad, being an engineer, helped her build a contraption that she would wear under her dress that would come up through the back of the dress at the neckline to hold up the bucket. For the bucket, she spray-painted a plastic one silver because a metal one would be too heavy. Halloween day, her parents allowed her to drive to school. The costume would have drawn too much unwanted attention on the bus. School was different. She was used to it there. Usually, she was only allowed to drive to and from work, to the store, or to the places nearby within ten miles or less. Because her school was across town, and she had only obtained a provisional license, how far she could drive unattended was restricted.

She ran into Sophia. She was not someone she wanted to see first thing in the morning. “Hey Aiko! Great costume!” “Hi Sophie. Thanks. Who are you supposed to be, little Miss Moffat?” “No silly, Little Bo Peep.” “Oh, cute.” “Are you going to enter the costume contest?” “I hadn’t thought about it. Why?” “You should. You might even win. Plus, the winners get a giant tub of candy and a one hundred dollar gift card.” “I’ll think about it.” The first bell rang. “Well, talk to you later.” “Okay, bye. Think about what I said.” Aiko didn’t want to reply to that. “Bye Sophie.”

Throughout the day, her costume received mixed reception from onlookers, from on the fence, to big fans, down to the completely appalled, all of which didn’t matter to her one way or another. As far as she was concerned, it was just more of the same. It was no different than how people treated her when she was just herself, which is why she chose that costume. Much like Carrie, she was ostracized at school, and much like Carrie, she fought back. The costume contest took place in a brief assembly in the auditorium during the last period. There was entertainment from the band, dance club, and the thespian club put on a short horror play. After which, the principal announced that the contest was to begin. She began to read off the names of the contestants. Each person who was called had come down to stand in front of the stage. “Aiko Pierre.” “What the fuck?” she said loud enough for a few people around her to hear. Embarrassed, she was not. She couldn't care less if anyone heard her. She was puzzled because she decided not to enter the contest. A few fans of her costume sitting around her nudged her to get up and join the rest at the stage. As she headed towards the stage, she spotted Sophia in the audience smiling, clapping, and cheering for her. It became clear that it should have been "who the fuck" that she spoke aloud. Sophia was the fuck who had entered her name into the contest, and she was the fuck who she would have a stern conversation with later. She wound up winning first place for the most original category. She walked away with ten pounds of candy and a one hundred dollar gift card she could use at any store in Silver Circle mall. That was perfect because she worked at the mall, so she could shop during her breaks.

After dismissal, Sophia caught up to her at the locker. She threw her arms around her neck hugging her. Aiko stiffened her body and pulled away. "What's wrong?" "Don't get me wrong Sophie, I'm glad that I won, but don't ever go behind my back like that again." "I'm sorry." "It's okay, water under the bridge, just don't do it again. Okay?" "Okay, but can I ask why you shut yourself out so much? You're awesome. You shouldn't be ashamed to show it." "I'm not!" she shouted slamming her locker door. Sophia appeared to be hurt and surprised at Aiko's reaction. "Sophie, I didn't mean to yell. I'm sorry. It's just complicated, okay. I'll explain it to you one day. Now is not the time." That seemed to appease her. "Listen, since you entered me into the contest, I feel it's only fair that I give you some candy and treat you to something on the gift card tomorrow. I'll pick you up." "I would love that!" "Open your book bag." Sophia did what she was told. Aiko scooped about two pounds of candy into it. "Thanks big sis!" "You're welcome. Be ready tomorrow." "Sure thing!"

The next day, Aiko kept her promise. She used her free employee passes to the movies at Silver Circle mall to see "Pulp Fiction", and treated her to a manicure and lunch on the gift card. That left her with seventy dollars she could spend on herself. She decided to save that for another day when she was alone. She had a good time with Sophie, and by good time meaning she rolled her eyes a few less times than she usually did when Sophie was around. There was still something about Sophie that just didn't add up.

In the weeks that followed, Sophia became clingier. Aiko began to regret ever taking her out to the mall. Somehow, Sophie equated that moment as them becoming friends. Aiko did not consider her a friend yet, after all, they were still on a trial basis. Sophia followed her around, watched her reapply her makeup in the bathroom, and even tried to dress like her. On some occasions, she would sit in the back of the bus watching her, but it seemed that it was only on the days that Vaughn wasn't there. She lived on the same side of town as their school, so there was no need for her to catch that bus. She made the excuse that she was visiting family on Aiko's side of town, but she didn't buy that. To say that she was annoying was an understatement. She had become like an itchy, irritating rash or ugly growth on her skin that wouldn't go away. Aiko valued her individuality. She didn't consider it to be flattering or a compliment to have a copycat stalker. It was time to cut her loose. The question was how. She didn't want to hurt her feelings, and Lord knows she didn't need another enemy. Until she figured it out, she would try to avoid her, though that would be hard. She knew her schedule, and which restrooms were her favorites. So, she would have to change things up a bit. She could switch restrooms and take the staircases on the opposite end of the building from her classes. It was more of a hike, but it was pertinent to her plan.

The next weekend, Vaughn picked her up for a date. He wanted to accompany her while she used the rest of her gift card, but he made her promise not to use any of it on him. He felt that she should enjoy the rest of it to herself. She agreed. After all, he couldn't stop her from buying something for her mom or Karla. He would be none the wiser. It was all girly stuff to him. On the ride to the mall, Aiko was lost in her thoughts and didn't say very much. "What's wrong baby?" "Nothing, just thinking." "About what?" "Don't worry about it. I'll figure it out." He hated when she shut him out, and instantly became infuriated. "How many times have I asked you not to do that?" "Do what?" "Shut down on me." "It's not important." He pulled over on the shoulder and put the car into park. "Tell me now Aiko!" "Fine. It's Sophia, my little sister at school. She's mimicking me and it's really plucking my nerves. I need to drop her, posthaste. I just don't want to hurt her feelings." He sucked his teeth, put the car in drive and merged back into traffic. "Is that all? You should feel flattered." "Well, first, I told you that it wasn't important. So, now you've just wasted your time and mine discussing it. And, second, for you to say that I should be flattered just tells me that you don't know me as well as I thought you did, because that shit doesn't flatter me. It annoys me." "You're right baby, my mistake. So who is this girl anyway?" Aiko began describing her. Vaughn interrupted her. "Wait, you mean Sophie? She's dark skinned, about five foot six, and dresses fancy?" "Yeah, how did you know?" "A few weeks ago, she started coming into my cousin's store while I was working. I think she likes me too." "Oh my God, please don't say that! No wonder she's clinging to me! She's trying to get to you and throw me off her game. That little bitch has crossed the line!" "Chill out. She might not even know that I'm your boyfriend. It could be just a coincidence. Besides, it's just a puppy crush. I don't pay her any attention. I love you." "I don't see how she couldn't know. Your name is doodled on my notebook. She wants everything else I have. Who's to say that she wouldn't want you too. I want you to stay away from her." He laughed out loud. "Look at my baby being all jealous." "It's not funny Vaughn." "I know. It's just that you're so cute when you're jealous." "Vaughn, I'm serious. Please stay away from her." "Okay baby, I will. I promise, but I can't stop her from coming into the store." "Well then, someone else can wait on her when she does, as long as it's not you." "Okay baby, I'll see what I can do." "Thank you." She made up her mind that she was going to meet Sophie at her locker on Monday to straighten this out.

Monday couldn't arrive fast enough for her, but finally, it did. She gave a lot of thought over the weekend as to what she would say, but nothing seemed to fit. Either it was too harsh, or not harsh enough. The best way to approach it was to just speak from the heart. Sophia greeted her in the usual perky way. Aiko responded neutrally as she always had. Sophie had on a similar outfit that Aiko had worn last Wednesday, adding fuel to the fire. Instantly, she detected that Aiko had something on her mind. "Hey, what's wrong?" "You." "Me? Why?" "For starters, you smother me and you cramp my style. While I should take it as a compliment that you dress like me, wear your hair like me and put your makeup on like me, I don't, at all. I find it annoying. Create your own unique style. Be a leader, not a follower. Do you understand?" Sophie's face was expressionless. "Okay. Is that it?" "No. There's the matter of you crushing on my boyfriend. In a word, stop! That is so disrespectful to me. There's a whole school full of boys right next door. Take your pick. Just leave mine alone!" She slammed her locker. "Fine." "Fine? That's all that you have to say? Wouldn't an apology be appropriate?" That sinister look that Aiko saw on her face on the first day they met resurfaced. "I only apologize when I'm sorry." "Oh, is that how you want to carry it?" "I just did." "You're barking up the wrong tree little girl. I'm not the one to cross, as I'm sure you've heard." "Then, bitch it's on!" Aiko threw her body up against Sophie, pinning her against the locker, mindful not to throw the first punch. She just wanted to make her point for now. She got in her face close enough that they could kiss. It didn't take long for them to draw an audience. Someone in the crowd shouted, "Loco Lady is about to fight ya'll!" "That's right. I am a bitch, a crazy one. You're about to find out just how much." Aiko conjured up something dark and sinister of her own. It was part of an automatic defense mechanism that she had developed. At times, she seemed zapped out. It felt almost as if she was watching herself from outside of her body. She looked Sophie directly into her eyes so that she could see and feel the pure, unadulterated hatred she now had for her. "I am going to take great pleasure in tasting your blood on my cold, metal shank after I gut you like a fish with it." She pulled over her right lapel to expose a seven inch, jagged edged knife. Tears of fear started streaming down Sophie's face. Aiko spread and evil, self-satisfied smile across her face, mocking Sophie's terror. "Now what was that you said? 'Bitch, it's on?' " She moved even closer to her. "Don't tempt me, bitch!" As she turned away to head to homeroom, she spotted a few bystanders who felt sorry for Sophie consoling her. The crowd around them parted like the Red Sea to let Aiko pass, but their jumbled whispers still surrounded her. Her "Loco Lady" label wasn't going away anytime soon after this. She played into it to scare Sophie. Even if it resulted in a suspension, she had no regrets. If it came down to it, she would cut Sophie, but only under a life or death, self-defense situation, not over her identity, or a high school boyfriend. As long as Sophie thought otherwise, then her point was made.

To her surprise, she was never called to the office, not that she was fretting over it. She figured that those who witnessed it were too scared to rat her out for fear of her vengeful wrath. Word about it had traveled fast. As rumors go, the details of the event morphed into something different by the time it circled back to her. She didn't feel the need to correct it, unless someone asked her directly. As far as everyone else, they could believe what they wanted. She had already embraced her infamy a long time ago. No matter of debate over details would be worth her time.

She couldn't wait to get home to call Vaughn. By the time she did, Sophie had already gone to his job crying to him. Once again, she begged for him not to give her the time of day, especially since she made her intentions to steal him from her very clear. Vaughn didn't understand why she was so upset. As far as he was concerned, his reassurance to her that he only had eyes for her should have been enough. His nonchalant attitude infuriated her. This was a situation that she needed to talk to Cierra about in person.

Cierra was more than happy to be her shoulder. She opened the door before Aiko had a chance to ring the doorbell. "Hey Ko! Come on in." "Hi. Thanks." "Did you walk or drive?" "I drove. Why?" "Because it's going to be dark when you leave. If you were walking, I didn't want you walking alone." "Oh." "I'm making some cocoa. Want some?" "Yeah, sure. I'm going to say hi to Kenny real quick." Kenny was in his room watching cartoons. "Hi Kenny!" "Hi Miss Koko! Are you getting your hair done today?" "No, not tonight. I'm just having girl talk with your mom. How are you doing in school?" "Good. I like all of my teachers this year." "That's awesome! Keep it up." "Okay, I will."

Cierra had the cocoa with marshmallows already hot and ready on the kitchen table. "Okay, so tell me what happened." Aiko took a sip of cocoa first. "Whoa! This is strong, still good, but strong. What did you put in this?" "Peppermint Schnapps. I felt you needed something to relax you. Sip slowly. I have somebody bringing us some KFC. I don't want you drinking on an empty stomach." "Thanks, I think?" Cierra laughed. "You'll be fine. I won't let you overdo it. Now, come on talk." Aiko shared every single, sordid detail from the moment she met Sophia until that day's event, including Vaughn's reaction. Cierra listened attentively. Aiko could sense that the gears were turning in her head. After she finished her emotional tale, Cierra, who was lost in her thoughts, waited a few minutes before she spoke. Aiko sipped her cocoa and waited patiently for her response. Finally, she spoke. "I need to put on the radio." She turned on 95.5 FM, which was playing slow jams. Luther Vandross "Wait For Love" was playing. She returned to the kitchen, plopped into the chair then took a deep breath. "Alright, here it is. I'm not worried about Sophia. You can handle her. It's Vaughn that concerns me. He is not respecting your feelings. He's just blowing you off and doing what he wants. Might I add, he's making you look like a fool to Sophia, which is why she is so comfortable challenging you and running to him afterwards. I have a feeling that there's more to the story that he's not telling you, Koko. Let things cool down then you should talk to him in person. You need to look him in his eyes when he's talking to you. Even if his mouth lies, his eyes will tell you the truth." "Yeah, you are so right. I was thinking that, but it's nice to get confirmation from someone else." "This may be hard for you to hear, but I think you should start to date other guys, older guys. You're mature for your age, and you're going to always have to deal with crap like this from teenage boys. Plus, you're too young to be committed. You should be having fun, playing the field, and exploring. You have to face the fact that you may have to let Vaughn go." "That's easier said than done." "Why?" "Because he's my first." Cierra sucked her teeth. "Oh girl, please. Dicks come a dime a dozen. He may be your first, but I can promise you that he won't be your last. And, as you go, you'll also learn that he damn sure ain't the best either. You'll get over him real quick. The best way to get over a man is to get under a new one." The doorbell rang. "And there's no time like the present." Cierra got up to answer the door. She took a long time to come back to the kitchen, about ten minutes or so. Aiko could hear her talking to someone in the hallway, but she couldn't make out what they were saying. When she finally came back, a man was with her holding the bucket of KFC they were expecting. He wasn't very tall for a man, about five foot nine, light-skinned with dark, wavy hair, and marble black eyes. He had a gold tooth that peaked when he flashed his gorgeous smile at her, but it didn't distract her much from his ripped body, which he underscored with light blue jeans and a black, long sleeve muscle shirt. "Aiko, this is my friend Clay. He lives in the next court. Clay, this is Aiko." "Hi Clay." He sat the bucket of chicken and sides onto the kitchen table. "Hey mama, it's nice to meet you." He kissed the back of her hand, while staring into her eyes. Aiko heard the clink of the lock on her floodgates detach. His charm and sexual vibe were strong and magnetic. It was no mistake that Cierra called him over. She knew what he was about, probably firsthand. She also knew that he was just what the doctor ordered for a broken heart. Cierra started to make a plate for Kenny to eat in his room so that they could have some privacy. Clay, being a gentleman, offered to fix Aiko's plate. Cierra walked back into the kitchen just in time to see him placing the plate in front of her. She smiled to herself, confident that her plan was working. She fixed her plate and sat down with them. "Aiko, I hope you don't mind, but I filled Clay in on your situation." "Not at all, I welcome a man's perspective." Clay took his cue to speak. Well, I think that the advice Cierra gave you was spot on. A man who is really all about his woman would bend over backwards for her, defend and protect her honor, and shun anyone whom she feels is a threat, regardless of whether he agrees. You're beautiful. From what Cierra tells me, you are intelligent, talented, ambitious and loving. Any man would be lucky to have you. If dumbass, pardon my French, can't see that and do whatever it takes to make you happy, then he doesn't deserve you. You've got the whole package mama. Trust me, if you let him go, you won't be single for long." "Well, I wish I could believe that last part. Haven't you heard? I've got issues. They call me 'Loco Lady' at school." "That makes you all the more irresistible. You're strong. You fight back. And, if you've got to fake the funk of crazy to survive, then so be it. That just adds resourceful to your resume." Aiko couldn't help but smile. This dude really understood her. It was obvious that this situation wasn't the only story about her that Cierra shared with him. That didn't upset her. If it weren't for her sharing with him, his advice probably wouldn't have been as sound.

Cierra polished off the rest of her food, then excused herself from the table to check on Kenny, leaving Clay and Aiko alone. He cleaned up behind the three of them. Mary J Blige "I Don't Want To Do Anything" came on the radio. Clay pulled her to her feet. "Dance with me mama." He walked her into the living room, where only the moonlight and the glow of the buttons on the stereo illuminated the room, creating a romantic atmosphere. He held her close. Their bodies touched as they moved, but not in a sexual manner. It was sweet and tender. He kept his hands above her waist. He stroked her hair and grazed her ear and cheek with his lips. He made her feel like a desirable woman again. They danced to two more songs before he escorted her to the loveseat. She tried to avoid taking control of the conversation, or dumping any of her personal problems on him. She let him lead the conversation, allowing her to shut down internally. After a while, he caught on to what she was doing. “Why do you do that?” “Do what?” “Hide.” “What do you mean? I’m right here.” She knew exactly what he meant, but she played dumb anyway. “I mean you hide inside yourself.” “It’s safe for me there.” “There’s nothing to be afraid of with me.” “No offense, but we’ve just met. There’s no way for me to know that for sure just yet.” “I understand, but sometimes you’ve got to let go in freefall mama. Life’s more exciting that way. You’ll cause yourself to miss out on a lot being afraid.” “I’m not afraid.” “Then what are you?” “I’m careful and calculating.” “I get it. Less chances of you getting hurt or making a mistake. But what if you calculate and make a mistake anyway?” “Then at least I know I weighed my options first instead of making a move blindly. The other way around, I would always beat myself up for not thinking first.” “Okay. That makes sense. But I still think you should loosen up a little.” “Opinions are like assholes, everyone has one.” “Except Coneheads.” “Coneheads? You mean from the movie?” “Yup.” That broke the tension and made her laugh. “You have a beautiful smile. You glow from the inside out.” “Thank you.” “You’re welcome mama. Can I ask you something?” “Sure.” “Can I kiss you?” “Why ask me? Just do it Mr. ‘live for the moment’.” “Because I wanted to give you time to calculate Miss ‘checks and balances’.” “Somebody else with jokes. I swear I..." Before she could finish, he leaned in and kissed her. The kiss wasn't bad at all, but it was lacking the spark that being in love brings. The rest of her body didn't need that spark. It reacted just as naturally as if it were Vaughn she was kissing. Clay lifted her blouse slightly, running his hands along her lower abdomen. She had a belly pouch that she was extremely self-conscious about and didn't let anyone, not even Vaughn touch. "Stop, please." "Why?" "Because I just don't like being touched there." "There's nothing wrong with your body. You think you're fat don't you?" "Me and the rest of the world." "I personally think you're sexy as hell. I don't like skin and bones." Aiko forced a tiny smile. "Thanks." "I don't get you. How can someone as fierce as you, who can make someone cry from the words you speak be so uncomfortable in your own skin?" She shrugged her shoulders. "I'm complicated I guess." "I think you should try to get over your insecurities about this." "I'll try." "Then let me touch you there." She took a deep breath. "Okay." He began caressing her belly. Her body tensed up and she wasn't even sure if she was breathing anymore. "Clay, this is embarrassing." "Shh, just relax." Evidently, he was enjoying himself because his breathing was quivering, and a bulge grew in his pants along his right thigh. "Seriously? This turns you on?" He kissed her again "Mmm hmm." She kissed him back and let him touch her anywhere he wanted as long as it was through her clothes. He had a point. She could only imagine how much more strong and fierce she would be if she had more confidence outside of her anger and defensiveness. She closed her eyes and cleared her mind of Vaughn, Sophie, and everything and enjoyed the moment. She heard movement coming from the hallway. Through her cracked eyelids she saw Cierra peeking around the corner watching them, but she didn't let it stop her. It actually turned her on to have a voyeur. In her mind, Cierra was touching herself behind the wall. Clay stopped abruptly. "What's wrong?" "I'm getting too excited." "Meaning?" "Meaning, I don't want to go too far. Not tonight. You're hurting. You're not ready." "Okay. You're right. Cierra, you can come out now." Cierra surfaced from behind the wall. "So, did ya'll have fun?" Aiko sent Cierra a look that read 'as if you didn't already know.' "Yes, I look forward to spending more time with her." "Me too. Thanks for everything." "You're welcome mama. See you next time." He gave her a good bye kiss. It was one for her to remember him. "Cierra, I'll catch you later." "Alright, bye Clay. I'll call you in a few." He gave Cierra a nod then left the apartment. "I suppose you already have all of the details?" "Yup. You needed that." "Thanks. By the way, where's Craig?" "After you called, I told him not to come over tonight." "Oh, I'm sorry about that." "Don't worry about it. He's been getting on my nerves lately anyway. He's too insecure and clingy. Come on, I'll walk you to your car." Cierra sat in the car with her and talked while it warmed up. "You know, Clay was right about a lot of things. One thing he was definitely right about is that you are beautiful." "Well, thanks Cierra." she replied bashfully. "You're welcome. Good night." Cierra leaned in and kissed her directly on the lips and held it for a few seconds. "Call me when you get home." Aiko, still stunned, just nodded. When she got home, she debated whether to call her, but she did anyway. There was no answer. As much as she dreaded the conversation that would have taken place, being left with unanswered questions was much worse. It leaves her to draw conclusions, which she was sure to spend too much time mulling over. Very little issues crossed her mind as just a fleeting thought. If she felt something was worth it, she would put it through her mental strainer. For the moment, she would just shove the kiss that Cierra gave her into the back of her mind. There are more pressing issues for which she needed to use her brainpower.

CHAPTER 9--TRACK 7-- 211°F

A few weeks had passed and Aiko never had a chance to talk to Cierra about that kiss, though they did have short conversations about other subjects. She was still battling Vaughn about Sophie. Since their encounter, Sophie took her advice in the worst way, except for finding her own man. She found a new dark, evil, Gothic look. It was not that Aiko thought the look was bad, but it was just that in her opinion the Gothic look worked for some people if they did it right. It wasn't for Sophie. It was the message that Sophie was trying to send to her that bothered her mostly. She was pretending to be as sadistic as her by reflecting it in her dark apparel as a way to intimidate her. Her effort was weak at best. It would take more than black clothes to put fear in her heart. It was another sad attempt to mimic her. Sophie also formed herself a posse. Some of the members were gained from Sophie's sympathetic bystanders from their public altercation. Clearly, Sophie was the ringleader.

The day before Thanksgiving break, students were filled with excitement for the long weekend. The shrieky chatter of gleeful girls echoed through the halls, interrupted only by the metal clanking of lockers slamming, and the loud vibrations of the morning bell. Besides lunch time, homeroom was the only other period Aiko could zone out and go into herself at school. After the morning announcements, she did just that as she sketched in her notebook. A soft voice from her left snapped her out of it. “Nice sketch.” “Thanks.” “What is it? “Don’t know yet.” “Oh, okay. I get it. Let it take form as you go along.” Aiko was not thrilled to be talking at the moment. “Yup, that’s the plan.” “I’m Kendra, by the way. I have a few classes with you. I usually sit in the back though, so you might not know who I am.” “You’re right. I don’t.” This conversation seemed very familiar to the first one she had with Sophie. That automatically put her on guard “Well, I know you.” “I’m sure.” Her indignant tone came across like venom from a snake. It didn’t get past Kendra. “Before you get your fangs out, I just want to say that I don’t think you’re loco. Well, I do, but only when you have to defend yourself. I don’t see anything wrong with that. You’ve got the guts to stand alone, unlike these conforming, sniveling, sneaky little bitches around here. Believe it or not, I’m not the only one who feels that way.” For the first time of the conversation, Aiko stopped sketching, lifted her head, and looked at Kendra. “Careful, you’re putting a target on your back socializing with me.” “Aw, who cares? I’m not worried about it. If anybody bothers me, I’ll just get you to kick their ass.” They both laughed out loud. “Okay, I’ve got your back.” “Cool.”

Before long, the second bell rang announcing the end of homeroom. Aiko and Kendra walked out of the door together engaged in friendly chitchat. Unlike the negative vibes that she got when she first met Sophie, Kendra seemed genuine, once she started opening up, but only time would tell. Just as they reached the first set of lockers, Sophie and her posse were waiting for her. She attempted to ignore them and kept walking, but they blocked her path. “Well, hello Aiko.” “Goodbye Sophie.” “Not so fast. My Vaughnie tells me that you don’t want him to talk to me.” “Your Vaughnie? Ha! And they call me crazy. Are you so desperate that you’ve crossed the line to delusional too? Poor Sophie can’t find her own man. Aw, that’s such as shame.” “Vaughn will be mine. It’s just a matter of time. We’re from the same country, we talked the same language, and we have a lot in common. Face it Aiko, I’m not going anywhere! You are!” “You’re such a waste of my time and of space. Go somewhere and wither and die.” “Make me bitch!” That was all she needed to hear. She reached into her blouse to grab her trusty jagged edge knife and put it up to her throat. She could faintly feel the beat of Sophie’s heart resonate on the blade from the vein in her neck. In that moment, she believed that she could actually take a life. She could watch the blood squirt from her throat and the life leak from her body and not even flinch. She began to slide the dagger across her skin. Kendra intervened. She grabbed her arm with both hands, only because that’s how much strength she needed to do so. “No! Aiko, she’s not worth it! Come on, calm down. Give me the knife. Come on. Give it to me.” It was now her own heartbeat that she felt, pounding in her ears. Hesitantly, she lowered her arm never breaking her deadly stare at Sophie, keeping her grip on the knife as Kendra cupped her hands around hers. Sophie checked her neck for damage as did her posse. The blade broke her skin, but not deep enough to draw blood. “I’m going to report you to the office for this.” It was Kendra that responded. “Go ahead. I just tell them that it was self-defense because you and your cult members tried to jump her.” Sophie scoffed at her. “You’re her only witness versus my four.” A voice emerged from the crowd. “Make that two witnesses.” Then another came forth, “Three.”

One after another, voices counted out themselves as witnesses on Aiko's behalf. She was so filled with fury that she hadn't noticed that half of her homeroom class was around them. "Oh, I see that the Loco Lady fan club is here. It doesn't matter. The only person I'm concerned about telling is Vaughn anyway. He's definitely not going to want you after this." Kendra got in the last word. "Fuck off Sophie! Or, would you rather me let go of her hand?" Sophie waved a dismissive hand at them then disappeared down the hall in a cloud of black with her devoted followers in tow. Kendra gently grabbed Aiko's face, which was beaded with sweat, and turned it towards hers. "Are you alright?" "Yeah, I think so. Thank you. Thank all of you." A few of her witnesses patted her back, and a few hugged her as they offered encouraging words. It blew her mind how much support she had gotten. "Okay now, can I trust you to put this up and not take it out for the rest of the day?" "Yes, she's not worth getting suspended for. I never had a suspension and I'm not starting now." "Damn skippy! You've got to get into your first choice college. Don't let that bitch mess up your chance." "Why are you doing this? You know, sticking up for me?" "You said that you've got my back right? Well, I've got yours too. I know what it's like to have to fend for yourself. I'll tell you about it someday." They started to fast walk to the next class, to avoid being late. "I was really surprised at how many people stood up for me." "I told you that I wasn't the only person who understood you." "Yeah, but up until now, nobody said anything." "They just needed a reason to. Sometimes, the best weapons are secret ones." "Well, I hope some of my 'secret weapons' catch my bus. I don't put it past Sophie to wait there for me." "Don't worry about it. That'll work itself out too."

She made it through the rest of the day without another incident. Kendra offered to walk outside with her to the bus. Within minutes of them walking to the exit, Sophie and her group came out behind them. They stood across from them staring and gossiping. "Aiko, just ignore them." "Maybe I should just get on the bus now." "And what? Be a sitting target? If they're going to try something, they'll do it no matter if you're here or there. Just give it a couple of minutes. I'm right here with you." "Alright, if you say so." A couple of minutes were all that had passed before Craig's car pulled up in front of the buses. Cierra jumped out before the car came to a complete stop. She was wearing a white T-shirt, a gray leather jacket, a grey mini-skirt hiked up to just below her butt with biker shorts underneath, tennis shoes and a black baseball cap that hung low enough to cover her eyes. It was entirely too cold for that attire, but she was not dressed for the weather. "Hey Ko. Hey Kendra. Where dat bitch at?" Kendra pointed her out. "CiCi, chill!" Aiko moved to stop her, but Kendra grabbed her arm. "So, you're Sophia. Damn, you're an ugly bitch! I hear you've been fucking with my girl Aiko and her man." "Bitch, who are you and why is it any of your business?" "I'm the bitch who ain't got nothin' to lose when I beat your ass!" "Bitch, it's five of us. What are you gonna do?" Aiko shook her head. Sophie still hadn't learned that numbers don't always mean strength, especially when dealing with crazy. Cierra socked her dead in the mouth on her left side with a right hook. Sophie dropped to the ground like a brick. Her so-called strength scattered like roaches leaving her right cheek down on the gritty, cold concrete. Cierra turned towards Aiko and Kendra. "C'mon y'all. Let's go." The three of them jumped into Craig's car. "Cierra, I don't know what to say. Thank you, but you could go to jail for assaulting a minor." "She ain't gonna press charges." "How do you figure?"

“Because she’ll be too scared to. Plus, she doesn’t know who I am.” “Yeah, but she knows that we do.” “So, you’ll deny it, simple as that.” “Okay, I can do that.” “Cool, end of discussion.” “How do you know Kendra?” “What? She didn’t tell you? That’s my little cousin.” “Kendra, why didn’t you tell me?” “You know now. That’s all that matters. I already felt the way I did, but when Cierra put me down on the details, and the fact that she was cool with you, I was on board for looking out for you.” “Well, I guess I should be grateful to have y’all gangsta bitches on my side.” They laughed out loud. Even Craig joined in on the laughter. “I have one question though, Kendra. How did you get those girls from homeroom to back me up?” “I didn’t. Well, I discovered three of them were already secretly team Loco Lady, but the rest acted on their own.” “Wow!” She wasn’t as alone as she had thought. Most likely, they were girls who had the same social issues that she had, and probably just as crazy as she was too, though not as open with it as she was. The reasons didn’t really matter to her as long as she had support. For the first time in weeks, Aiko smiled from happiness from deep within.

Craig turned up the radio to blast “Mr. Wendal” by Arrested Development. His stick shift rocked the car back and forth to the beat. They dropped Kendra off first since she lived closer to the west side of town. “Ko, do you want to go home, or come to my place for a while?” “I’m going home. I need to talk to Vaughn, asap.” “Okay, well call me and let me know how that goes.” “As soon as I hang up the phone with him, I will.” She couldn’t wait to square the situation up with Vaughn once and for all. She kept going over in her head what she was going to say and how she was going to say it. The fact that he kept talking to Sophie was enough to get her blood boiling alone, but she found out that he had been repeating their personal conversations to her too. She was so hot with anger that her skin could sizzle off of her bones.

Vaughn answered on the second ring. “Hey baby!” “Oh, so I’m baby now?” “You’ve always been my baby. What is with the attitude?” “Sophie and her friends tried to gang bang me outside of my homeroom today. You mean to tell me that she hasn’t come crying to you yet?” “No. What happened?” Cierra must have done Sophie in more than she had thought. “You heard me the first time. She threatened me, so I put a knife to her throat, but don’t worry. Your little girlfriend didn’t get hurt, at least not by me. Not yet.” “She’s not my girlfriend. Why do you keep saying that?” “Because you keep acting like it Vaughn! She repeated to me what I discussed with you in private, which means that you have continued to go behind my back talking to her! And, she made it very clear that she’s certain that you are going to drop me for her because you two have so much in common. Just exactly how much time have you spent with her Vaughn? She can’t be just pulling all of this out of the sky.” Vaughn went silent on her. “Well, I’m waiting.” “We talk a lot, but I don’t have any romantic feelings for her.” “How much is a lot?” “It’s a couple of times a day, every day.” Her heart sank. “See, that’s not right how you’re doing me. How do you think that makes me feel? If I was doing that, you’d be upset too, and you know it!” “How am I doing you wrong? I told you that I don’t have feelings for her.” “You still went behind on my back. You still disrespected me, and you made me look like a fool to her. Why else would she be so comfortable coming to you?” “Damn it Aiko because she’s my friend, alright! I like talking to her. We do have a lot in common, and it does feel good to talk to someone from my country. That doesn't mean that I am disrespecting you or doing anything wrong." "You just don't get it do you? So you're not going to cut her out, not even for me?" "No. You're just going to have to trust that we're just friends and that I won't let her break us up." "It's too late! We are broken up as of right now! Go to hell Vaughn!"

CHAPTER 10—TRACK 8-- 212°F

She pushed the off button then slammed the phone down on the base. The dramatic slam-hang up in one motion was lost because of the cordless phone, but he got the point. She wanted to cry her eyes out, but she couldn't. She had reached the level of anger that triggered emotional numbness. As she paced the floor between the living room and dining room, she replayed his words in her head repeatedly. Her thoughts were scrambled again. She felt as if her head would implode from her loosening grip on reality. The telephone kept ringing back to back from Vaughn's desperate attempts to talk to her. As far she was concerned, he needed to suffer, and she needed to get away from the house for a while. Her home girl Karla was just who she needed. She rarely gave advice, but she was a good listener.

Kody answered the door. "Hi Kody. Is Karla home?" "Not yet. She went to the store with our mom. She'll be back in an hour or so." "Oh, okay." Kody noticed something was bothering her. She never could hide her feelings from her face. "What's wrong?" "Nothing. I should go. Tell Karla to call me when she gets home. I need to talk to her." "You can talk to me until she gets home." "I don't think so Kody." "You look like you could use a friend. We are friends, aren't we?" "Well, yeah." "Then, come in. I'll warm you up some tea and food and we can talk and chill until Karla gets home." "Okay. I suppose it couldn't hurt." Aiko waited at the dinette set in the basement. He microwaved some fried chicken and French fries left over from dinner the night before, and fixed her glass of ice water and a cup of tea. She explained the situation to him as she ate. He listened attentively, though she couldn't quite read his mind as his face remained expressionless.

She muffled a tiny belch. "Excuse me. That was good. Thanks. Tell Mrs. Lynn she put her foot in it." "Hey, why don't you come sit on the couch and drink your tea? It's closer to the fireplace." She agreed. She took her shoes off and put her feet on the couch. Kody sat next to her, put her legs across his lap, and started massaging her feet. "Kody, you don't have to do that." "Does it feel bad?" "No, it feels good, but…" "Then shut up, relax and enjoy it." She didn't respond, which left an awkward silence looming over them. "So, finish telling me." "That was it pretty much. I still can't believe I broke up with him. He was my first." Kody remained silent. "You don't have anything to say? I just spilled my guts for nothing." "What do you want me to say?" "What you're thinking, something, anything." "He was in the wrong, whether his intentions were innocent or not. You did what you had to do. Live with it, or swallow your pride and fix it." "I'm not sure that I want to, especially if he won't see things my way." "Well then, there you go. Have fun and do you for now." "Yeah, you're right." "Feel better?" "Actually, yeah I do. Thanks." "Yeah, it's all good. Guess what I heard?" "What?" "I heard this fine ass sista named Aiko is single now." She playfully kicked his knee. "Shut up Kody." He lifted her legs, scooted himself between them, and put his face within inches of hers. “Make me. Put your tongue in my mouth.” “Ew, no!” She mushed his face away, but that just made him more determined. He got even closer, and followed her eyes with his, while caressing her thighs. “You know that I really like you, right?” “No shit?” He smacked her thigh. “Stop getting smart girl.” “Would you expect anything less? That’s how we do with each other.” “Yeah, but I want more.” “I’m not sure that I can give you more. I may have broken up with Vaughn, but I still love him.” “That doesn’t mean that you have to put your life on hold either. Do you really think he would put his life on hold for you? Hell, he couldn’t even cut that girl off for you. He’s probably with her now.” “Kody, stop. I don’t want to hear that right now.” “Well, it’s the truth, and you need to hear it. Where is he now Koko? Can you answer that without a doubt that he’s not with her or on the phone with her instead of you right now? Bottom line, he ain’t here, but I am, in the flesh, looking straight into your eyes and telling you that I *do* want you. All I need is the chance to prove it.” Aiko’s emotions fought their way back to the surface from where she tried to bury them, and tears overflowed the wells of her eyes. Kody gently brushed the tears away with his thumbs and kissed her on the cheek right next the corner of her lips. He peered into her eyes again to check for any sign of objection or resistance. When he found that there was none, that was his green light to proceed, and he kissed her again, this time directly on the lips. She recalled Cierra’s words “the best way to get over a man is to get under a new one.” Truth be told, she had a crush on Kody too, but she never acted on it. Being newly single, there was nothing to stop her, except thoughts of Vaughn and the pain of their breakup. As much as she tried to push them down, she couldn’t. She pulled away from Kody’s lip lock. “Kody, wait.” “What’s wrong?” “I’m struggling with putting the whole Vaughn thing out of my mind. I want to be free and enjoy living in this moment with you, but I'm just so hurt and angry that I want to throw or punch something or scream at the top of my lungs to release it!" "Take it out on me." "What?" "I said, take it out on me." "How?" He grabbed the back of her head and kissed her passionately, swirling his tongue in her mouth. She kissed him back without hesitation, hoping that the more they kissed the more her pain would subside. He slid his hands under her blouse to unsnap her bra. "What are you doing? Stop!" He ignored her plea. "I said stop!" "You want me to stop? What are you going to do to stop me?" Kody gave her a sneaky, sexy glare. "What's that look for?" "Figure it out." He continued to work on her bra and groping, caressing, and kissing her upper body. She shoved his shoulders as hard as she could, which didn't accomplish much because of his sturdy, broad, muscular frame. He gave her another smile that was gratified and sly. "Now you're getting it. Take it out on me." It became clear that Kody wanted her to convert her anger and pain into passion and lust. Her inhibitions unhinged and she adhered to the arising sensual force of nature overcoming her. She grabbed him by the collar of his hoodie, yanked him down to her and bit his bottom lip. Caught off guard he flinched, but only for second, and he became more aroused and aggressive, kissing and biting her neck. The bites were painful, yet surprisingly pleasurable. After removing her blouse and bra and leaving red bite marks down her body, he slid off her jeans and panties. He wasted no time plunging his face into her center, eating her like a ravenous beast. Since no one was home, she moaned and screamed in pleasure freely.

Once he quenched his thirst from her juices, he lifted her up and sat her down on to his large, hard and veiny dick. The move was swift and seamless, leaving her no time to protest. The only sound she made was the short, shrieking heave she released from the shock of him entering her body. As far as length and width, he had Vaughn beat by at least an inch in both. It only took a few strokes for her to adjust. What Kody was about to discover was that although she had been with only one man, her skills were exceptional. Her moves were as natural to her as breathing. She loved being on top. The only thing she loved more was the control she had. She grinded and twirled her body with confidence, giving Kody a look of superiority. He reached for her hips. She whacked his hands away without losing her rhythm. She pushed his shoulders against the back of the couch and grabbed his face "No touching until I say so!" she commanded. "Damn, that's sexy bitch." he replied with his voice breaking. There was no offense taken by his derogatory name-calling. She knew that he wanted to keep her fired up to take her aggression out on him. The crack of her hand slapping his face echoed through the basement. "Mmm, give it to me again baby." She smacked him again. "Don't tell me what the fuck to do!" "Can I grab your hips now baby?" "Yes." He grabbed her hips firmly, keeping her from moving. He began to thrust upward forcefully, delivering direct blows to her G spot. Unbearable pleasure rippled through her body. She leaned forward, dug her nails into his upper back, and bit his bottom lip until she drew blood. He kissed her so that she could taste the blood she drew. It was like an aphrodisiac for them both. He lifted her up and turned her over to her knees, facing the back of the couch. He then reentered her from the back with urgency. A cracking sound echoed through the room again. This time, it was from Kody smacking her ass. He might've been in the dominant position, but she was determined to maintain her control. She twirled and winded her hips against his thrusts, giving it back just as forcefully as she was receiving. “Pull my hair nigga!” Kody obeyed his orders and grabbed her long ponytail. She glanced over her shoulder looking at him hungrily. The crackle from the fireplace was no match for their intense panting and grunting. The small storm window above her head began to fog. It could have been argued that it was from their hot and heavy encounter, rather than the fireplace.

The roar from the engine of Mrs. Lynn’s car approached the house. “Kody, they’re back. We have to stop!” He ignored her, stroking faster and harder. “Kody!” He pulled her ponytail bringing her ear close to his lips. “We’re going to finish this. We might get caught. Let that excite you.” She closed her eyes and let her imagination get carried away with scenarios of them getting caught. She could hear Karla and her mother’s voices and footsteps and the rustle of bags being moved. Her heart raced with fear, and the fear converted into excitement. She became more aroused, exploding her juices all over Kody’s dick, lower abdomen, and upper thighs. “Yeah, that’s what I’m talking about baby!” He kept going trying to get every orgasm he could out of her until he achieved his own. The footsteps and voices were now in the house moving around in the kitchen and bedrooms. “Cum for me one more time.” “Make me nigga.” she sighed out. “My pleasure.” He slowed it down and stroked her in a circular motion. Her body quivered as she exploded with another huge, milky orgasm. Kody took his cue to release his own, and sped up his pace again. When he finished, he collapsed onto her back and kissed her neck and shoulders. They took a minute or two to catch their breath. He pulled out and smacked her ass.

"Come on. We've got to get dressed." He only had to slip on his boxers and sweats. In addition to her bra, panties and clothes, she had to fix her hair and makeup. She got dressed as quickly as she could then headed to the bathroom to repair her disheveled face and hair. To help freshen up, she showered herself with body spray. When she came out of the bathroom, Kody was spreading a cloud of air freshener around. "Don't you think that's enough?" "I'm trying to cover the pu-dussy smell." She laughed out loud. "Okay, well crack the window. If anyone asks, just say that the fireplace had it too hot down here." "It was that hot ass of yours though." He kissed her lips then cracked the window. They sat in their usual seats, and not a moment too soon because Karla came running down the stairs calling for him. "Oh hey, Ko! Kody, mom wants you." "For what?" "Like you tell me, go see!" He walked past her and shoved her shoulder. She smacked him on the back of his head. He tried to dodge, but Karla was too quick. It was a skill that he and their brothers taught her that always backfired.

Aiko told Karla about what happened with Vaughn. As she suspected she listened, but didn't have much input. Before long, Kody rejoined them with some sodas and snacks. He and Aiko behaved as they normally did towards each other. The three of them enjoyed the first evening of their four-day holiday weekend together. Karla was none the wiser of the sexual indiscretion that had transpired in her absence. Aiko dreaded going home. That night she went from down in the dumps, to nothingness, to cloud nine. With Kody she had discovered the rough, dangerous, nasty and aggressive side of sex and how arousing and possibly therapeutic it can be. She knew that there would be Vaughn's phone calls to deal with, and given the night she had it could only be a buzz kill. Sure enough when she got home her mom told her that Vaughn had called umpteen times for her. She rolled her eyes, casually mentioned that they broke up, and requested that for the entire weekend at least that he be told that she does not want to talk to him.

The long weekend was fun and leisurely with the exception of Vaughn's incessant calls. For that reason, she convinced her parents to let her drive her car across town to school for a while so that she could avoid Vaughn popping up on the bus to corner her. Her plan worked, but only for week. The following Friday, while unwinding to Jodeci in her room, she heard a familiar tap on the window. *Oh my God, no he didn't!* Frustrated because of Vaughn's unwelcomed surprise visit, she yanked open the curtains and window. "What do you want to Vaughn?" "I want to talk to you." "Are you still involved with Sophie?" "Well, yeah but…" "Then, you and I have *nothing* to talk about! Go home!" Before she could slam the window shut, he blocked it. "Just give me ten minutes. Please?" "You've got five minutes then you leave." He climbed through the window and took his usual spot on the daybed. She remained standing. "I'm sorry for everything baby. I'm working on weaning her away. I just need more time." "I gave you enough time. It's too little, too late now." "I'm doing this for you!" "Is that supposed to make me feel better? I talked to you until I was blue in the face about the situation with her, her harassment and threats. You wouldn't listen to me. I had to break up with you in order for you to see the light? And now, you tell me that you're doing this for me? So, no! You're doing this for yourself because you lost me. If you hadn't, you would have let me continue to go through all of that so you could have your cake and eat it too." "I still love you." "You don't love me enough to put my needs above your selfishness. I'm done Vaughn! Your five minutes are up. Leave!" He stood up in front of her. "You may be done, but I'm not. I'm going to win you back." She stared at him emotionless. He leaned down to kiss her, but she turned her head away. He gently grabbed her chin and turned her face back towards his. "You still love me too. Deny it if you want, but I know it. For now, can I have one last kiss?" "No. Leave." "Please baby, just one?" "One, then you leave." He leaned in slowly. When their lips connected, a spark of familiarity overcame her. His lips were soft and moistened with the coconut lip balm she loved to taste on him. The kiss he gave her was tender and passionate. It felt like the first kiss they shared. He made sure not to push too hard to avoid her shutting down on him, but,as long as she didn't pull away, he had no plans to stop. Her body began to awaken. It was a natural response to his kisses that betrayed her stubborn anger towards him. As usual, he was perceptive to her body's silent signals. He slid his hands under her blouse. She moved his hands, but never broke the kiss. That was a green light for him to try again in a few minutes. A part of her wanted to let him make love to her for old time's sake. It was just a week ago he was her boyfriend and her first real love, but he was no longer the only man she had been with sexually. Since her romp with Kody was just days ago, a part of her wanted to sleep with Vaughn so that she could have a fresh comparison. The fact that she thought of that as justification made her feel sleazy. After much debate with herself, she chose the pitchfork over the halo and let Vaughn make love to her, but still standing firm on their breakup. To Vaughn, it was a step in the right direction to win her back. As far as the comparison, the score was one to one. Both were very good, just different.

In the weeks that followed, the situation at school seemed to calm down. Aside from the dirty looks and whispers from Sophia and her followers in passing, nothing out of the ordinary drama occurred. Vaughn was persistent in his efforts to win her back. He showered her with lavish gifts and dates at expensive restaurants. Her plan was to string him along for long as she could. She enjoyed being single and free from the insecurities that came with being in a relationship that was constantly threatened. Of course the 'no strings attached' wild sex she had with Kody every chance she got was an added bonus. If she got back with Vaughn, that would have to come to an end. She wasn't quite ready to end it. During Christmas break, she snuck in as many sessions with him as possible. Her diary was filled with juicy, tawdry details of her sex-capades with Kody. For that reason, she purchased a box with a lock in which to hide her diary. More so than her family, she was fearful that Vaughn would see it. Whether they got back together or not, she had no intention of him ever finding out. Chelsea was the only person she told to avoid bursting at the seams for holding in such a big and juicy secret. She ate every word Aiko spoke like they were a thick, juicy steak. Gossip is what Chelsea lived for, especially anything that tarnished Aiko's goody two shoes aspirations. That annoyed her about Chelsea, but in this case, her enthusiasm gave her the courage to stick to her actions.

Another New Year's Eve had come. It had been six weeks since she had broken up with Vaughn and first slept with Kody. Aiko planned on bringing in the New Year down Karla's house watching the countdown of the top one hundred videos of nineteen ninety-three. Vaughn insisted on spending the holiday with her. As a compromise, she agreed to go to a late dinner with him, as long as he had her home by ten so that she can keep her plans with Karla. He took her to her favorite restaurant downtown. She ordered a sushi platter for an appetizer, and for the entrée a surf n turf with steak and endless shrimp. Whenever Vaughn wasn't looking, she snuck shrimp into a one gallon freezer bag in her purse to bring to Karla and Kody for their get together later. He did notice how quickly her plate got empty after each refill. "Damn baby, have they been starving you?" "No, I just didn't eat today and I'm trying to get your money's worth." "My money is long baby. Don't worry your head about that." "Okay." "So, when are you going to be mine again?" "When I'm ready." "And when is that going to be?" "I don't know Vaughn. I know you're trying. I just have trust issues right now, and I really don't want the drama to start up again at school. If we don't get back together, we can at least be friends right?" "Yeah, but I want more than that. I want you in my life forever. I want you to be the mother of my children." "Whoa! Slow down now. Let's just take it one day at a time and work on seeing if we can get back together first. "I want five kids." "Three tops, nigga! Now, can we go please?" She didn't want the gallon of shrimp in her purse to go bad.

He dropped her off at Karla's house. The curtain in the bay window was peeled back as if someone was peeking through them. She was sure it was Karla on the lookout for her arrival. "Bye Vaughn. Thanks for dinner." Vaughn gave her a long, passionate kiss goodbye. "You're welcome. Happy New Year baby." "Happy New Year Vaughn." Karla opened the door before she had a chance to knock. "Hey Karls! Grab a bowl and some cocktail sauce." "For what?" She pulled the bag of shrimp out of her purse. “Oh my God, no you didn’t! Girl that is so ghetto! I didn’t know your boujee ass had it in you.” “Shut up. Is everybody downstairs?” “If by everybody you mean Kody, then yeah. My other brothers went out and so did my parents.” “Hey, I’m cool with that. We always have fun.” When they got downstairs with the shrimp and cocktail sauce, Kody was on the couch with a huge chip on his shoulder. “Hi Kody!” “Hey Ko.” She turned to Karla and asked, “What’s wrong with him?” “I don’t know. Maybe he’s mad because he had to stay home and babysit us.” Aiko shrugged her shoulders. “We’ll cheer him up.”

As the night went on Kody seemed to lighten up some, but it was still evident something was bothering him. Ten minutes before midnight, Karla bundled up to go on the roof to see the fireworks. Aiko declined, using the cold weather as an excuse to stay inside. Really, she wanted to find out what had Kody in a bad mood . “What’s wrong with you?” “You know what’s wrong with me!” “Um, no I don’t. That’s why I asked.” Kody didn’t respond. “Fine, be that way! I’m going outside with Karla.” She rushed towards the coat rack. He was right on her heels. He grabbed her left arm, swung her around and pinned her against the wall. “I saw you kissing him!” “For the record, he kissed me. I was honest with you that I still love him, but he and I are not together as a couple. He takes me out and stuff as a way to win me back.” “Is it working?” “Why do you care? You and I aren’t a couple either. We’re just fucking, remember?” “Are you still fucking him?” “Only once since we broke up, and that was five weeks ago.” “Right after we did?” “It was about a week after.” “Slut!” She slapped the piss water out of him. “Don’t you ever talk to me like that again!” “What, like calling you a hoe?” She slapped him again, this time harder, if it were even possible. “Bitch!” She geared up to slap him a third time, but he grabbed her wrist. He stared at her intensely for a few seconds then he kissed her hard and aggressively. She tried to push him off, but he pinned her arms against the wall as he kissed and bit her lips and neck. That aroused her, and she started kissing him back. He yanked off her jeans and panties, and lifted her up. She wrapped her legs around his waist, and wrapped her arms around his neck while he slid down his sweat pants and boxers. They slammed against the wall as he entered her body. Fireworks whistled and cracked through the air announcing the arrival of the New Year. Out of all of their encounters, this one was the roughest and most sexually charged. She was definitely going to have a migraine in the morning from her head banging against the wall.

Afterwards, she gently rubbed his face. “Are you hurt?” “No. How’s your head?” “I’m fine, for now.” “Sorry I called you those names.” “I know, but you made it up to me.” “I want to see you later today.” “Why?” “So we can get in our first session of the new year.” “Didn’t we just do that?” “Nope, that was the last one of last year.” They laughed out loud.They did their usual cover-up and waited for Karla to come back down. “Ya’ll missed it.” “We’ll live.” “I see you’re back to your old self smart ass.” Aiko grabbed a plate of food and flopped in her favorite chair. “Your parents said that I can stay till two AM right?” “Yup!” Well, let’s get it in! Turn up the TV. Kody, can you get me a soda please?” “I’ve got something better.” He handed her and Karla bottles of Heineken. Aiko looked at him then looked at Karla with her mouth open, catching flies, as her grandma used to say. “We won’t tell if you won’t.” “I’ve had beer before. I’m just surprised at you Karls." "Then, I guess we both have seen a new side of each other tonight." "Alright then, cheers and Happy New Year!" They toasted the neck of their bottles and took big swigs. If Karla only knew that Aiko had a side to her that was secretly sleeping with her brother, it would probably be the end of their friendship.

After she ate, she started to feel queasy. Karla noticed. "What's the matter? You look a little green." "I'm a little nauseous. I think maybe I ate too much shrimp." Kody handed her a bottle of water. She took slow sips. "Is that better?" "Yeah Kody, I think so…" It wasn't better. In seconds, her mouth was filled with chunky, acidic, shrimp and beer flavored vomit and she took off to the bathroom. "Are you alright Ko?" "Yeah, I'm fine now. I think I should go home and rest. I think that the combination of food I ate didn't agree with me. See y'all later today." She snuck a wink at Kody before she departed.

Later that morning, she threw up again. She decided to stay away from shrimp for a while. That was a bummer because she loved shrimp a lot, but shrimp wasn't the only food making her ill. Just about everything she ate made her woozy. It wasn't until two weeks later when she was over Chelsea's house telling her about her illness that she got a clue. "Aiko, when was the last time you had your period?" "I was supposed to get my period about two weeks after Thanksgiving I think. I never got it, but since I've been on the pill, my periods have been light to nonexistent." "But, you've never been sick because of it, right?" "Right, I haven't." "You're pregnant." "Get da fuck outta here with that Chelsea!" "The pill is only ninety-nine percent effective. Did you use condoms with Vaughn or Kody?" "No." "Then bitch, you're pregnant!

And you don't even know the father is!" "You would love that wouldn't you?!" "Hey, don't get me wrong, it tickles me pink when your Dudley do right ass has a little drama." Aiko rolled her eyes. "Well, glad I could amuse you." "*But* you're my friend and I care about you. I don't wish any harm on you, and this is definitely not a situation I ever wanted to see you in. If you are, you have some big decisions to make. First, we've got to get a home pregnancy test. We'll get two brands just to be sure."

Aiko drove them to Rite Aid and they returned to Chelsea's house. After taking both tests, it was confirmed that she was pregnant. She stared at the tests in disbelief. The moment seemed almost surreal. She felt the blood drain from her head and trickle down until she felt as if she were going to faint from the drop in blood pressure. There was no question that she would keep the baby. What scared her most was the disappointment her parents would have. Surely, they would assume that her life would be destroyed. She didn't share that point of view. Life would be more difficult, but in no way did she feel that having a happy, successful existence would be beyond her reach just because of a teen pregnancy. She would make sure of it. Although deep inside she wished that the baby was Vaughn's, either way, she would be on her own. Vaughn was no longer her man and Kody never was. Once Vaughn finds out that she slept with his arch enemy, there would be no turning back for him. She would lose him forever. Quite possibly, she would lose Karla as well. As close as they were, she wasn't sure if Karla would be able to forgive her for keeping such a big secret from her, especially since it involved her sibling. For now, no one else would be told. She needed time to get her game plan together.

CHAPTER 11—TRACK 9—OVERBOIL

Another month had passed. Valentine's Day would have been her and Vaughn's one year anniversary. She had no desire to engage in any festivities relating to their would -be anniversary or the holiday. There was nothing to celebrate. Vaughn insisted on taking her out. She agreed to go only if it was a double date and he would bring a friend for Karla. She would drive her car and meet him there to avoid Kody spying on them again. Karla and Vaughn's friend Andre hit it off well. They barely seemed to notice the tension between Aiko and Vaughn. Aiko didn't really want to be there, and it was evident. She retreated into her shell, avoiding eye contact and conversation with Vaughn as much as possible. Besides stuffing her face, it was the only way she felt that she could hide the guilt of being pregnant with a baby that Vaughn was not the sole father candidate. Despite the awkward atmosphere, Vaughn was very patient. "Are you alright baby?" "Yes, I'm fine. I'm just tired." "You look it, no offense." "None taken." "You need to slow down on the food baby." "Well, I'm hungry." "Yeah, but you said you've been sick lately, and you're eating to catch up is starting to stick to you." "What the fuck is that supposed to mean? Are you calling me fat?" Karla and Andre were sucked out of their little world and into the tension. "No baby, you're not fat, but I noticed a little more weight on you." "Well, since it's bothering you so much, I'll just take my fat ass home! Come on Karla." Karla exchanged numbers with Andre and excused herself from the table.

The ride home was silent between the two of them at first. Tevin Campbell's "Can We Talk" bopped through the speakers. Karla wasn't afraid to speak her mind, but she knew all of Aiko's red buttons. This wasn't the time to push any of them. Comedy was always her method of choice in these types of situations. Phrasing her comments carefully meant the difference between a peaceful dialogue and a meltdown. "Do you want me to get my brothers to kick his rasta ass?" Aiko forced a crooked smirk. "Seriously though, what happened?" "He said that I was gaining weight and that it bothered him." "That's funny because that's not what I got from what he said." "Oh, so you were listening." "Yeah, and?" "And that's the way I took it. It doesn't matter what you got from it." "Maybe not, but he was right. You have gained weight, and you're moody and throwing up. Got something to tell me?" "No. Not anymore." Aiko had planned to come clean with Karla, but she considered changing her mind when she took Vaughn's side. "Oh my God, are you pregnant? Does Vaughn know?" Aiko didn't respond. "I already figured it out, so you might as well tell me." "No, he doesn't." "Well, you should tell him he's going to be a father. That's the right thing to do." "It's not that simple Karla." "What's complicated about it? He's the father, so you tell him, unless you're not going to keep it?" "I'm keeping the baby." "Then what else is there?" Aiko took a deep breath and conjured up the nerve to tell her as much as she could. "He may not be the father." Karla's mouth flew open, then peeled back into a huge smile. "You undercover hoochie! How many possible fathers are there?" "Just two." "Well, who is he? Do I know him?" "That's not important right now." "The hell if it isn't! He deserves to know just as much as Vaughn. I want to know because I'm your friend and I want to help you." "Trust me, you don't want to know." "C'mon, tell me." "No." "Tell me!" "No!" "Damn it, tell me!" "It's your brother, okay! It's Kody!"

A look came over Karla's face that Aiko had never before seen from her. It was a combination of shock, disappointment and hatred, all of which she never wanted to be the cause. Her heart sank to her feet from the weight of the guilt. "How could you do that to me? We're supposed to be friends, and you fucked my brother behind my back!" "Karls, I'm so sorry. I didn't plan it. It just happened." "Oh, so you just tripped and fell onto my brother's dick, huh?" "It was something like that. He was consoling me the day I broke up with Vaughn. One thing led to another and…" "And y'all fucked. Was that the only time?" "No." "How many times was it?" "I don't know. I wasn't counting. Why would you want to know that anyway?" Karla was seething with anger. "I don't want to be around you right now. Pullover, I'm taking a bus home." "Karla, I'm not letting you out. It's cold and late. You can hate me in the car." "Let me out now! I'm not playing!" "No Karla!"

The next thing Aiko felt was a sting on her right cheek. Karla had slapped her. Before she could respond, more blows flew at her. Because she was driving, there wasn't much she could do. She felt that she deserved Karla's wrath, but it wasn't the right time or place for it. She tried to block as many of her blows as she could while keeping her eyes on the road until she could find a safe spot to pull over. In their scuffle, Karla inadvertently unbuckled Aiko's seatbelt. Neither of them was aware of it. The area was wooded, dark and eerie. The roads were still slick and icy from the snowstorm from four days before. It was too much of a risk to wait. She needed to pull over immediately. The problem was that there was no shoulder, but given the circumstance, it would have to do until Karla could calm down.

"Karla, I need you to stop so that I can see!" Karla was too angry to adhere to her plea. Instead, she continued attacking her in a fit of rage with most of her blows landing on Aiko's face, hindering her vision. As the car was turning a curve, the tires beneath them lost traction and began to slide, causing the car to veer onto the opposite side of the road. Aiko reacted quickly turning the wheel into the spin. Karla's anger instantly changed into fear, and she screamed frantically as she gripped the dashboard with both hands. The car spun in circles three times before it came to a screeching halt on the other side of the road facing the direction they had just come from. They both were panting heavily trying to get their breathing under control. "Are you alright Karls?" "Yeah, I think so." "Scared the shit out of you didn't it?" "Hell yeah! My life flashed before my eyes!" "Shit, and it wasn't much life for either of us yet." "Well, let's get our black asses home so that we can live out the rest of it." "I'm with you on that." She started to turn the car around to head back in the right direction. Out of nowhere, a dark car came around the curve at least twenty miles above the limit. The driver laid on the horn with no intent to slow down. Rather, he expected Aiko to complete her turn- a-bout at lightning speed to get out of his way. The dual cone band of illumination from his headlights grew larger as he approached. Streaks of yellowish-white bounced across her dashboard and raided her eyes to blindness.

Screech! Boom! Shatter! Darkness. Silence. Light, red and blue. Light, red and white. Faces, unknown. Voices, distant. Heartbeat, weak. Breathing, faint. Darkness. Silence.

“Koko, wake up. Baby, it’s me. Wake up.” Aiko opened her eyes slowly to a dimly lit room. Her eyes were watery and her vision was blurry. She tried to focus on a brown figure sitting by her bed. After a few moments she realized that it was Vaughn smiling ear to ear at her. “Vaughn?” Her voice was weak and cracked. “Yes baby, it’s me.” “Where am I?” “You’re in the hospital?” “Why? What happened?” “I have someone you need to meet.” “Who?” The low coo of a baby came from a bassinet to the right of Vaughn. He smiled at her again then picked up the baby. “I want you to meet our son.” “Our son? Are you sure?” “Yes baby, I’m sure. He looks just like me.” “I want to hold him.” He gently handed her the baby. Instantly, she felt the connection to him. Her heart swelled with elation and her eyes flooded with tears. The little version of the love of her life looked up at her and squeezed her finger as if to say “Hi mommy.” “He’s beautiful. He does look like you. Does he have a name yet?” “His name is Christian.” “Christian. That’s perfect. Thank you. Hi Christian. I’m your mommy. I love you so much. I promise that I’m going to be the best mommy for you.” Vaughn reached over and took Christian from her. “Say bye-bye to mommy. She needs her rest.” “No, I want you and Christian to stay longer.” “We have to go. Goodbye mommy. Bye.” “No, Vaughn wait! Don’t go!” Vaughn and Christian disappeared into the dark corner of the room. Their departure seemed so final. It tore her through her core and she began to sob uncontrollably. Desperation set in and she tried to get out of the bed to go after them. Unbearable pain shot through her body. Blood spread across her hospital gown around her abdomen. She had torn a few stitches from the C-section. In a panic, she pounded on the call button, but no nurse responded. Instead, her grandfather appeared through a bright light from the left corner of the room. She had lost him eight years prior to cancer. They were very close and he adored her. There was no hiding that she was his favorite of all of his grandchildren. She took his death hard. There was not a day that went by that she didn’t miss him.

“Hello sweetheart.” “Hi granddaddy! What are you doing here?” “I’ve been watching over you. I wanted to tell you that I love you.” “I love you too granddaddy. I’m sorry I wasn’t there to say goodbye.” “It’s alright sweetheart. You’re going to have to be strong, okay. Promise me.” “I promise.” “Good. I have to go now.” “No, not you too! Please, don’t go?” “You know that I can’t stay sweetheart.” “Well, can I come with you? I don’t want to be alone.” “You’re never alone, even when you think you are, but you can’t go with me. You have important things to do.” “Okay, what am I supposed to do?” “You’ll know when the time is right, but you’ve got to go back to find out.” “Okay. I miss you so much.” “I miss you too sweetheart. My time is up. I have to go, and so do you. Remember what I told you.” “I will. I promise. Goodbye granddaddy.”

"Goodbye sweetheart." In an instant, her grandfather and the light disappeared and she was left alone in the dimly lit room. Within minutes the dim light faded behind her eyelids as she fell asleep. Darkness. Silence.

"Code Blue! Hurry up, we're losing her!" "Okay. Stand back! Clear! One, two, three, Clear! One, two, three…Clear!" "Doctor, I've got a pulse!" "Okay, administer three CC's of Aldactone, stat!" "I'm on it!" "Brain is activity normal. Pulse is still weak." "Doctor, Aldactone is in the IV." "Blood pressure is one sixty over ninety. Patient is stabilizing. Let's get her cleaned up for recovery." Once in recovery Aiko remained unconscious. She could hear the voices of her family, friends, coworkers, classmates, and the unfamiliar voices of the doctors and nurses. During moments of silence, her mind wandered to distant memories and hopeful futures. At times, it was hard to tell one from the other and realities from fiction. They all seemed to run together in one long dream of which she couldn't break free, at least not on her own.

"Ko, I'm so sorry. It's all my fault. I overreacted. I shouldn't have attacked you like I did. If I had kept my cool, maybe you wouldn't have…" Karla choked over her words and broke into tears by Aiko's bed side. She heard every word. It was painful to hear her best friend blame herself. As far she was concerned, she was the only guilty party. Every part of her being yearned to console Karla and to make things right between them. She just needed to conjure the strength to speak. "Karls." "Oh my God Aiko! Are you awake? Can you hear me?" "Yeah." "Can you open your eyes?" She blinked several times and attempted to open them, but the light was too strong for her weak eyes. Karla quickly caught on. "Hold up, let me dim the lights. Now try. Is that better?" "Yes. Where are we?" Her voice was raspberry and cracked. "The hospital." "Hospital? Why?" "We were in an accident on Valentine's Day. Remember?" Aiko strained trying to put the scattered pieces of memory and images together. "I think so. I had just told you about Kody and me and the baby, then the car spun out of control and a car was coming towards us and…" She sucked in a deep heap of air. "Oh my God! My baby!" She grabbed her abdomen and desperately searched Karla's face for the fate of her unborn child. Karla's face broke down into pure sorrow. She managed to choke back tears enough to say "The baby didn't make it, Koko. You miscarried on the night of the accident. I'm so sorry." Aiko began shaking her head from side to side in disbelief. "No, no, no, no, no, no, no, no!" She felt so empty. Tears streamed down her face. Karla, who was then crying again, grabbed a Kleenex from the box on the nightstand. Ignoring her own wet face, she began to gently dry Aiko's face. "Karla, I need to know everything." "I don't know if I should right now." "My baby is dead. Nothing you tell me can be worse than that." "What's the last thing you remember?" I remember the car spinning out, then headlights coming towards us." "Okay, well somehow your seatbelt was unbuckled. You were thrown from the car through the windshield." "How's my car?" "It's all fixed now. There was just body damage, nothing serious. Tony has been starting it up for you." "Okay. Continue." Karla lifted her brow in amazement at how well she was taking the news so far. "You were flown to shock trauma. I was taken in an ambulance." "Okay, and?" "And, this is hard for me to say." "I know, but give it to me straight." "You flat lined on the operating table. They revived you, obviously, but that's when you lost… him." "Him? The baby was a boy?" "Yes." Aiko retreated into her thoughts, unnerved by the disturbing correlation between her dream of a baby boy and her deceased son. “Is my son’s body still in the morgue? I want to see him.” “Aiko, it was a miscarriage. It doesn’t work like that. Plus, he was still so tiny.” “I get it. He’s at the bottom of a biohazard trashcan. They could’ve at least waited so that I can have a chance to say goodbye.” “Well they can’t hold on to that for weeks.” “Weeks?” “Koko, you’ve been in a coma for little over a month.” “A coma? I see.” “You can still say goodbye. We can have a memorial service.” “I want to say goodbye to him on my own when I’m ready.” “Okay, whatever you want.” “I think that I should tell the nurse that you’re awake now. I’m sure they’ll want to look you over.” “Okay, in a minute. First, I need to know how you and everyone else are doing.” “I’m recovered. I just have a few bumps and bruises still. As far as everyone else, they’re worried but hopeful. Everyone’s been visiting and praying.” “How’s Vaughn?” “He’s been up here every day with me and your parents.” “How much does he know?” “He knows everything.” “You mean everything, everything?” “Yes, he knows about Kody too. Kody knows about nothing other than the accident. I’d like to keep it that way.” “I suppose you told Vaughn.” “Well, yes and no. He and your mom were in the waiting room when the doctor told them about the miscarriage. Your dad was getting coffee in the snack room, thank goodness. As soon as I was able to have visitors, they both bum rushed me with questions after my family left. I was heavily medicated, and I guess it was a truth serum. I would have told them the truth regardless. There was no sense lying about it at that point.” “I understand. I just don’t know how I’m going to face him now.” A gentle tap on the door interrupted them. “That must be your nurse now.” The door was opened cautiously. On the other side wasn’t the nurse, it was Vaughn. Karla leaned into Aiko’s ear. “Speak of the damn devil. Here’s your chance to face him. Make it count.” “Hey Karla.” “Hi

Vaughn. Look who's awake!" "I see! Hey baby!" "Hi Vaughn." "I'll give you two some time to talk before I let the nurse know that you're awake." "Okay thanks Karla, for everything." "You bet."

She noticed the flowers in Vaughn's hand. "Are those flowers for me?" "Yes." "Thanks." He placed them on the nightstand. "I'm so glad that you're awake now. I missed you baby." "You and everyone else from what I can tell. It looks like a florist shop in here." "Most of them are from me." "So, I guess that you missed me the most, huh?" "In my mind I do. I love you enough to try and show it." "I don't know why. I don't deserve it after what I did." "It's not your fault. It's mine. I drove you to it." He started choking over his words. "I didn't listen to you. I wasn't there for you, not the way you needed it. The price was the loss of our son. But, I'm here for you now the way you need, and I promise that I am going to never let you down again." For the first time Aiko saw Vaughn break down and cry. Under normal circumstances, her heart would have melted. She would have even considered getting back into a relationship with him. But, this wasn't a normal circumstance. Remorse for the loss of her unborn child was the only emotion that she could feel. She couldn't force herself to feel sorry for Vaughn, or connect with him emotionally, even if she wanted to try. Her heart had shut him out. To her, he was the blame for everything and no amount of pleas, promises, or tears would convince her that he deserved another chance, or fill the deep, dark void now taking residence in her soul. She turned to her left side and lay still and quiet. Vaughn could sense the distance she had created between them. "Baby?" "Vaughn, I think that you should leave now." "But what about us?" "There is no us anymore." Her voice was emotionless and calm. "But baby…" "I'm not your baby. We have no baby. We have no us. I'm letting you go and setting you free. You can do whatever or whomever you want. You don't have to feel guilty anymore." "But Aiko…" "Vaughn just go please." "Fine, I'll go, but I'm not giving up. I love you and I know you love me too. You know where to find me when you're ready." With that, he left the room closing the door behind him.

CHAPTER 12—TRACK 10—REBOUND

Aiko was released from the hospital a few days later. They kept her for observation to make sure she recovered from her coma. Not surprisingly, she passed her tests with flying colors. With the exception of a few residual cuts and bruises, she received a clean bill of health and could complete her recovery at home. However, her scars ran more deeply than just the physical. Emotionally, she was devastated over the loss of her baby and the demise of her relationship with Vaughn. She let him go not because she wanted to, but because she felt that she had to in order to get her head together. She felt lost and she needed time to get back on track without distraction, though it was hard not to think about him and the baby. Kody was very supportive and didn't pressure her about picking up where they left off until she was ready. The fact that he didn't know about the baby made her wonder if he'd be scared away if he did. She needed his friendship and support, so telling him was not an option. Thankfully, she had lots of schoolwork to catch up on to keep her busy and take her mind off of her problems. Her supervisor at work was gracious enough to let her come back, so that helped as well. Plus, she always had her music to give her peace. She started taking a liking to classical music. Some of her favorites were Pacelbel's "Canon," Beethoven "Fur Elise," Chopin "Nocturne" and Debussy "Clair de Lune." She had no shame in blasting the classical music as much as other genres. Tony and Dante frequently complained about the classical music more so than the others. She would sharply tell them that they needed a little class in their lives and turn it up even more until they gave up complaining. Tattling was an option, but they knew that she needed an outlet to use to cope with her recent ordeal, so they didn't bother.

Since her return to school, she had gained a few new members of the Loco Lady fan club. Word had spread fast about her coma, so those who had sympathy found themselves viewing her in a different light. To them she was now less crazy and more tangible as a person. Aiko couldn't care less either way, and she made a point to behave no differently. With junior prom approaching, the halls were buzzing with girlish excitement about dresses, shoes, hairstyles, limousines, dates, and after parties. As much she hated to admit it, she really wanted to attend, but the only person she wanted by her side was Vaughn. He would go out of his way to treat her like a queen and make her prom experience like a fairytale. Sadly, she had to let him go, and with him her hopes for a perfect prom night. Without him there was no point in going, but her mother insisted that she go to avoid having any regrets. Her cousin Tony volunteered to escort her. Against her instincts, she agreed.

The night of the prom Karla and Chelsea will right by her side encouraging her. Even after designing a dress, getting it tailor-made, dying shoes, and hours in the nail and hair salons, she wanted to bail out even up to the last minute. Cierra called to wish her well and extended an open invitation for her to stop by her place and hang with her and Clay afterwards if she needed to talk. When they arrived at the prom, Tony insisted on getting their photos taken right away claiming it was so that it was best to take them when they were still looking fresh. It was a good idea. No sooner than the flash of the last photo blinded them that he took off by himself to Mac on the other girls. She rolled her eyes, found an empty table in a dark corner, and watched him from afar flashing his clip-on gold tooth at every chick that looked his way. He left her alone and never looked back. For two hours she sipped punch, ate finger food, and chair danced until she had enough. She wasn't having fun, and the longer she sat there, the angrier she became, not just at Tony's abandonment, but at herself. In hindsight she could have swallowed her pride and asked Vaughn to escort her, making it clear that it wasn't any indication that she wanted to rekindle their relationship. Knowing Vaughn, he would have agreed without hesitation, if for nothing else, for the chance to see her again. She,started to track down Tony so that they could leave. Since she drove, he had no choice but to leave too. When she found him, he was up close and personal with a girl that was finally giving him the attention he was seeking. She interrupted them and yanked him away by his arm. "We've got to go." He resisted all the way to the car. Finally, he yanked his arm away. "Hey, what's your problem?" "I'm ready to go." "But I was about to get that girls number." "Oh trust me, I did you a favor. That bitch was ugly." "The only bitch I see around here is you!" "You can thank yourself for that! You left me! And for what? So that you can pick up jailbait? Is that the only reason why you volunteered to come?" Tony's guilt rendered him speechless. He couldn't deny that she was right. What he did was selfish. He just stood there with a dumbfounded and guilty expression. “Yeah, that’s what I thought. Just get in the car, jerk!”

On the way home, she decided to take Cierra up on her offer to hang out with her. She dropped Tony off, not bothering to change and headed straight to Cierra’s apartment. She instructed Tony to tell her mom where she was going and that she’d call when she got there. Aaliyah “Back & Forth” was blasting through Cierra’s door. She didn’t think that she could hear the doorbell through it, but the door swung open after one ring. “Oh my God! You look so beautiful! Clay, get my camera out of the kitchen utility drawer for me please?” Clay came with the camera within five seconds. “Hey mama? Wow, you are breathtaking!” “Thanks. Is Kenny still up? I want to say hi.” “No, he’s over his grandma’s for the weekend.” “Is Craig hanging with us tonight?” “No girl. He’s still plucking my nerves. I told him to stay home. Did you eat?” “Yeah, finger food.” “Don’t worry. I got you. We ordered a bunch of Chinese food, and I got your favorites! First, let me get some more pictures then I’ll get you a T-shirt to cover your dress.” “Okay, cool. Can I use your phone to call my mom?” “You don’t have to ask that. Just go ahead.” “Thanks.” Her mom was okay with her staying as long as she wanted. It was prom night and she was just a few minutes down the road. Aiko took a few pictures with Clay and Cierra then threw on the T-shirt. The three of them dug into the Chinese food once it arrived twenty minutes later. Aiko attacked the beef yat gaw mein first. She debriefed them on her cousin’s selfish behavior and the miserable prom night she was having. “Well shit girl, the night ain’t over yet! We’re going to have some fun and erase all of that!” Cierra got up and made some margaritas. She served up the drinks and sat down again. “Before you ask, they are not virgins so take your time.” “I will with the next one. After the night I’ve had, this one’s going bottoms up with the quickness.” She took the drink to the head like a pro. “Oh shit Cierra, I think you’ve created a monster!” Aiko slammed the glass down, gave Clay an intense, devilish look then growled at him. Clay and Cierra burst into laughter. They were happy to see Aiko having a moment where she wasn’t taking herself too seriously. Clay grabbed the pitcher and gave her a refill. “Alright monster, take it easy on this one.” She gave him a warm smile. She enjoyed how he made her feel whenever she was around him. Paired with Cierra, they always made her feel special to them. After the night she had up until that point, it was amazing how quickly they turned it around for her in thirty minutes. That was just the beginning. Clay danced with her to all of her favorite songs making her feel like the princess she had hoped to feel that night. It didn’t compare to Vaughn, but she’d take it. Cierra jumped in on the upbeat songs being the life of the party as usual. Once they tired themselves out from dancing, they relaxed in the living room with some more drinks. Cierra and Clay kept exchanging strange looks. Cierra nodded and stood up. “Ko, I’ve got something I want you to try. I’ll be right back.” She returned with a plastic baggie, a bong, and a lighter. “Seriously, weed? You do realize that I’m a minor right?” Clay chimed in, “I thought you were a monster?” “I am, but this may be pushing it.” “Girl please, did I let you overdo it with the alcohol?” “No, I don’t think so.” “Then I’m not going to let you overdo it with this. Here, put your finger there and inhale.” She followed Cierra’s instructions. She felt like the smoke was suffocating her. She started coughing and choking. Clay patted her on the back. “Hold the smoke in a few seconds longer next time.” She looked at him, still coughing and eyes watering with a 'nigga what?' expression. Cierra passed the bong to Clay while she got Aiko some water. She sat down, took a hit then passed it back to Aiko. "No, give it to Clay for second. I'm still recovering from the first one." They laughed at her. Clay teased her before he took his second hit. "Wimp." He knew that she had a big ego to defend and said exactly what it would take to challenge it. "Gimme the damn bong, nigga." She snatched it from him and not only took one hit, but two hits. "Oh shit! The monster is back!" "Stop teasing her Clay. Hand it here Koko." She watched Cierra take her second hit then passed it to Clay. When she did her arm stretched like a rubber band. Clay took his hit, threw his head back, and blew out the smoke. His lips swelled up like balloons on his face, and the smoke turned into bubbles. "Clay! What's wrong with your face?" "What?" "Your lips, they're really huge!" Clay grabbed his mouth and looked into the wall mirrors. "Girl, ain't nothing wrong with my face." Cierra grabbed Aiko's face with her arms stretched out long enough to jump rope with, and looked into her eyes. "Are you alright?" Cierra's eyes bugged out at hers like cartoon characters, and her pupils danced around like the beaded eyes of an old fashioned doll baby. Aiko yanked her body away from Cierra in terror. "Yo Cici, I think she's trippin'." Cierra started snapping her fingers at her. To Aiko it sounded like a hammer hitting sheet metal into a microphone. "Koko, are you trippin' girl?" Aiko was too busy fidgeting and blinking her eyes trying to regain her bearings to respond. "Yeah Clay, she's trippin'. You laced it didn't you?" "Yeah, but just a little bit." Cierra reached her long, wobbly arm behind Aiko and smacked him on the back of his head. His neck stretched out two feet and his head popped forward, snapped back, and bounced back to his shoulders. "I told you not to do that! That's too much for a first time!" "Damn, my bad. I'm not going to do it again." "Hopefully it wears off soon. Get your dumb ass up and fix a cold rag for her for head!" Clay did as he was instructed. Cierra forced her to drink more water while she held the rag to her forehead. Within thirty minutes or so, the hallucinations wore off, but she was still high. That's when the munchies kicked into high gear. She ate a little more Chinese food, and poured herself another margarita. "See, look at her. She can handle it." "Shut up Clay! I'll deal with you later. How are you feeling Ko?" "I'm high, if that's what you're asking, but I'm fine." "Are you sure?" "Yeah, your eyes were funny." She pointed at Cierra's eyes and giggled. Then she turned to Clay. "And your lips were this big." She threw her arms out really wide to show him, giggling until her stomach hurt. After the giggles came the uncontrollable sobbing. She went through ten tissues until she finally cried herself to sleep. A half an hour later, she woke up extremely dehydrated and thirsty. She gulped down the rest of her water and sat on the couch. Marvin Gaye "Sexual Healing" was playing on the stereo. Because the room was dark, it took a few minutes for her eyes to adjust. When they did, she saw Cierra and Clay making out on the couch right next to her left side. She watched for a few minutes before she spoke. "What are y'all doing?" Cierra got up and sat to her right. Clay scooted over to her and started kissing and touching her. Cierra watched him for a few minutes before she joined in, rubbing Aiko's back and thighs, and kissing her neck and shoulders. Clay slipped her T-shirt off, exposing more of her skin from her low-cut prom dress. He and Cierra both honed in on a new piece of her flesh to devour. Under normal circumstances, she would have felt weird, but her inhibitions were lowered from the alcohol and marijuana. Clay stood up, pulled her to her feet, and guided her towards the bedroom. Cierra followed. When they reached the bedroom, Clay undressed her and laid her down onto Cierra's queen sized bed. Still standing, Cierra undressed herself then lay next to Aiko's left side. Clay removed his white polo shirt and jeans and plunged his face into her pussy. Cierra joined in by sucking and twirling her tongue on her left nipple and caressing her body. She tapped Clay on his right shoulder signaling him that she wanted a turn. Clay moved aside and took her right nipple into his mouth while Cierra took his place between her legs. Her technique differed greatly from Clay's. She was gentle, slow, and skillful, whereas Clay was more firm, rushed and sloppy. It wasn't that Clay didn't make her feel good, but she preferred Cierra's style better. Because she was a woman, Cierra knew exactly how to please another woman as she would want to be pleased herself. In that moment it became evident that Craig knew about Cierra's bi-sexuality, which is why he was always so insecure.

Cierra continued to partake of her center. She wondered when she would come up for air. Her body began to quiver, and an overwhelming sensation to pee came over her. "Cierra stop. I have to pee." "That means that she's doing a good job down there, mama." Clay's comment was almost comical to her, but he was dead serious. "No, I can't do this." She wiggled around trying to break free. "Just relax and enjoy it." Clay held her down. He kissed, licked, and sucked all over her upper body, leaving no inch untouched as a way to calm and distract her. She closed her eyes and let go of all of her tension, and with it an orgasmic explosion. Realizing she had accomplished her goal, Cierra got up and lay beside her again. Giving her no time to recover or object, Clay mounted her and slipped his rock hard dick inside of her. Cierra masturbated as she watched. As far as size, he was even with Vaughn. As far as control and skill, he had Vaughn beat. Considering he was older and more experienced, that came as no surprise. He performed with the perfect blend and balance of making love and fucking. It was as if Vaughn and Kody were morphed into one man. It bothered her that Cierra was right about older men. She didn't want her to be right because that meant that she had to face some truths about herself that could possibly eliminate any residual desire to reconcile with Vaughn. At the moment, Vaughn was the furthest thing from her mind. The countless orgasms Clay was giving her took the forefront. Only his endless stamina could compete with them as he made love to her for hours. He leaned down to her ear. "Are you ready to have the biggest orgasm of your life?" She responded with a breathless "Yes." He lifted her legs and moved in closer, angling her body for direct blows to her G spot. Thrusting with the resolve to prove himself, he hit his target with bull's-eye precision. She yelped with pleasure uncontrollably. Her body locked up with resistance from her fears of what was about to happen. "Relax mama." She tried, but it wasn't easy. Sensing her struggle, he tightened his grip on her legs and delivered longer, harder strokes. She couldn't budge or fight it. It was happening. She felt pleasure beyond her wildest imaginations, and she didn't think that she could take it. Her yelps turned into cries as she begged him to stop. The more she begged, the harder he worked at his mission. Tears streamed down her face as she reached her climax. As promised, it was the biggest orgasm of her life. Her body collapsed from exhaustion. Her head flopped to her left towards Cierra who was just finishing an orgasm of her own. She grabbed some of Aiko's juices onto her fingers, licked them then tongue kissed her so that she could taste her own sweetness. Clay gently turned her face towards him and sampled another taste of her from her tongue. She flashed him a tiny, tired smile then gave into the weight of her eyelids and drifted to sleep.

The next morning, she woke up well rested but disoriented. For a second, she didn't know where she was. She shielded her eyes with her hand from the sunlight beaming through the drapes. The smell of pancakes, maple sausage, and cheesy eggs crept into the bedroom. Cierra and Clay had already gotten up and were playing music. Her prom dress was neatly hanging on the bedroom door. The intense sensation to pee came over again, but this time she really did have to pee. When her feet hit the floor, her legs felt like they were made of Jell-O, and she wobbled to the bathroom. She pee'd for what seemed like five minutes straight. When she went to the kitchen, she assumed that Cierra was cooking. Much to her surprise, it was Clay at the stove. Cierra danced at the table. His face lit up when he saw her. "Good morning beautiful!" "Beautiful is not the word to describe how I look right now." "Oh girl please, you're glowing." "If you say so. Is it okay that I grab a shower?" "Sure. The towels and stuff are in the linen closet in the hallway, and there's a pack of toothbrushes in the bathroom drawer."

After she showered she joined them in the kitchen. Clay served her up a plate and a big smile. "Before you even ask, I've already called your mom and told her that you were too sleepy to drive home and she was okay with you spending the night." "When did this happen?" "Last night after you passed out on the couch." "Oh, well thanks." "No problem. I'm going to fix your hair before you leave." "Okay." "So, did you have a good time?" "Yes Clay, I did. Thank you." Clay winked at her. "You're welcome mama." "Thank you too Cierra." "It was my pleasure." "In more ways than one." Clay snidely remarked. "Shut up Clay!" Cierra scorned. "Oh my God Clay, you're embarrassing me." "We enjoyed you too. No need to be embarrassed mama." Aiko let him get the last word. He couldn't possibly understand the mixed emotions she was feeling. What she had done betrayed her beliefs. She felt guilty for indulging in it.

After breakfast she rushed home to call on Karla to come to her house. Karla was there in five minutes and out of breath from rushing. "Ko, what's wrong?" Aiko looked around for her family. "Come on, let's go in the backyard. I don't want anyone to overhear." They sat on the top of the picnic table as she explained every sordid detail that happened between her, Cierra and Clay. Karla listened in shock. There was a minute of dead silence before Karla responded. "So, do you think that you're gay now?" Dead silence returned. Aiko didn't really have to give that answer any thought. Being gay never crossed her mind, but she examined the question anyway. "Hell no! I'm not gay. I'm strictly dickly for life!" "I heard that." They gave each other high fives and switched the conversation to the prom. That's what she loved about Karla. She didn't over analyze, and she knew how to ask the right questions to get her to think things through and come to her own decisions. Talking to Karla was easy, but facing God with this sin wasn't going to be. She was too ashamed.

CHAPTER 13—TRACK 11--INTERLUDE

About ten months had passed. The rest of nineteen ninety-four went by so fast it was almost a blur. Aiko was hiding from God in her shame. Going to church went from almost every week to almost never. She and Kody picked up where they last left things. On occasion, she got together with Clay. She remained friends with Cierra, but turned down any invites for the three of them to hang together alone. Her goal was to eventually chock up that night to life experience, and that meant no repeats. As for Vaughn, he was still around, but his pursuit of her had waned. She heard through the grapevine that he was dating someone. Her guess was that he was with Sophia. After all of the months that had passed, the thought of Vaughn being with Sophie still hurt her. She could deal with him being with anybody but her. Trying not to think about it wasn't hard. Between Kody, Clay and her friends she was occupied. Plus, she had a new friend named Ricky. He was a scrawny Caucasian and African-American dude with light skin and hazel eyes. Light bright brothers really weren't her taste, but he was funny and he gave her lots of attention. For someone twenty years old, he was kind of on the immature side. Considering he shared an apartment splitting bills down the middle, his immaturity otherwise wasn't a deal breaker. They met at work. He was her trainee, but they didn't hit it off right away. His playfulness plucked her nerves, and he danced on them every chance he got. What changed her mind was six months prior when she walked into the coat room and found him on the floor sweaty, shaking, and semi conscious. She found out that day that he was a diabetic and his blood sugar level had dropped tremendously low. Weakly, he pointed to his book bag. She almost broke the zipper trying to pry it open. She handed him his syringe and cringed as she watched him stick himself in the belly. Then, he grabbed a candy bar and ate it in less than a minute. From that day on, she tolerated his playfulness a little more. He was a very sick young man, and she knew that he laughed to keep from crying. It wasn't too long after that they became somewhat of an item. It wasn't official, but they did everything real couples do. She wasn't ready to fall in love again. There was no point. She was going away to college in the fall and didn't want any boyfriend attachment.

So far, the year had been going good for her. She lost twenty pounds which built her self-esteem. She was still a force to be reckoned with, probably even more so. Her confidence was no longer derived from people's fear of her volatile temper, but from deep acceptance of herself, the good and bad parts. She changed her outer appearance to match her inside. She cut her hair into a Toni Braxton style and colored it auburn. It was bright and fiery just like her. To give herself more of an edgy look, she pierced her right eyebrow, and right upper earlobe to go with her nose ring. On her eighteenth birthday, she planned to get a fierce, growling lion tattoo on her left ankle.

One Saturday afternoon she had the house to herself. Chelsea and Karla came over to hang out with her. Before she had any fun she wanted to knock out her Saturday chores. As usual she had her music blasting to give her momentum. One of her favorite albums at the moment was "My Life" by Mary J. Blige. "You Bring Me Joy" was playing. Chelsea and Karla sat at the dining room table sipping lemonade and watching her sweep the kitchen floor. "So, who are you taking to senior prom?" Chelsea asked. "I'm taking Ricky of course. Why?" "Well, I mean, you do have several choices." Leave it Chelsea to stir the pot. "No I don't." "Sure you do. There's Ricky, then there's Clay, Kody, and that Indian guy who likes you that keeps coming into your store. What's his name? Oh yeah, Ahote. If you *really* want a memorable prom, you could always take Cierra." It took all of the restraint she had not to smack Chelsea across her face with the broom. "Wait. Koko you told her about Kody?" "Well, I had to tell somebody. It was a big secret and hard to keep for long, and who I could tell was limited." "Yeah, look what happened when she told you." "Don't puff your chest out. You only found out by default. She would never tell you anything that private unless she had no other choice." "What's that supposed to mean?" "It means, bitch, that you have a big mouth!" "The better to suck a dick with, bitch! Oh, but you wouldn't know anything about that, virgin! But Kody does, just ask Aiko." Karla remained calm, which was just before the storm. She stared at Chelsea and shook her head. "You still underestimate me don't you?" Chelsea smirked proud of herself for getting under her skin.

"Karls, don't hit her. Please? "I won't." She didn't, but she did throw her lemonade in her face. Chelsea sat there with her mouth open in shock and her eyes bloodshot from the burn of the fresh lemons. Aiko burst into laughter until her stomach hurt. She handed Chelsea a damp towel to clean herself then sat down. "So ladies, ready to have fun?" Karla and Chelsea were still fuming and they both gave her the stink eye. The CD changer queued up TLC's "Creep." Chelsea mumbled under her breath, "That's your theme song Aiko." Karla slapped her five on that. "Oh, so ya'll are buddies when it's time to gang up on me? I see how it is." "Shut up and deal the cards, hoe." Chelsea slapped Karla five on her comment. "I can't stand ya'll bitches." In unison they responded, "We love you too bitch." They all giggled. Aiko dealt the cards and they spent the rest of the day peacefully having fun.

Senior prom was just a few weeks away. Despite Chelsea's snide remarks about her date choices, Ricky was her only option. She planned to drive to his place the next day. There were a few details about their plans for prom she wanted to finalize. When she got there his roommate Byron was in the kitchen wearing a white wife beater, cotton print boxers, and a scarf on his head tied in the front. He was fixing a snack for him and his boyfriend Percy, who was in the bedroom watching TV lying on his side with tight red underwear on, and his butt facing the bedroom doorway. "Hi Byron." "Hey Koko! Ooo girl, your outfit is fabulous! I want to be you when I grow up. Honey, Ricky ain't worth all of that. You need to get yourself a real man with your fly self." She laughed. "Byron, you are a trip." "You're laughing, but I'm serious honey. You know that you got a steak appetite. I don't know why you keep wasting your time with somebody who can only give you Vienna sausage, and I know that's all you're getting. Ha!" Ricky walked into the room overhearing the last bit of Byron's comment. "Shut up Byron! Hey baby." "Hey." He kissed her on the lips. Byron was repulsed by him kissing her when in his opinion he wasn't worthy. "Mmm, that's such a shame. Think about what I said Ko." Ricky was even more irritated and let Byron know that he had overstayed his welcome. "Bye Byron! Don't you have an ass to pump or something?" He grabbed his perfectly prepared snack and headed towards his bedroom, but not before he got the last word. "I'm just calling it like I see it. Koko, call me girl." He smacked his lips and rolled his eyes at Ricky and switched into his room. Aiko turned to Ricky "Are you sure that he's gay?" "I would say yes except that he seems to be into you too much for me." She chuckled. "You have no worries. The only dick lips I want to taste are my own." They retired to his room. "Okay, so about prom." He covered her mouth with his forefinger. "Shh, not now. Later." He moved closer and passionately kissed her, making her body melt. Most of the time, he gave her abbreviated foreplay, but this time he was more attentive to her body's needs. It was a nice change, though she wasn't holding her breath that anything else would get better. Byron was right. Ricky wasn't working with much. By far, he was the smallest she's had, which wouldn't have been a problem if he knew how to work with it. Every time they had sex doggy style, he would slip out a dozen times before she got frustrated and got on top. That position requires long and deep strokes, and Ricky was nowhere near equipped for it. The only plus was that giving him head was as easy as sucking on a blow pop. He kissed her earlobe. His quivering breath tickled her. "Grab my big dick." An image of a can of Vienna sausage popped in her head. She thunderously laughed out loud right in his face. “What’s so funny?” She could hardly compose herself long enough to answer him. She didn’t have the heart to tell him that his dick was big only in his imagination. “I’m sorry. I’m just not used to you talking dirty. It caught me off guard.” “Do you like it?” “I don’t know yet.” He took that as a no, but he didn’t let it stop him from trying to score.

After they made love, she thought it would be a good time to try to talk again about prom. He agreed to everything she wanted, but he had a request of his own. “Hey, I wanted to ask you something.” “Okay, shoot.” “Well, I care for you a lot. You’re smart, beautiful, and hard-working.” “Thanks.” “And, I was thinking that on prom night we can start trying for a baby.” “What? Boy, you must have bumped your head!” “No, I’m serious. You know that my diabetes hasn’t gotten any better. I want to leave a legacy just in case something happens to me.” “I understand all of that, but I’m going to college in the fall, remember?” “Yeah, but I was thinking that you could postpone that for a year.” “No, absolutely not!” “Why not?” “Do you really have to ask that?” “I don’t see what the problem is.” “And that’s the problem.” She jumped out of bed and started to get dressed “You’re leaving?” “Yes. This discussion is over.” As she stormed out, she noticed Byron peeking through his cracked bedroom door. It was evident that he had heard them arguing. He knew better than to approach her when she was that heated, but he intended to get the scoop in a day or two. As for Aiko, she wasn’t sure if there spiff meant that she needed to find an alternate prom date. She planned to recruit Clay as a stand-in as soon as possible.

She got a hold of Clay the next day. He was more than willing to escort her. Evidently, Byron was too anxious to wait another day to speak to her because he rang her cell phone off the hook.

For the sake of her nerves, she finally decided to answer. "Yes Byron. What is it?" "Oh, you're snippy today. Gee, I wonder why? Ima let you slide with that because I expect nothing less from your crazy ass." She couldn't help but laugh. He always made it hard to get upset with him. "I know you heard the argument last night. That's why you're calling right?" "It's one of the reasons, but I didn't hear everything. What was it about?" "He wants me to ditch college and have his baby so he can leave a legacy or some shit." "That nigga is crazy!" "That's what I told him." "Well listen, there's more that you need to know, but I can show you better than I can tell you. Can you come over right now?" "I really don't want to run into him." "He's not here. Are you coming?" "Yeah sure, I'm on my way." When she got there, Byron was waiting in the doorway. "Okay, what is it that you have to show me?" "Shh, come in and be quiet." He grabbed her hand and led her towards Ricky's room. "What's going on?" "Shh." He put his ear on the door then waved her over to do the same. What she heard was the familiar sound of Ricky's squeaky bed. She searched Byron's eyes for confirmation of what she was thinking. He nodded at her then opened the door. Her eyes saw what her ears heard. Ricky was having sex with another woman. Their entry startled her and she jumped off of him and covered herself with the sheet. "Aiko, I can explain." "No need to. What I just saw explains it." "You can join us if you want. It wouldn't be your first threesome now would it?" Byron didn't give Aiko a chance to respond. "Asshole! What makes you think she wants to fuck you and this little girl?" "At least I'm woman enough to give him a baby." "That's what makes you a little girl. You have no idea what you're getting yourself into. How old are you anyway?" "I'm fifteen." "Ha! Case in point. If Aiko was willing to give him a baby, your stupid ass wouldn't even be in his bed. He's using you. Put your clothes on, go home and do your homework little girl before I put you across my knee and beat some sense into you!" "My momma don't even beat me!" "That's the problem, but when I'm done with you, she won't have to. Go home!" The base in his voice resonated like a sonic boom. It took both Ricky and Aiko by surprise. The little girl had no choice but to obey his orders and she scampered out of the room dressing. Aiko took a deep breath. "Ricky, it's over. Lose my number." "Wait!" He jumped out of bed naked and ran over to her. "C'mon, one last goodbye romp? Maybe we'll score. I prefer to knock you up over her anyway." That's when time seemed to stand still as she watched Byron's right fist head straight for Ricky's left eye. It made contact with a loud cracking sound like the fake sound effects in action movies. Her mouth flew open as Ricky fell to the floor in slow motion, but the thump his body made was in real time. Byron stood over his limp body heaving with anger. He turned around, grabbed her by the hand again and led her to the front door. They sat on the front stoop of the apartment building for a few minutes in silence. She wanted to give him the same courtesy to calm down as he did her the day before, though he didn't need as much time. "Thank you Byron for standing up for me." "No problem." "Why?" "Why what?" "Why do you even care?" "Because we're friends right?" "Yeah, but I have never seen a gay dude dot a nigga's eye like that for a girl before. It was bizarre. I didn't think that you had it in you. I mean, you switch your butt and shit." "Aiko, first let me tell you something that you should know. I'm bisexual not gay." "Okay, and?" "And, I switch by choice, if and when I feel like it, but I'm still a man. I was born of a woman. I love women. I respect women, and any man that disrespects them in front of me will get his ass kicked, simple as that." "Damn, that's sexy." He laughed. "Shut up Aiko." "For real though, some all the way straight guys ain't got the resolve or the balls to do that. I respect you for that." He lowered his voice to a sexy baritone. "You want me now don't you?" They laughed out loud. "I would, but now that I know gay niggas can fight, I don't want Percy beating my ass for stealing you away." They laughed out loud again. "Promise me something Ko." "It depends on what it is." "Promise me that we'll be friends for a long time." "We will as long as you promise to kick some ass for me now and then." "Bitch please, you forget I know how you do too. I may need you to kick some ass for me." "Then it's a deal." Percy came out with some beers and joined them. "What's he doing in there babe?" "His stupid ass is in his room with a pack of frozen peas on his eye." "His stupid *and* broke ass had better cook and eat those peas when he's done too." Byron rolled his eyes with fresh annoyance over the thought of Ricky wasting food. The three of them enjoyed each other's company with beers, jokes and laughter for a couple of hours more.

Senior prom came and went. Clay was almost as good of an escort as Vaughn would have been. She continued to keep herself busy with work. She picked up a few more hours a week once summer came. In addition to the movie theater, she had been working a part-time job at a dollar store at the mall since a little before Halloween. As much as she hated to admit it, she wasn't ready to let Ricky go, at least until it was time to leave for college. She liked the arrangement that they had. It was relationship like without the relationship. Letting him go earlier than she anticipated was easy, but what was hard was being alone. She wanted a man she could hang tight with over the summer to take his place. Clay was a good candidate, but he wasn't ready to be joined at the hip with anyone. She and Kody's continued rendezvous were still a secret. If Karla found out that they were still at it, more hell would break loose. For the moment, working to pass the time away to avoid loneliness was the alternative.

CHAPTER 14—TRACK 12—AHOTE OLIVIER

She was on her ninth straight day of working. She picked up an extra shift at the store after she finished eight hours at the theater. Although she was tired, the money was good. Because she was assistant manager at the store, she could sit down when she wanted to, or keep busy making sure the store was faced and cleaned. She didn't have to worry about the back to back, face-to-face customer contact that she did at the theater, which was a relief. She wasn't really in the mood to be social. She decided to work in the candle isle so that she could smell them while she took inventory. A familiar voice pounded on her eardrums. "Hello beautiful." His voice was deep and sultry. Paired with his unique accent, it was lethal. It was the voice of Ahote. She had met him in the fall when she was working a concession stand shift at the movie theater. He was the most beautiful man she had ever seen. She stared at him so much that it bordered rude, but she couldn't help herself. He was magnetically attractive, and he seemed to glow and float as he moved. He flashed his sexy smile at her, winked and disappeared down the hallway through the theater doors with his popcorn and drink. Since then, he frequented the theater almost weekly. In her mind he was coming to watch her drool over him. Whatever his reasons for coming so often, she was glad to get another glimpse of that magnificent hunk of man. He was a twenty-one-year-old, six foot two, two hundred and thirty-five pound Native American man with titian brown skin that glowed like a summer sunset, and long, silky, coal black hair. His body was chiseled like a Greek god, which was accentuated by his navy blue wife beater hugging every curve of his muscles. This man could best be described simply as gorgeous. She was almost afraid to turn around to look at him. He had a way of leering at her as if to undress her with his equally coal black eyes. She could feel his every sordid thought. The hairs on the back of her neck stood up, but not without reason. He had walked up behind her gently blowing slow, deliberate puffs of hot breath against her skin. She was on a stepstool stocking candles. The sensation made her disoriented and weak in the knees and she lost her balance, though she was never in danger of falling. Ahote was too much into her personal space for that to happen. He wrapped his russet colored pythons around her upper body just below her breast line. His cologne was intoxicating and teased her senses with hints of spice and musk. He smelled earthy, but in a good way. She closed her eyes and let his scent take her to the most beautiful, picture-perfect forest. His scent alone could seduce off her panties. “Whoa! Are you alright?” Still lost in her imaginary forest, she didn’t respond. He leaned in close to her ear and softly sang her name, “Aiikoo.” “Hmm?” He gently shook her to get her attention. “Earth to Aiko.” She snapped out of it and attempted a play off that failed miserably. “Oh um, I was just in shock from my near-death fall. You know, lightheaded and stuff.” She cleared her throat to occupy the awkward silence. “You know, you’re beautiful even when you lie through your teeth.” She buried her face in both of her hands. “Oh my God, I'm so embarrassed." He moved her hands away and looked directly into her eyes. She could see her reflection in his black, shiny pupils. "Don't be. There's no reason." "Okay, I'll try. How did you know that I was working tonight?" "Well, if it weren't from the stepstool, I wouldn't have." "Short joke, ha ha ha." "Well, good things come in small packages." "And how would you know?" "I don't, but I intend to find out." His stare was so intense that it made her uncomfortable. For some reason, she couldn't break away from it. It was as if he was Dracula and she was his helpless prey. Her boss's interruption rescued her from his ocular grip. "Aiko, are you done inventory on the candles?" "Um, almost." "Well can you wrap it up soon? I need you in the party goods isle next." "Alrighty, I'll be there as soon as possible." She turned back to Ahote being careful not to lock eyes with him again. "Well, I have to get back to work." "Have dinner with me tomorrow night." "I don't know Ahote, I…" "You what? Have a boyfriend? Are you working?" "No, but…" "Got a hot date with someone else?" At that point she was a little annoyed. "No!" "Let me guess again. You're washing your hair? But, that shouldn't take long." Clearly, that was a cheap shot at her now shorter haircut. "Go to hell Ahote!" "Only if you go with me." Now fully annoyed, she darted away from him mumbling under her breath. "Oh come on. It was a joke." He had to bring himself to a light jog to catch up to her despite his long legs. He grabbed her right arm and swung her around towards him. Instinctively, she yanked her arm back giving him a pestilent glare. "I know you're crazy!" "I'm crazy about you." "You don't know me like that." "But I know enough that I want to get to know you more. Just give me a chance. Please? I promise you won't regret it." "Yeah, well I've heard that before." "But never from a man like me. I can live up to it." "We'll see." His face lit up. "Does that mean you'll go out with me?" "I guess so. Pick me up at eight." "Seven, I have something special planned." "Okay, seven. Now would you leave please before get into trouble?" "Okay love. For now, I bid you farewell." He kissed the back of her right hand as he stared into her eyes giving her implications of the night ahead. There was nothing sexual about the messages he was sending her, yet it still gave her chills. It was more deep and mysterious, but not in a way that made her feel in danger of anything malicious, at least not physically. To describe it would be to say that it seemed that he wanted to tear down her barriers. That made her very uneasy. Her barriers were her safeguard. No one, not even his fine ass was going to level her fortress leaving her vulnerable. With that, she decided to do whatever it takes to block his every attempt.

The next night as she prepared for her date with Ahote she listened to The Fugees "The Score" album and Nine Inch Nails "Head Like a Hole." Music set her mood and mind for whatever occasion of which she was preparing. In this case, she needed music that put her into a strong, yet cool and relaxed state of mind. She felt that her music selections were suitable for that. Chelsea wasn't really into rock music, and she curled her lip from the first note that played. "I don't see how you can stand it." "Stand what?" "This music. It's like nails on a chalkboard." "It's not that bad." "You're an Oreo cookie." "No I'm not. I'm just open-minded and appreciate all types of music." Karla saw an opportunity to take a cheap shot. "Well Chelsea, if you don't like the music you can always just leave." "I wouldn't give you the satisfaction." "Then shut up about the music." "Both of y'all shut up or both of y'all can leave!" Karla was offended. She didn't like being put in place alongside Chelsea, and Aiko rarely snapped at her. "I know you're not talking to me bitch!" Once again, Chelsea and Karla found common ground in the midst of their animosity. "Mmm hmm, retract your claws kitty. It ain't that serious, and it ain't nothing new when it comes to me and Karla, so stop trippin'. " Karla tagged back in, "What's with you anyway? Your tribe of men ain't putting out any dick lately?" Chelsea found her moment for a cheap shot this time. "That could be it. Let's call Kody and ask." Aiko gave Chelsea a look that could kill. Nothing that came out of Chelsea's mouth usually surprised her. She expected her to be a stink stirrer, but this was venomous. Essentially, she was dry snitching that Aiko and Kody were still screwing each other. This was a strategized attempt to start some more trouble between Aiko and Karla for her personal entertainment. She knew that after the car accident, their relationship was somewhat on shaky ground. The subject of Aiko and Kody was still a spark for Karla's temper, so all she had to do was light the match. For someone who was always the epicenter of other people's drama, she always managed to mask her dirty hands and avoid any drama of her own. She was truly a puppet master. Eventually karma would catch up to her if she didn't focus on controlling her impulse to cause discord. Aiko didn't want to raise Karla's suspicions, so she decided to keep her cool and her mouth shut until she could corner Chelsea about it later. She was not going to let Chelsea ruin her perfect vibe for her date, or her friendship with Karla.

Ahote arrived ten minutes early, but that didn't impress her nor did she rush. She made him wait simply because she was worth waiting for. She was casual, but absolutely gorgeous. She wore tight, dark blue jeans with holes at the kneecaps, a black wrap front tunic top with a plunging neckline, and four inch heel open toe black sandals. Her hair was freshly done in her fiery red spiked tresses topped off with a shine from oil sheen. The makeup she chose to go with was to accentuate her eyes, which she felt were the strongest feature on her face. She kept it simple with black eyeliner extended at the edges for the cat eye effect, mascara, and clear lip gloss. To accessorize she had long dangling silver earrings with a matching necklace, and silver rings and bracelets. If Ahote was annoyed by his fifteen minute wait for her, she couldn't tell. His face lit up like a Christmas tree when he saw her. As a true gentleman should, he got out of his black 1994 Volvo 850 Turbo and opened the passenger side door for her. Once he got into the driver side, he opened the moon roof. Clearly he wanted to show off a little bit. "Nice." "Thank you. You look beautiful." "Thanks. You look good too." He was wearing a crisp white T-shirt draped in a gray blazer, light blue jeans, and gray leather hushpuppies. His only accessories were a silver herringbone necklace and a silver wristwatch. "So, where are we headed?" "You'll see." "I'm not good with surprises." "Well with this one, you will be." "You're confident." "Yes I am." "I've got to say, that's a turn on." He laughed out loud. It was loud and hearty and compared to what Aiko imagined that God's laugh would sound like. "Then my plan seems to be working thus far. But, the night is still young, which only gives me more time to prove myself." "Go for it. I'm game." He turned the radio station to Aiko's favorite station. Method Man and Mary J Blige "You're All I Need to Get By" was playing. "What do you know about that?" "More than you thought apparently love." She couldn't help but blush. She felt the need to skip the subject so that she could regain her composure. Because he was older, she didn't want to act like a doting school girl around him. "So, this is your car. Did your parents buy it for you trust fund boy?" His parents were loaded. She knew that for sure. They owned a string of casinos in the Midwest and Mountain states. "Actually, I bought this with my own money." "Really? What do you do for a living?" "Well, I'm a therapist. I worked as an intern during my undergrad. So when I graduated this year, a year early might I add, I was offered a full-time job. I start studying for my Masters in the fall then I'm going for my PhD. After that, I'll start my own practice. And, yes I may ask mom and dad for the startup money for that." "I'm impressed. How do your parents feel about you not taking over the family business?" "They weren't happy at first, but I made a deal with them." "What was that?" "I told them that I would take over once they are ready to retire, at retirement age or longer, but no sooner. In the meantime, I'd sit on the board only showing my face for major decisions. Once I take over, I'll either sell my practice or scale it down to part-time out of my home." "Wow, you've really given it some thought." "I had to. As much as I want to follow my dreams to make myself happy, making my parents happy is just as important to me." "Sounds like all of you are lucky to have each other." "Yeah, thanks. Plus, my mom threatened to put a head shrinking curse on me." "Well, your head could use an inch or two off." "The one on my shoulders maybe, but not the other one." Her mouth flew open in shock. "Ahote, stop playing." "No, seriously. Why do you think my dad is still hanging in there? Partly love, partly fear." She laughed out loud. "So that's the secret to a lasting marriage, get them by the balls, though that's not what I thought that saying meant." "Yeah well, either way is not pleasant and I wasn't chancing it. My mom is very sweet until you get on her bad side." "I wish my mom had a bad side. She's too nice and people take advantage of that." "We should schedule a play date for our moms so they can rub off on each other." "Okay, it's a deal."

She began to recognize the route he was taking led to the Baltimore inner harbor. There were so many sights and sounds and restaurants down there that she didn't bother to try to guess where he was taking her. "Can you tell me now?" "Nope. I want you to stay in suspense until the last moment." "Then it better be good." "I don't think you'll be disappointed." Before long, he pulled into a parking garage that was a few blocks walking distance from the harbor. Parking was expensive, but considering his car was new and money was no object for him, the garage was the safest place to park. He held her hand the whole way to the harbor. It was a perfect, warm 83° night with clear, starry skies peeking from between the tall and picturesque buildings that framed the heart of the harbor. The moon's rays twinkled off of the ripples in the water. The air was filled with hints of seawater and a hodgepodge of yummy food scents from nearby restaurants. People from all walks of life, mostly couples were out enjoying the sights, sounds, and smells of the Baltimore harbor. Vagrant musicians set up camp on random corners pedaling for cash in their guitar cases, hats, or buckets in exchange for their amateur entertainment. The bright, colorful lights of storefronts were alluring and enticed people to spend their money on over priced items. The atmosphere swelled with a type of excitement that could lift even the grumpiest of moods. Ahote remained a gentleman performing acts of chivalry from the grand gestures to the small sentiments, including walking on the side of the trail closest to the edge of the water. Despite the beautiful surroundings and present company, her curiosity began to get the best of her, and she became anxious to find out where he was taking her. In an attempt to get her way, she stopped in her tracks and folded her arms like a tempered two-year-old. "Love, what's wrong?" "I'm not taking another step until you tell me where we are going." "Is that how it is?"

"Yes, that's how it is." "Well okay. Have it your way." In one swift motion, he lifted her and continued to walk as if she was the weight of air. She was somewhat aroused by his move and strength, but she didn't want him to know that. "Mutha fucka, you must have lost your mind. Put me down!" "For such a beautiful woman, you curse like a sailor." "And I fight better than one too. Now put me down!" "Oh, I might as well since we are already here." Once her feet hit the ground, she lightly whacked him on his shoulder. "You play too much." He laughed out loud. "But you like it. Admit it." "I will not. So where exactly is here?" She looked around scanning for which restaurant they were nearby. He chuckled at her innocent ignorance of the obvious large ship in front of which they were standing. "Well, it's this, the ship. It's a dinner cruise." "A dinner cruise? Wow! I have to admit, it's different." "And yet, it's just the beginning. After you my Lady." He slightly bowed and gestured for her to lead the way. Instead, she rested both of her hands in the crutch of his arm. "I prefer that we walk together." He smiled at her. "As you wish." "You're too much." "You want me to stop?" "Hell no! I'm just saying. It's been a long time since I felt well, girly, for lack of a better word. It's nice. Thank you." "You're welcome. Shall we go in now, together?" "We shall." The maître d' greeted them as soon as they walked in, "Welcome Sir Olivier and Madam Pierre. Your table awaits." The setting was beautiful. The lights were perfectly dimmed, low enough to set the mood and light enough to enjoy the simple, yet classy decor. Smooth jazz gently oozed from the sound system serenading them at the perfect volume. Candles flickered on every table, adding romance. Aiko was so captivated by the ambience that she almost didn't notice that they were the only people there. Once they were seated, she waited a few minutes staring at the entrance anticipating more diners. "Ahote, are you sure about this place? I mean, it doesn't seem very popular. Nobody else is here." "That's because I paid for a private night." Her mouth flew open in disbelief. "That must have cost you a fortune!" "A fortune is what I have. I spare no expense." "This is unbelievable! I feel like I'm a princess in a fairytale or something." "As every woman should feel. You are no exception." She covered her face with her hands to mask her blush. He tilted his head staring at her curiously much like a puppy would. "Why do you cover such a beautiful smile?" "It's called being bashful. Yes, I do have those moments occasionally, but don't get used to it." "No, you had better get used to blushing. I'm going to have you as red as your hair." "Don't count on it." "Well so far, it's me one and you zero." She smirked at his wit. The maître d' popped up out of the shadows like Dracula. All of his hair, including facial were shiny and perfectly slicked down, appearing to be drawn onto him. "Pardon me sir, madam. I have the champagne you've requested." He held the bottle in front of Ahote for him to examine for approval. Ahote nodded in confirmation. "Will the lady be having champagne? She appears to be rather young Sir."Ahote casted him an agitated glance, then reached into his pocket and grabbed a one hundred dollar bill. "How young does she look now?" The maître d' had no hesitation in grabbing the money and slipping it into his handkerchief pocket. "That is none of my concern Sir. I'll be back momentarily to take your order." He snapped his fingers signaling for the waiter to serve the champagne then disappeared into the shadows from whence he came. "I don't know whether to feel sorry for him or impressed by you." "Why?" "Well, you kind of used your money for power." "And you see that as a bad thing?" "In a way, yeah. The truth is that I am under age. He was looking out for me." Ahote scoffed at her naïveté. "If you think for one moment that he had your best interest at heart, you're sadly mistaken. He wasn't thinking about you. He was protecting his business." "Oh, I didn't think about it like that, but I guess you're right." "I know that I am." "But, you were wrong for bribing him." "Maybe, maybe not." "How do you figure not?" "Because money is power, bottom line. It's why businesses acquire other businesses when the price is right. It's why the Yankees can hire the best players. It's why only companies that can shell out millions can buy thirty second commercial spots during Super Bowl for the exposure. It's why I got us a private evening here tonight. And it's why garcon over there served champagne to a minor. I offered him money and he willingly accepted. I didn't force him. He could have declined, but he made that decision to choose money over the right thing to do." "But, had you not offered the money, there wouldn't have been a choice to make." "Don't you get it? He was looking for that choice. That's why he mentioned your youth in the first place. There's nobody here to witness it and I already paid for secrecy and privacy. What need did he have to bring it up? Think about it." "Hmm, you make a good point except for one thing." "What's that?" "You don't have the power and neither does your money. Seems to me that garcon has all of the power. He managed to take what I can only imagine was an exorbitant amount of money from you for this night, but also weasel another one hundred dollars out of you. To think, it's still early in our date. I'm curious as to what else he's going to do." He became lost in his thoughts with a furrowed brow. She could almost hear the gears grinding in his head. "You know what, you're right, but you're still supporting the fact that money is power." "Okay, I'll bite. How so?" "In this instance, he used *my* money for *his* power." "That makes sense." She raised her glass of champagne. "To having unlimited power." "I'll drink to that." Their glasses clinked and Aiko took her first sip of champagne. It was a night of many first. Ahote ordered caviar and escargot for appetizers. Surprisingly, she found them both very delicious and had no hesitation in giving them a try, despite their otherwise unappetizing common names. For the entrée it was à la carte, and she had choices of everything she could imagine from Maryland blue crab to steak, duck, rack of lamb with mint jelly and more. She sampled a little everything she had room for in her stomach.

Their conversation was fun and intellectual all at the same time. It aroused and intrigued her in a way on which she could not quite put her finger. By the third glass of champagne, her inhibitions began to fall apart, which was the complete opposite of her plan. She ordered a glass of ice water to help bring down her buzz. Before she could take more than a few sips, Nat King Cole's "Unforgettable" floated through the speakers. Ahote stood up and extended his hand. "May I have this dance my lady?" She placed her hand in his. "Yes, you may." He pulled her close, placing his right hand in the small of her back. She placed her right hand in his palm. There wasn't much space for full ballroom dancing, but he made due with the space he had. He danced with fluidity and elegance. She felt as though they were levitating two feet from the floor. He stared into her eyes with an overwhelming intensity that she could not handle. She broke the stare by looking at the cheesy nautical themed wall clock. He quickly and gently grabbed her chin guiding her face back towards his. He pulled her closer to him. He began to sing the lyrics. His voice was like an instrument, carrying a tenor range. She would have never imagined a voice like that could come from his mouth. It seemed to emerge from the depth of his soul. As much as she tried to avoid it, she was falling under his spell, at least in that moment. Whether it would have a lasting effect remained to be seen. There could be nothing good that could come from it in her opinion. A man this perfect and mesmerizing could be addictive, and that's dangerous, if to nothing else her barricade that she worked so hard to build. From the corner of her eye she saw the maître d' and waiters watching them with doting grins. Normally she would have been annoyed, but Ahote's serenade held her captive. For the ending he spun her around, dipped her and leaned his mouth within a fracture of an inch of hers. His warm, quivering breath gently grazed and heated her lips. Her heartbeat was in her ears and her breathing quickened with anticipation of a kiss. He stared into her eyes, this time with less intensity as if he were searching for something. By this time, they had drawn a crowd from the staff. They were bunched up in the kitchen doorway leering at them mindful to keep a respectful distance, though their whispers, coos, and pointed fingers still invaded their moment from across the room. Ahote smirked with amusement. "Should we give them what they are waiting for love?" "That's up to you." He leaned in closer as if to kiss her, only he sharply turned his face to her ear instead. "Not yet love. In due time." He lifted her upright. There were a few "Aws" and disappointed mumbles and the crowd scattered back to their stations. Aiko caught a sudden head rush and her knees buckled. Ahote reacted quickly and caught her almost as if he anticipated her stumble. He helped her to her seat and signaled for the maître d'. He scurried over to the table. "Yes sir. Are we ready for dessert?" "Yes. We'll have two orders of tiramisu, if that's okay with you Aiko?" "I've never had it. Is it a good?" Before Ahote could answer, the maître d' gave his opinion. "Oh Madam, I assure you it's to die for. You'll love it." "Okay, I've tried everything else new tonight. I might as well." "Very well then. Would you two care for some coffee too?" Ahote spoke for her again. "Yes, bring two coffees please." He returned in less than ten minutes. He was right about the tiramisu, and the coffee was the perfect complement to it. She and Ahote took their time with the desserts engaging in light and fun conversation. He summoned garcon once again for the bill. The maître d' returned with a check and two dinner mints. He placed them both on the table "In case you need these for later Madam." He gave her a suggestive wink and a smile. She blushed. Ahote settled the bill and left a two hundred dollar tip for the maître d' and one hundred dollar tips for every member of the staff. "Where are we going now?" "You'll see." "Another surprise?" "Are you complaining?" "Nope, I'm just asking. Are you getting smart with me now?" "No never. I don't want my ass kicked." "You had better act like you know." He smiled at her and grabbed her hand. It was late, yet the harbor was still lively. Most of the shops and boutiques were closed by then with the exception of restaurants, sports bars, and sub shops. Although full from her gourmet meal, the smell of Pollack Johnny's foot long hot dogs and fried onions tempted her senses and aroused her appetite. She made a mental note to visit the harbor again in the near future to grab one of those foot longs with the works.

The ride to the next destination was over thirty minutes. They filled the time with conversation, laughter, and good music. They arrived at Luskin's Hill, named after the former electronic store that used to be there. It was a popular spot to see fireworks. Her parents used to take her and her brother along with their cousins there every year. The last time she was there, she remembered getting her hair caught on the wire of the flagpole. Nobody bothered to rescue her. It was a good thing that she untangled herself. Needless to say, she was bitter at everyone the rest of that night, and they all dismissed her hurt feelings. Being that her last memory there wasn't a pleasant one, she was less than thrilled to be there. It took no time for Ahote to notice. "What's wrong love?" "Nothing, it's just that I have a bad memory here." "Oh really? Perhaps I can turn it around for you." "You can certainly try. I can't promise it'll work." "Then we shall see." He opened the moon roof again exposing the cobalt blue sky and sparkling stars. "It's beautiful isn't it?" "Yeah, I guess." "Tell me what happened." "No, it's not important. It was a long time ago anyway." "Clearly, it has some importance if it still affecting you this way. Tell me." "Fine, where's your couch doc?" "Just talk." She opened up to him about the memory. He listened in silence, churning his gears again. "Well, there you have it." He didn't respond. "Um, hello? I just spilled my guts here! Are you going to say something?" He casted her a look of concern . "You know what I think?" "I would like to. That's what I've been waiting for." "I think that in that moment you realized the concept of every man for himself. You shed your princess gown and found your strength and independence. I think it shattered your sheltered view of the world, and left a tiny scar that has gotten reopened time and time again since then." "Wow! You got all of that from a ponytail stuck in the flagpole story? I really don't think it's that deep." "Yes, because watching loved ones ignore your plea for help because of their being absorbed in their own happiness made you realize that you only have yourself to lean on. If family won't help, who else will? Every time you've gotten hurt since then, your idea of humanity became disillusioned, making you more self-reliant. That's good in a sense, but if you don't watch it that bitterness will overtake you. You'll wind up afraid to ask for help when your own strength just isn't enough." "I hear you, and for your information, my sheltered view of the world was shattered a long time ago, but that situation made it worse. Can we not talk about this anymore? I don't want our night to turn into a therapy session." "As you wish." "You sound like Wesley in 'Princess Bride'." He chuckled. "Yeah, I kind of do don't I? I'll try to stop." "You don't have to. It's cute." He smiled at her. For a moment, she saw a bashful side of him. He turned up the music on the radio, got out of the car, and went around to her side to help her out of the car. He effortlessly hopped onto the hood and patted the spot beside him. "Join me?" She knew that she couldn't hop up there with as little effort as did he, so she took her time sliding onto the hood trying to still look cute and ladylike. He threw his arms behind his head and lay back against the windshield. Isley Brothers "Voyage to Atlantis" was playing.

He gazed at the stars lost in his head again. "It's almost unfair how vast and beautiful the universe is, yet we're stuck here. Sometimes I wish my spirit could roam free, leave the cares of the physical world behind for a bit, and see all that's out there." "Um, you'd be dead." "I know that. I'm just saying to imagine if it were possible to come and go as we please." "Yeah, I guess I can see what you mean by that. Life is hard sometimes, for me a least, but you have good looks, money, a career, and power. What's there to escape from?" "Money doesn't equal happiness Aiko." "It damn sure helps." "Again, you're thinking in the physical. Open your mind love. Think supernaturally." "Okay, you're getting weird on me." "Am I?" "Uh, yeah." "No I'm not. I'm not talking about anything that you don't already know about. You are a Christian right?" "Yes, but what does that have to do with it?" Ahote sensed her offended tone. "Wait, hear me out. As a Christian, you believe in life after death. You worship and believe in a deity of whom you have never experienced on the physical level only spiritually and emotionally, yet you know He's real and you maintain your faith in the midst of his abstraction." "Yup, all of that!" Her response still had an offended edge. "So what I'm talking about is no different. It would be connecting on a spiritual and emotional level to the universe and all things in it, including people." "Oh okay, but what would be the purpose? Connecting that way to God changes my life for the better, not to mention it feels good." "This would be no different. God created everything in the universe, so connecting to the things in the universe is connecting with him." "I can see your point. Give me an example." "Okay, take connecting to another person for example. Have you ever felt the exhilaration of making love with a man that you're spiritually connected to?" "I can't say that I have." "Well, allow me to describe it to you." "Oh no Ahote, you really don't have to." "But, I want to." He turned his body towards her to make direct eye contact. "Imagine the feeling in your heart on the first, highest drop on a roller coaster. It's scary initially, then fun and breathtaking. Your arms go up and you let go feeling free like you're soaring around the bends and loops. Your senses are stimulated and you feel alive. Now translate that feeling into making love. You and this man are experiencing this together simultaneously. Your bodies are intertwined and hot and sweaty. There is electricity shooting between you as you passionately breathe into each other's mouths exchanging love. Your souls become one in sexual bliss. Because your senses are heightened, your orgasms are unbelievably explosive, blowing your mind and elevating the moment to an out of body experience, though every thrilling sensation of the physical remains." Aiko was captivated by his description. There was not much she could do to hide it. “How do those flies taste?” She quickly snapped her mouth shut like the Venus fly trap she was at the moment and cleared her throat. “Well that was interesting, but I don’t believe you.” “I’ll have to prove it to you one day.” “What makes you think you’ll ever get that far with me?” “I know because I can see that burning desire in your eyes for something that’s beyond your wildest dreams. You’re bored and you crave for something new and exciting. You just don’t know how to get it. That’s where I come in.” “Oh really?” “Yes really. Why do you think I chose you?” “Chose me? You need to go somewhere with that bullshit, chief.” “Oh I will, and I intend to take you with me.” He turned over to his back again. “As for now, the only stars you’ll be seeing are the ones up there.” She chuckled “I knew you were going to be dangerous for me.” “You have no idea how much, but in a good way. I promise.”

They spent the rest of the time chatting, listening to golden oldies, and gazing at the stars. Ahote walked her to the door and ended their date with a long, firm hug and an endearing peck on her left cheek. “Good night love.” “Good night. Thanks for everything.” “You’re welcome. I’ll call you tomorrow.” She turned around to open the door and caught a glimpse of the mini blind stuck in a cracked position from her mom peeking through them. As soon as she walked through the door, her mom rushed from behind the dining room wall smiling from ear to ear. “So, how did it go?” “It went well. I’m kind of tired though. Can I tell you about it in the morning?” “Sure.” “Thanks Ma.” “No problem. Sweet dreams, because honey, he is so fine!” Aiko blushed all over herself. “Okay mom, good night.” For the first time in a long time she went to bed with no music. She turned on her red light and laid on her back staring at the ceiling consumed with Ahote's words. She closed her eyes to first imagine flying free through a rain forest in the Amazon breathing fresh air and grazing leaves with her fingertips. The dew drops on them burst into tiny particles from the gentle force as nature's soundtrack of exotic birds, monkeys, and insects soothes her soul. She can feel the energy of the earth flowing through her body. It is intoxicating and she wants more. Fueled by that energy, she bursts through the top of the trees, soaring higher into the sky. The clouds tickle her skin as she passes through them. Curious as to how they taste, she sticks out her tongue. Just as she had imagined as a little girl, the clouds taste like cotton candy. Up into space she continues to soar. The earth is even more beautiful and perfect than any pictures she had ever seen. It is quiet, serene, and cool up there. She explores every planet. Other than Earth, Saturn was her favorite. Its rings are not only beautiful, but they dubbed as a giant, circular sliding board for her. When all of her exploring is done, she rests on the handle of the Big Dipper sipping on a glass of Milky Way from its scoop, counting the stars in vain. She ends her trip back on earth in a remote meadow under one lone, huge oak tree. No other trees or structures are around as far as the eye can see. The grass is bright, picture-perfect green standing six inches high and blanketed in splashes of pretty, colorful wildflowers. The leaves of the tree rustle in the light breeze. A tranquil calm overcomes her. In that moment surrounded by the wondrous creations of God, she fells His almighty, yet gentle presence. She always felt that nature brings people closer to God, and this is confirmation. The birds begin to chirp as if announcing His arrival and singing His praise. Overwhelmed by the love and peace His presence bestows upon her, she begins to weep. It came from the depths of her soul and brought with it all of the pain she had buried, but in a good way. It was a release, and a release was exactly what she needed to begin healing. Before long, morning arrived. She couldn't tell at which point her thoughts melted into her dreams. The bird song welcomed her to the new day. It was uncanny how it sounded much like the oak tree dream. She took a deep breath and smiled. Her heart was filled with pure joy. Surely, God wanted her to make that connection to remind her that the love, peace, and joy went beyond just a dream, but such is her life, that remained to be seen. Those things everyone had the right to have, yet it was still a mystery as to why some have them so easily and others spend a lifetime searching for them. One day, she hoped to solve that mystery and share her discovery with the world. In the meantime, she had to deal with a ton of questions from her mom, who was sure to barge into her room at any moment to commence a grilling session about her date with Ahote. She planned to spare no detail. It was a perfect, fairytale first date. Once her mom hears about it, she will be 'Team Ahote' for sure. She knew that it would come from a good place. Her mom just wanted her to be happy.

For a week after that she hadn't heard from him. That really shouldn't have bothered her, but it did. Admittedly she missed him, but since he disappeared on her, she would just go on business as usual. Allowing herself to think about it would only make her angrier. It wasn't because she had feelings for him. It was too early for that. It was simply because he was behaving like a typical male. After their date, she thought more highly of him than that. It was disappointing that he managed to break down the pedal stool she had placed him on so quickly.

That Saturday she only had to work at the store. She considered picking up a shift at the movie theater since she had no other plans that night besides chilling with Karla if she felt up to it . She couldn't decide, so she would leave it up to how she felt after her shift at the store. The day seemed to drag on despite how busy the Saturday traffic of teenagers and stay-at-home moms wasting money on snacks and cheap toys. Her lunch break couldn't come fast enough. When it did, all she wanted was to be alone. She had to cover the register for someone who called out of work. Face to face customer service was exhausting because no matter how crappy you feel, you have to keep a smile on your face. It was time to take off the mask. The loading dock was the perfect place to do just that. She pulled out her portable CD player and played Mary J. Blige "Mary Jane." That song always put her in a good mood. Every time she thought about Ahote's disappearing act, Toni Braxton's "7 Whole Days" would play in her head. She wanted to drown it out with another song. The dock was quiet. All of the shipments had already been delivered. She leaned back on the steps, closed her eyes, and let the warmth of the sun sooth her. The moment was quickly interrupted by the ring of her cell phone. Her heart jumped with hopes that it was Ahote. "Hello. Oh, hey Karls! What's up?" "Hey, what are you doing after work?" "I was thinking about picking up a shift at the theater. Why?" "Well, I'm bored. My brothers are all out, and I miss your crazy ass." Okay, I'll come over after I'm done at the store, and I miss you too. I've got to go. My lunch break is almost over." "Okay. We can start planning your birthday party too. See you later, Ko." "Bye Karls." She resumed her chill out until lunch was over. It wasn't until she was deep into work again that she realized she had forgotten to eat. She had a coworker ring her up a snack size box of Slim Jim's to hold her over. She would call

Karla after work to see what she had a taste for, and pick it up on the way to her house. By the time she got off of work, she didn't much feel like doing anything but veggie out in the den with her music, but she could do that with Karla there. Karla understood her like that. She headed to the parking lot. Although it was well lit, she always found the parking garage creepy and she hated walking through it alone. She called Karla to let her know she was picking up some Taco Bell. When she got to her car, Ahote was leaning against it holding a bouquet of flowers. His car was parked right next to hers. "Hey love!" "What are you doing here?" "I came to see you and to bring you these." "No thanks. You can go." "Look, I'm sorry that I didn't call you. I had to rush out of town. My dad had a stroke and I had to help him get settled back at home. Plus, I had to help run the business while he was recovering." "I'm sorry to hear that, but why should I believe you? I've never heard of someone recovering from a stroke in a week." "First of all, it was mild. Secondly, my dad is stubborn, so after a week, there was no stopping him from returning to work. Now, can you lose the attitude?" "Why should I? There are twenty-four hours in a day, and sixty minutes in each of them. There's no excuse why you couldn't have at least sent me a text message. Now, I need you to move so that I can get into my car!" "No." "No? Excuse me?" "You heard me. I'm not moving until you forgive me and drop the attitude woman." She was taken by surprise with his commanding tone. She didn't think he had it in him, but she was determined to get her way. By this time, she was seething with anger and she casted him a defiant glare, gritting her teeth like an attack dog. "I have plans with Karla. Now get the hell out of my way!" He was just as determined not to back down. "The only plans you have is with me. Who do you think got Karla to make sure you didn't pick up an extra shift?" "So now you're enlisting my friends as your henchmen? Is control that important to you? Well, you're not going to control me! Move!" He didn't yield. He didn't recoil from her wrath. He stared directly into her eyes. The marble black of his eyes had a strange gleam in them that made her feel nervous. It felt as if every facet of her soul was exposed to him. As much as she wanted to escape the clutches of his gaze, she was trapped by it once again. He managed to have that effect on her more often than she cared to admit. It was as if he had some sort of hex on her. "You are so beautiful when you're angry." He wrapped his arms around her waist and yanked her against his body. Still lost in his stare, her breath trembled as she awaited his next move. He traced her lips with his forefinger and leaned in for the kiss. Right before their lips connected, he paused looking deeper into her eyes and letting his warm, steady breath graze her lips first. She exhaled deeply and closed her eyes. His lips met hers at the very second she thought he was going to pull away. His big, strong hands rubbed up and down her back squeezing and massaging every inch, hill, and valley. Normally that would make her uncomfortable, but she let go of all of her personal hang ups so that she can enjoy her first kiss with him. His kiss was soft, very slow, and he twirled his tongue around hers and her lips at the same pace. One thing was for sure, he wasn't in a hurry. If the kiss lasted only five minutes, he could make it seem like fifteen minutes. It had been her desire to run her fingers through his silky, black hair since the day they met, and this was her chance. She grabbed his hair with both hands. It was just as she had imagined it, soft, smooth and fun. She could play with his hair all day. His breathing became heavier and he kissed her more intensely. Apparently, her playing with his hair had struck a chord that excited him. He grabbed her hands and put them on his chest, but she wasn't finished. She reached up and grabbed his hair more forcefully. She loved how his long locks glided between her fingers. He moaned, confirming her suspicions that it was a major turn on for him. After a few moments, he grabbed her hands again and broke away from the kiss. “What’s wrong?” “Nothing. Nothing at all. You were doing everything right.” “So, what’s the problem? Why did you stop?” He shifted his body as if he was uncomfortable. She glanced down to see that he had a full woody, and it was huge. Her eyes bugged out of her face. “Wow! Hello!” He nervously chuckled at her snake charming greeting to his privates. Without asking permission, she reached down to grab a handful. He stopped her in her tracks. “No not like this. It’ll be in due time, just not right now.” “Well, it seems to me, he would beg to differ.” “Well, he is not the brains of this operation, the one on my shoulders is.” “I think that you should let him know that because he’s ready to come out and play. By the way, does he have a name?” “His name is Ahote just like me.” “You couldn’t have been more creative?” “Well my name does mean ‘restless one.’ There’s no other name more befitting.” “Oh my goodness! I think I’m in for some trouble.” “That you are, love, but the best kind possible. I assure you. Now, ready for our date?” “Sure. Where are we going?” “Right here.” “Here?” “Yes, we are catching a movie then going to dinner. I figured that this time we would do a classic date.” “Okay, but isn’t it supposed to be dinner first, then a movie? You’ve got it backwards.” “Not really. If we do the movie first, we have the movie and anything and everything else to discuss at dinner. It adds to the conversation.” “Hmm, that’s true and makes sense. I’ve never thought of it that way.” “I know, that’s why I’m here. Shall we?” He extended the crutch of his arm to her. She placed her hand in the crutch and let him lead the way. “Can I ask you something?” “Sure. Shoot.” “How long did you wait to get that parking space next to mine?" "Not long. Just two hours." "Two hours! Yeah, you're 'special'." "Yes, I am. You just have yet to find out how." They saw "Batman Returns" and dined at Bennigan's. He insisted on paying for the movie tickets even though she could have gotten them for free because she worked there. It was by far the best classic date she ever had.

From then on, Aiko and Ahote were joined at the hip. He spoiled her with fine dining, jewelry, and fun and adventurous dates from go carts, baseball games, and the amusement parks to the romantic dates like one day trips to New York City for Broadway shows, buggy rides through Central Park, and hot air balloon rides over Niagara Falls. He was considerate enough to make sure she still had time for herself, family, and friends. He even paid for some of her outings with Karla and Chelsea, spoiling the three of them with the elegance of the finer things money could buy. Each time, he demanded that they take a limousine on him. Who could argue with that? It was not that Aiko didn't try, but he always won. Although the luxury and extravagance that Ahote gave her was lovely, it was the conversations between them that she valued the most. They discussed everything from current events, fashion, careers, money, love and relationships to religion and the mysteries of the universe. She learned so much about him and from him. The fact that he was so candid with her made her feel trusted and in turn she trusted him. It was the most free she had felt in a very long time and it was exhilarating.

CHAPTER 15—TRACK 13—DUE TIME

It was already mid-summer. Her birthday was in six weeks. One week after that she would leave for college in New York City. Between planning her eighteenth birthday party, buying school supplies and dorm room necessities, and packing, the next six weeks were going to be crunch time. Ahote planned a picnic in the park for them. It struck her as odd that he was very anxious about it. Normally he kept his cool. He made a point to remind her how special it was going to be. As if she didn't already have a ton to plan for, she had to add to it how to put together a comfortable, yet sexy outfit for the picnic. She called in her troops Karla and Chelsea to assist. They put on TLC's "Diggin'On You," poured glasses of ice cold lemonade and went to work. It fit the occasion so she played it a few times on repeat, which had Chelsea's eyes rolling. As usual, Karla had to check Chelsea's impatient attitude. Obsessive music repeating came with the territory of hanging with Aiko, and anyone that expressed an intolerance for it she had no problem showing them the door. After the usual highs and lows of the dynamic between the three of them, Aiko's look came together to perfection. Outsiders looking in could say what they wanted about them, but they were truly friends accepting the good, bad, and ugly about each other, and they were one hell of a fashion team. It may have taken a few years, but Aiko's sense of style had finally rubbed off on Chelsea. The end result was a short sleeve red and white striped drawstring tunic top, dark blue jean formfitting capris, and red strappy sandals with two inch heels. They were high enough to give her some height to accentuate her shapely legs, but low enough to be comfortable walking in grass. Of course, they accessorized. Her makeup was light and natural, top eyelid eyeliner only, mascara, and red tinted lip gloss. Since her hair had grown some over the summer, they put a feathered and swooped bang over her right eye. It had bounced and body giving her the ability to run her fingers through it or toss her head flirtatiously to capture Ahote's attention. To finish, she had a cropped jean jacket that came just below her bust line, which gave length to her torso and drew attention to her breasts. It would also come in handy in case it got chilly since the picnic was going to be by a lake.

Ahote was punctual as usual. He seemed to put as much thought into his outfit as she did. He had on blue jean shorts, a medium brown polo shirt which had enough buttons open to expose his smooth, glowing, orange tanned chest, and brown closed toe sandals. For accessories he had a gold herringbone necklace, gold watch, and a brown cowboy hat with his hair in a ponytail. When they arrived at the lake there was no work to be done. Their spot was private and sectioned off with no neighbors as far as the eye could see. There was no doubt that he dropped a bag of cash for it. Their spread was already set up, blanket, food, and music. He helped her down to the blanket and joined her. He appropriately chose smooth jazz to set a laid back mood. Duke

Ellington and John Coltrane's "My Little Brown Book" was playing. The sun seemed to know its role in the scene, hiding slightly behind the white, fluffy clouds providing just enough light and warmth. The clouds were scattered enough not to white wash the blue of the sky, giving way to the perfect summer day. Ahote popped a bottle of champagne that was chilling on ice. They toasted to absolutely nothing out loud, but in their eyes they toasted to each other. Ahote had the chef prepare a spread of all of her favorite foods from ones that were already on her list to the foods she discovered on their dates. A breeze carried in from the water whizzed by and blew her bangs into her face. He reached over and gently brushed her hair from her eyes. He then glided the tips of his fingers down the contour of the right side of her face. "You are so beautiful." "So are you." "Hungry?" "Yes, I'm starving." "Well then, let's dig in." They dined, laughed, and conversed for hours indulging themselves not only in the delectable cuisine, but in each other. His choice of music was designed around their mutual preferences and included legendary and modern jazz artists with selections of songs like Pat Methany "Last Train Home," Miles Davis "So What," Herbie Hancock "Maiden Voyage," and Dave Brubeck "Take Five." She made him promise to buy the CD's for her as a birthday present. As dusk approached, they watched the aesthetic orange and magenta sunset. He snapped his fingers and all of the trees surrounding them illuminated with the soft, white glow of string lights. It was absolutely breathtaking. The air began to chill. She put back on her jean jacket. Ahote lit a fire, which added to the ambience. Miles Davis's "Au Bar Du Petit Bac" came through the speakers." He pulled her to her feet. "May I have this dance?" "Of course you may." They began to dance together. Her spun her around, dipped her and spun her around again. He got behind her, wrapped his arms around her waist, and rested his chin on her left shoulder, as they continued to sway to the sultry song. "Go away with me, just for a week." "I would love to, but how would I explain that to my parents?" "Well, you just tell them that it's a senior trip that you and your friends planned at the spur of the moment." "Hmm, I don't think that they'll go for that." "Well, your mom is on board, at least that's what she said she'll be telling your dad." "What?" "Yeah, she told me that you would've lied to go anyway. She might as well be in on it. At least she knows that you'll be safe." "Wow that shocks the hell out of me!" He laughed out loud. "Your mom seems to know you very well. You're just oblivious to it." "Maybe. I don't know whether to be happy or not about that. I mean, I like to keep some mystery about me." "With moms, never. Accept that." "No, I choose to remain oblivious for a while longer. It's an ego thing." "Yeah, don't I know it." "Hey!" She elbowed him in his rib cage." "Ow! I'm sorry love. I was just kidding." "You had better be." "Or what?" She aimed her elbow again. He nervously laughed. "Okay okay, you win." She turned around and faced him. "I win? Oh goody! What's my prize?" "This." He gave her a long, slow, passionate kiss under the bright, twinkling stars, which were no match for the sparks flying between them. He released the kiss and caressed her face. "Come on, I'll take you home. The mosquitoes have feasted on both of our asses long enough tonight." "Hell yeah! You thought of everything except the bug spray." "How big of can would I need for you to go away?" "Oh, you've got jokes now. Come here!" He took off running towards the car. She playfully chased him around until they both ran out of breath.

The next week was all about her week long get away with Ahote. Despite her incessant pleas, he refused to tell her where they were going until they reached their destination. She packed outfits for every possible occasion he could have planned and squeezed them all into one suitcase and a carry-on bag. The fact that they were traveling by airplane was all she knew. He sent a driver to pick her up to meet him at the airport. When she arrived, she started to feel uneasy. The airport was small with very little people or travelers around. He greeted her with a big grin. He was oozing with excitement. “Hi love! Are you ready to go?” “Um yeah, except that I’m worried about this airport. It’s small and it’s a ghost town. Are you sure about this place?” He laughed at her unwarranted discomfort. “What’s so funny?” “It’s a small airport because it’s used for private jet and charter planes only. Not to worry love it’s perfectly safe.” “Oh okay. I feel kind of silly now though.” “There’s no need to feel silly. Come on, I want to show you something.” He walked her to a large bay where their plane was being checked. The bay could have easily fit three aircrafts, but only one was there. “Meet Suletu, which means ‘one that flies.’ It’s my dad’s private jet.” It was a huge Boeing 747 with all of the latest bells and whistles. Either it was new or barely used because it was squeaky clean and the paint was nowhere near weather worn. “Wow, she’s beautiful! Is she new?” “She’s three years old. He just takes good care of her.” “Well if this is any indication of how your dad takes care of your mom, she’s one lucky lady.” “And the apple doesn’t fall far from the tree.” He winked at her. She blushed all over herself. “Come on, we can board now. She’s just about ready.” He signaled for the pilot to lower the stairs. He gently pulled her out of the way. Stepping inside of the plane seemed more like entering a home. It was unbelievably spacious, modern, and very well decorated. It had a fully equipped Butler's kitchen straight ahead and a bedroom in the back. Off of the bedroom was a master bathroom with a walk-in shower. The seating area had a black and beige color scheme with every double wide seat upholstered in soft, plush, Italian leather. Ahote walked over to the stocked up mini-bar and popped the chilled champagne prepared for them. "Have a seat love. Our luggage is being loaded. We'll be leaving shortly." "Okay. Ahote, I have a confession to make. This is my first time flying. I'm so scared that I could piss on myself, but I'm not trying to destroy this leather." He chuckled at her and handed her a glass. "Then you're really going to need this. Now, drink and relax. It'll be okay. I promise." "Can you tell me where we're going now?" "Nope." "You suck." "Like a vampire." "I don't know how to respond to that." Taking a sip of champagne, he stared at her mischievously over the glass rim with the intent to get inside of her mind and spark her curiosity. Her loss for words and restless shifting in her seat proved it was working.

The pilot's voice belted from the loudspeaker announcing their departure and giving the emergency routine instructions. He failed to mention their destination, surely under the command of Ahote. The plane took off, jolting Aiko into immediate panic mode. Her heart jumped to her throat, and she was sure she had stopped breathing. Ahote wrapped his arm around her whispering comforting words in her ear. It impressed her that he didn't have to think twice about reacting to comfort her. As soon as the plane stabilized in the air, he dimmed the lights, poured more champagne for them and turned on some oldies slow grooves including Smokey Robinson "Quiet Storm" and Earth, Wind, & Fire "I'll Write A Song For You." Somewhere between her third glass of champagne and the tenth song she fell asleep. “Wake up love. We’re here.” She jumped up to discover that he had moved her to the bedroom. “You moved me?” “Yeah, your neck was crooked. I wanted you to be comfortable. Does it hurt?” “Does what hurt?” “Your neck.” “Oh duh, yes it does a little.” “I’ll get you some aspirin.” “No, I’ll be okay. I’m ready to go.” He was just as excited as she was to get going. The staircase was lowered awaiting their exit and their luggage had already been loaded into the limousine. “So, can you tell me where we are now?” “Yes love. Welcome to Colorado, my home state.” “Really? I’ve always wanted to visit Colorado!”

On the ride to their quarters, she couldn’t help but stick her head out of the sunroof. The air in Colorado was fresh, clean, and crisp. The pillowy white clouds had no threats of rainfall, and the sky was the perfect hue of blue. It reminded her of the dream she had in the meadow. Ahote gave her time to take it all in before he demanded her attention, grabbing her by the waist and pulling her back into the car. Her hair was in disarray from being blown by sixty-five miles per hour wind. He finger combed her hair back into place. “I’m glad that you are enjoying yourself so far.” “That’s not saying much. We haven’t done anything here yet.” “Oh, it’s coming.”

In about an hour they arrived at their destination. It was a big, beautiful, modern cabin nestled in the woods. There was a long path leading up to the house. It was the center of about five acres of land that included a ranch with horses and livestock. He gave her a tour of the house then had the personal chef prepare breakfast. Since they were two hours behind in the Mountain time zone, it was still early. Their whole spread of biscuits with butter and jelly, bacon, eggs, and chicken and waffles was all made from scratch and harvested from the ranch. After breakfast, he took her on a daylong tour of the town. Being true to a tourist, she got souvenirs and took a ton of pictures. Evenings in Colorado were chilly even in the summer, so after a long day of sightseeing they snuggled by the fireplace in the living room sipping on wine and listening to jazz. She fell asleep in his arms and woke up still in them in his California king bed underneath silk sheets. He was flipping channels on the television. “Good morning sleepyhead.” “Good morning. You moved me again?” “Yes. It’s not like you’re heavy.” She made a ‘yeah right’ face at him which didn’t get past him. He flexed his right python at her. “Not to me.” She hung her head bashfully. He lifted her face by the chin and gave her a reassuring kiss. “Are you hungry?” “Yes.” “What do you have a taste for this morning?” “Um, definitely those homemade biscuits again, slab bacon this time, fried eggs, okra, and grits with a little ketchup and butter. That should make me heavy enough.” “Nope, I’ll have you burning it off by noon. I’m going to take a shower.” He slid out of bed bare naked. Every muscle in his back was strong and defined. She traced them with her eyes down to the small of his back and to his round, full, toned butt which was just as tanned as the rest of him. *His sexy ass tans in the nude*. “Damn.” The moment it slipped off of her tongue she realized that it was supposed to be an inner thought too. He looked over his left shoulder at her smirking with confidence. He knew that his body was enticing. That was nothing new to him. He could get any woman he wanted with that body, or his money, or both, but his sights were set on Aiko. There was something about her that drew him to her other than her obvious beauty and intelligence. What he knew for sure was that her stubbornness and instinctive self preservation were attractive challenges. Part of his motive for the week long trip with her was to solve the mystery of her.

After breakfast, he took her on a tour of a few of his parents' casinos. They gambled on the machines and the blackjack table and caught a couple of live band shows. In total she won twelve hundred dollars which she would put towards books. At lunch, he took her to the penthouse of their main casino. Awaiting them were his parents. Both of them were gorgeous. It was clear that he was destined to be good looking. His father was an older, more distinguished version of him with long salt-and-pepper hair. His mother was a goddess about ten years her husband's junior. Her presence could demand the attention of any room in which she stepped. She was as beautiful as a perfect oil painting figure that walked off of the canvas. Her features were well defined, yet soft and feminine. Her deep, dark eyes seemed to see through the dimensions of the world or a person's soul. Her full, long, black, wavy hair cascaded down to the back of her knees. Surprisingly, they both were dressed in the latest fashions. That shouldn't have surprised her at all. It was the 1990s. She pictured them in loin cloths and headdresses. She was offended that she was thinking like a caveman. Clearly, she hadn't educated herself more on the modern Native American and that annoyed her. After all, she was dating one and she should educate herself for that reason. Being a person who loved all cultures, she planned to put that on the top of her to do list. "Mom, Dad, I'd like to introduce you to Aiko." His father bowed to her. "Osiyo." Ahote whispered in her ear, "Do the same." She bowed back. "Osiyo." His mother chose to greet her in a way more familiar to her. She stepped forward and extended her hand. "Hello, nice to meet you Aiko." "Hello ma'am. It's nice to meet you as well." She stepped back to her husband's side. "You've done well Ahote. She's beautiful. Her hips will give you many sons." Every ounce of her blood rushed to her cheeks and every muscle tensed in her body. Ahote could sense his mother's comment unintentionally embarrassed her, and he gently rubbed the small of her back to put her at ease. "Etsi, howatsu!" "Oh atsutsa, I mean no harm." She walked over to Aiko and put her arm around her. "Come my dear let me show you around while the men talk." She showed her every corner of the penthouse then they joined the men at the dining room table. The spread consisted of baked salmon, fresh salad and fruit. They were eating lightly because a big feast was planned for dinner at his parents' house. Lunch turned out very pleasant. His parents were actually down to earth and funny. They were kind and generous towards her and even hugged her before she and Ahote departed. After their lunch had settled, he took her horseback riding on a path at his ranch. She was too afraid to ride one alone, so she rode behind him on his horse Onyx. He was a black stallion just as gorgeous as his owner. She made herself comfortable resting her head on his broad back and gripping his ripped abdomen. The three of them were connected as they drifted through the trees. The perfumed summer air traced their unified silhouette as they cut through it with speed. Once again nature's soundtrack serenaded her ears and her spirit. After the ride, Ahote let her brush and feed Onyx. "He's beautiful. I think that I'm in love with horses now." He chuckled at her amused at how unlike her that sounded. "Do you want to see him do a trick?" "Yes, of course." "Onyx, is Aiko a pretty lady?" Onyx shook his head up and down. "Well then, bow to the pretty lady Onyx." He bowed with one leg to the ground and one leg curled under his torso. "Now do a dance for her." Onyx trotted around in a circle, then side to side in place. "Good job boy! Take another bow." Onyx obeyed. "Ask him for a kiss and hug." "You're kidding right?" "No, try it." "Onyx, can I have a kiss and hug?" He leaned forward and nuzzled her cheek then rested his head on her shoulder. "Oh my gosh, he's amazing!" "Thanks, I trained him myself." "Wow! Remind me to hire you when I get a horse." "It's a deal."

They headed back to the house where they napped for a few hours before they had to be at his parents' house. When she awakened from her nap, Ahote had laid out a swimsuit, and a handmade Cherokee princess head chain and top for her. It was modernized, formfitting with a low-cut bust line, and very sexy. A few tweaks here and there and with the right shoes and jeans it could start a trend back in Baltimore, which she fully intended to set in motion. She held it up against her body admiring it in the full-length mirror when Ahote walked into the room already dressed. "I had them made especially for you." He was so stealth and quiet that she didn't hear him enter the room. She yelped like a scared puppy. "I'm sorry. Did I startle you?" "Yes, I damn near leaped out of my skin!" "Well, can you leap into your clothes? We are running late." She didn't like his tone and her expression let him know that she disapproved. He apologized with a kiss. She freshened up then put on her outfit. She had the perfect accessories to go with it and she topped it off with sandals that laced up the calf. She was cleaned and dressed in thirty minutes which seemed to appease him. His parents' house was half an hour away. They would due there by six PM and they were leaving in just enough time to be punctual. When they arrived, the two of them looked like royalty. His parents' house was a private lakefront mansion. There were no neighbors as far as the eye could see. All of their family members and friends from all walks of life were gathered in the back of the house, including Ahote's twin sixteen-year-old brother and sister. People were gathered around a giant bonfire by the lake singing and dancing. Others were either swimming in the lake or in the large in ground pool. The aroma of open pit grilled meat filled the air. Off to the side were tables set up for seating, and others were dressed in side dishes and fixings. Some food was traditional to their culture, and the rest was classic American grill. The younger folks played frisbee and badminton, while the older ones played cards and chess. Ahote took her off to the side. "Come on, I want to teach you how to shoot a bow and arrow." "Oh, I don't know. I'm not trying to miss and hurt anyone." "It'll be okay. I'm right here." They walked over to the outer edge of the woods where a target was mounted on a tree. He got behind her to perfect her form. Each touch of his was slow and seductive. He put his lips right her earlobe. "Now, focus on the target. Aim. Pull straight back and hold it. Now let go." The arrow whooshed through the air landing on the outer ring. "That's not bad. Let's try again." He moved in closer leaving very little space between their bodies. "Now focus. Pretend the bull's-eye is your most desired achievement or your worst enemy. Now let go." She got in inside the rings that time. "That's better. Let's get the bull's-eye this time. Mount up." She did what she was told. "Straighten your arm. Good." This time he pressed his body completely against hers and put his mouth to her ear again. "Now, that bull's-eye is the love of your life, the man who can give you love, the world, and the ultimate orgasm. Are you going to let him get away?" He started sucking on her earlobe and kissing on her neck. Her arm began to lower. He lifted it back into position "No, focus. A true warrior let's nothing distract them." "Ahote, I don't think that I can do this." He pulled her waist into his crotch, slowly grinding against her ass. "Ahote!" "Shoot it!" "You're kind of making it hard for me." He licked her from the base of her neck back to her ear. "Do it now!" She focused, aimed, and let go. The arrow whooshed more aggressively through the air and landed in the bull's-eye. He spun her around and planted a long, passionate kiss on her lips. "You did it love!" "Yeah, I surprised myself too. I'm really hot. Are you hot?" "Somebody needs to cool off, huh?" In one swift swoop, he lifted her up, ran over to the pool, and jumped in with her in his arms. They popped to the surface of the water together. He removed his shirt, exposing his muscular chest. The water dripped and glistened off of his golden, sun-kissed skin. Heat spread through her body like a wildfire. She could have boiled the pool. He gently lifted off her shirt, admiring every curve of her plump, smooth, caramel colored breasts. Hunger for her grew in his eyes. He seductively licked his lips as if he was tasting her body. She moved in closer to him and placed her hand on his chest, popping water bubbles with her fingers. “Ahote, stop.” “Stop what?” “You know what.” “No I don’t. Tell me.” “Stop looking at me like that.” “Like what?” She sighed deeply. “Like I’m on the menu.” “If you’re asking me to hide my desire for you, all I can do is try for now, but I will have my feast.” *Oh shit!* Suddenly, she began to hyperventilate. “Love, what’s wrong?” She motioned her fingers like pushing an inhaler. He jumped out of the pool, got her inhaler out of her purse, and rushed back to her. He stroked her back until her breathing was under control. “Are you all right now?” “Yes, thank you.” “I didn’t know that I had that effect on you.” “No, my asthma does.” He did have that effect on her, but she refused to admit it. “Look at you lying through your teeth. You can’t even look at me straight in the eyes.” “That’s because I’ve got chlorine in them, now shut up.” “Make me.” She smacked the water in his direction splashing water in his face and she swam away. Stunned only for moment, he darted after her. It didn’t take long for him to catch up to her. She wasn’t a fast swimmer. Treading water was tough because of her curvy body. Once he caught up to her, he pinned her against the side of the pool. “Try to run now.” “I could if I wanted. One knee to your groin and it’s all over.” “You wouldn’t.” “I would if I had a reason, but I don’t. I’ve got you right where I want you.” She wrapped her arms around his neck, pulled him closer, and gave him the most passionate, seductive kiss that she could muster. He had no complaints, and indulged in every moment. From the corner of her eye she saw his mom staring and smiling at them. She broke the kiss. He chased her lips with his trying to reconnect. “Ahote, your mom can see us.” “So, I’m grown.” “Yeah, but it’s awkward.” “Okay okay, to be continued love.” They joined in some of the other activities until they worked up an appetite. By the time they finished eating mostly their Native American friends and family remained. Everyone gathered around the bonfire. The elder men of the family begin a traditional Cherokee song and dance routine. Their voices were beautiful and mimicked instruments. After a few songs, it was the young men’s turn. Ahote joined them. The young men’s performance was more modern. To Aiko, it resembled the step dancing that the Greek fraternities do you at college events. If she didn’t know any better, she would’ve thought they were showboating like peacocks to impress the females. Ahote was fantastic, not to mention very sexy. She had no idea he could move like that, so fluid, flexible, and agile. For some reason she had always thought that muscles equated to stiffness. As she could see, there was nothing stiff about Ahote except his cock. She was completely aroused. If that was his goal, then it worked undoubtedly. Next, it was the young ladies’ turn to reciprocate. They were just as exciting and desirable to behold. These Native American women were beautiful, sexy, and exotic. A sense of admiration and envy overcame her. She couldn’t help but wonder why Ahote would take interest in her when he could have his pick of any of these women that were already friends of the family. Afterwards, it was a free for all dance. Ahote kept trying to coax her into joining them. Reluctantly, she finally caved. It wasn’t that it didn’t look fun, she just felt out of place. She could do her thing on the dance floor, but this was at an away game. Luckily, she caught on quickly and before long, she was in there like a pro. She could see that Ahote was impressed. After the dancing everyone gathered for storytelling and mingling around the fire. She and Ahote sat together on a boulder drinking beers to cool off. “So, did you have a good time?” “Yes, I did. My birthday party won’t be able to top this.” “Oh, your party will have its own brand of fun. It’s apples to oranges.” “I guess you’re right, but this is magical. I will remember it for the rest of my life. Thank you.” “I’ve got a surprise for you.” He reached into his pocket and pulled out matching hand carved necklace, earrings and bracelet. The design was intricate with impeccable craftsmanship. He let her put on the earrings and bracelet then he placed the necklace around her neck. She felt the sting of an evil eye on her. She peeked up to see a slender, tall and beautiful Native American woman slicing her up with a deadly and tear filled stare. She appeared to be of an upper-class, well dressed in contemporary attire. Her long, dark hair cascaded over her right shoulder down to her waist. It was strange how she hadn’t noticed her before. She stuck out just as much as she did, though for different reasons. She glanced up again to find that the woman had vanished. “I made them myself.” “Wow, they’re beautiful. Thank you.” “Anything for my lovely Sora.” “Sora?” “Yes, that’s now your official Native American name. It means ‘song bird.’ It fits you, don’t you think?” “Oh my gosh, it’s perfect. I love it.” She sealed her gratitude with a kiss. “Are you ready to go?” “Yup.” “Come on, let’s say goodbye to everyone.” They exchanged goodbyes and exited as the royalty that they arrived.

On the ride home her curiosity got the best of her. “Ahote, who was that woman staring at us when you gave me the jewelry?” “Oh, that’s just Ama.” “Well she seemed upset. I’m still bleeding from her stare.” He laughed. “She’s my ex-girlfriend. Our families go way back. We were betrothed at one time, but I called it off.” “Whoa, wait, you were engaged? Was it arranged, and do people still do that?” “You’d be surprised how many cultures still do that, but no, it wasn’t arranged. Our families were close and we grew up together. Everyone just kind of expected it, and it just naturally happened that way. I just wasn’t into her. She has a dark and dead spirit.” Aiko caught her mouth hanging open again. “Really? I mean, she’s gorgeous. You couldn’t work around the spirit thing?” “Nope. What’s the point of having a diamond that doesn’t have clarity and doesn’t shine?” “Oh, I get it. It ain’t nothing but a rock.” “Exactly!”

When they got back to his house, he drew a bubble bath in the hot tub that was in a cozy C-shaped room off of the master bedroom. There were uncovered, curved windows that hugged half of the hot tub. There was no risk of being seen in there as he had no neighbors nearby. Aiko sat on the edge of the bed getting undressed for a long, hot shower herself. Ahote came into the bedroom in a bathrobe, grabbed her hand, and led her to the hot tub. He had candles lit everywhere. The soft, flickering glow danced on the walls and the glass of the windows, which created the illusion of even more candles. He had wine chilling tub side and smooth jazz playing on the hidden, built-in surround sound system that was installed throughout his entire bedroom. “In A Sentimental Mood” by John Coltrane dripped from the speakers. She loved that song ever since she heard it on an episode of "The Cosby Show." "Take a bath with me." Before she could answer, he took the liberty of removing the rest of her clothes making the decision for her. After he helped her into the tub, he poured two glasses of wine, handed them to her, and got into the tub sitting between her legs. "I think my mom likes you a lot." "How can you tell?" "For one, she kept asking me when I'm bringing you back for a visit. She's never done that. And for two, she said so." She laughed out loud. "Well that makes me feel good. What about your dad?" "He's the one who suggested that I give you a Native American name, so that's a sign that he like you too." "So what you're saying is that it doesn't matter to them that I'm not Native American or rich?" "No, it doesn't, especially after my breakup with Ama." She mumbled under her breath, "Yeah, they'll be okay with it until the dark cloud bursts." "What?" "Nothing, it's something that happened a long time ago. Finish what you were saying." "Well anyway, they realized that I refused to be boxed in like that and they began to think differently. They actually agreed with my choice, which surprised the hell out of me. They didn't like her either. And anyway, have you looked in the mirror lately? You've definitely got some of us in your bloodline somewhere." "Well shit, you would know better than I would. Come to think of it, I've always thought that my grandmother looked Native American." "Well, there you go. You should trace that one day." "Yeah, one day I will. I'm curious." "Do me a favor love, wash my hair?" "You mean I can actually touch it now, Sampson?" "Yes Delilah, just keep the dagger away." She grabbed the shampoo and lathered his hair. After two washes and rinses, she had used three quarters of a bottle on his long, full mane. "Let me do yours now." "I don't think there's enough left for me." He reached into a drawer at the foot of the tub and got another bottle. "I stay stocked up." "You have no choice with all of this hair." He washed her hair and bathed her entire body. Never would she have imagined that having a man wash the crack of her ass could be so sensual. If anything she thought it would be awkward. His technique was gentle and smooth, and he distracted her with kisses and touches on other parts of her body. He kissed each toe as he washed between them. Squeezing the washcloth letting the water trickle down her back, he passionately kissed her. The sensation set her desire aflame. He wouldn't let her wash him. He washed himself just as sensually as he did her, forcing her to look but don't touch. It was torture, but in a good way. After the bath, they towel blotted their hair and bodies. Ahote lit candles around the bedroom. Aiko immediately went for some pajamas. "No, leave them. Come here." He sat on the bed with his legs stretched out facing the headboard. He positioned her on his lap with her legs wrapped around his waist while they hugged and her head rested on his right shoulder. He whispered in her ear "Do you know why I'm attracted to you?" "No, I've been trying to figure that out." "Well, besides your obvious beauty and sexy outer appearance, I'm attracted to your spirit." "What about it?" "It's tender, yet strong, pure and naïve, yet wise, open, yet closed, intuitive, yet blind, pained, yet hopeful. I could see it all through your eyes from the moment we met. Your spirit is like a rare, precious, delicate gem that could be destroyed if placed in the wrong hands. There's so much energy and power inside of you that you aren't even aware of. I want to help you tap into that and channel it in ways that will help you conquer anything that comes your way. Will you let me?" She lifted her head and stared into his eyes with tears streaming from hers. She was so touched by his insight into her being and his profound words that she couldn't find her own to speak. A faint whisper of "Yes" finally escaped her lips. He wiped her tears and gave her a soft, shallow pack on her lips. "First, you and I need to link spiritually. Do you trust me?" "Yes." He put his hands up. "Put your hands in mine." She followed his instructions. "Now, look into my eyes. Don't break the stare until I say so." "Can I blink at least?" "Yes, you can blink silly. Follow my breathing, slow and steady. Free your mind. Feel your energy flowing through your body. Let the negative energy exit through your fingertips. Pull the positive energy in from the atmosphere. Now close your eyes and keep doing it." Her energy felt like free flowing water coursing through her veins. After about fifteen minutes of silence, Ahote started his instructions again. "Now look into my eyes again. Feel my energy as I feel yours. Keep following my breathing." This time, the staring was deeper and more intense. She began to feel a connection to him. Maybe it was all in her head, or maybe it wasn't. She wasn't sure. All she knew was that she felt wrapped in a blanket of warm and breezy, soft and harmless flames. Perhaps it was his energy that she felt. He threw his head back and closed his eyes shaking off a fleeting shiver. She assumed that he was feeling the cool trickle of her energy. That was her cue to close her eyes and immerse herself in the moment. They remained lost in each other's aura in what seemed like an alternate universe where time stood still. Ahote let go of her hands and placed his on her face. He kissed her slowly and erotically, deliberately breathing into her mouth. She felt a rush much like a crack head's first hit of their preferred poison. Somehow, she knew that he was giving her a piece of his spirit and she reciprocated. He sucked in her air taking long, deep drags her as if to get high. He then commanded her to lie on her stomach. He proceeded to give her a long, sensual, full body massage. It felt so good and relaxing that she dozed off to sleep. He delivered a gentle smack on her right butt cheek to wake her. "Turn over." She didn't hesitate to do what she was told. He massaged every part of her front, kissing and licking in random and usually neglected areas of flesh. He finished her toes and worked his way upwards. Out of nowhere, he released a deep, hungry growl and plunged his face into her center. She arched her back, let out an uncontrollable heave, and clutched the sheets. Either it was the torturous buildup of anticipation, or this man had unparalleled skills because she never had her pussy eaten like that before. She felt as if she was dying from the pleasure, yet charged and alive synchronously. When she could take no more she begged him to stop. He ignored her plea and continued to feast on her center, pushing her mind to the edge. Only when he had his fill did he cease. He lay on top of her, giving her only minutes to regain her composure. He kissed her while looking into her eyes to reconnect their spirits. Once their spirits were back in sync, it was time for their bodies to join. He spread her legs while still lying on her, kissing her and looking into her eyes so as to not break the connection. He then slowly entered her body. She had an orgasm for every inch of his manhood as he penetrated. His slow, rhythmic strokes rippled pleasure through her body with countless, mind blowing orgasms. The fusion of mind, body, and spirit into one during intercourse created an experience beyond the physical realm with every pleasure of the physical still potent and relevant just as he had described.

For hours it was just Aiko and Ahote in the world. They melted into a fifth element just as essential to their world as earth, air, water, and fire are to the real one. When they were done, they drifted off to sleep in each other's arms. The next thing that she remembered was waking up to the smell of burnt out candles and fried food. The curtains were still drawn, leaving the room dark and cozy. The low hum of voices from the television broke the silence of her morning deaf ears until Ahote entered the room. "Good morning love!" "Good morning." Her voice was groggy and didn't come out as sexy as she wanted. "I brought you breakfast." He delivered breakfast in bed which consisted of chicken and waffles, grits, and homemade biscuits. "This looks yummy. I'm starving. Thank you." She noticed that he didn't bring anything for himself "Aren't you going to eat something?" "I already did." "You couldn't wait for me?" "Baby, it's eleven thirty in the morning. I waited for as long as I could for you to wake up, and I didn't want to disturb you." "It's that late? I'm so sorry." "It's okay. You needed to rest." She gave him a smile then dug into her breakfast.

Ahote had the whole day already planned. They took a nature walk on his property. There was a small lake with a waterfall halfway through the trail where they rested. The waterfall presented a tranquil atmosphere. They sat Indian style by the water's edge where he taught her Buddhist meditation techniques. Later that day, he took her out for a night on the town. They ate at a fancy restaurant, caught a Broadway show, then changed and went to a nightclub. She was too young to get in, but as usual Ahote played the money card to gain her access. When they returned home, they took a long shower together and lay in each other's arms watching television. "One thing I can say about you, you feed me good then make my thick ass burn it off and then some." They laughed out loud. "Well, it's not intentional. It's just that I love good food and good fun. The calorie burn is a plus." "Well either way, I like it. Thank you." "You're welcome." "So, just what kind of therapist are you anyway?" "I practice traditional therapy helping people with mental and emotional issues, and sometimes sexual issues, but I incorporate the best techniques from religions or beliefs from around the world." "What kind of techniques?" "I use mostly stress management techniques, or anything that relaxes or connects the mind, body, and spirit." "So, have you been doing that with me?" "Yes, I have." "So, does that make me your patient? And, how much of what you've done for me have you done for other patients?" "No love, you are not my patient. Only the techniques that I've shown you I've shared with my patients, and that was through instruction booklets, never hands on. Everything else that I've done with you or for you was strictly between me and you and on a personal level." "Okay. I'm glad to hear that." He gave her a kiss. That was all it took to get all four of her burners on full blast. They made love in a way just as beautiful and connected as the night before. This time, he introduced Kama Sutra to the mix. At times she thought that she was physically limited for such positions, but he was a patient and skillful coach. She managed to push her limits, exploring how limber her body could be. That was one of many things he taught her that week. He took her to a Japanese Zen garden as an ideal setting for inner peace, meditation, and mental strength. He arranged private yoga lessons to help increase her core strength and stamina. There was so much she learned not only about her body and sexuality, but her spirit as well. She felt stronger, sexier, smarter, and empowered. Her senses were keener, being more tuned into the planet and her surroundings. Her thought processes were clearer because her mind had been de-cluttered. Her intuition and insight were sharper. Most of all, her self-esteem had shot through the roof. Everything Ahote had taught her contributed to the boost of her self-esteem, but it was the way he treated her that helped most of all. If she could put her finger on exactly what was the most impactful, it would be difficult. If forced to choose, she would say that it was his appreciation of her inner beauty. That made her feel more beautiful on the outside, despite the list of nitpicky flaws she had for herself. Men are attracted to confidence, so it's been said. Somehow, Ahote sought and resurrected hers from the grave in which she had buried it.

The weeklong getaway had ended much too soon, but it was time to get back to the real world. She had a new attitude to flex and an eighteenth birthday party to plan. It put her at ease that Ahote attended school in Baltimore, so she was only saying goodbye to Colorado for now. Once back home, the change in her was noticed immediately. Her mom was first to speak on it. “Whatever happened out there, it did you some good. For once in a long time, you look happy.” “Thanks mom. I feel happy. I feel ready for my life ahead. Next step is college!” “So, are you he an item now?” “You know what, I don't know. We never talked about that." "Maybe you should ask him." "Maybe I will. I just have to find the right time." Feeling jet-lagged, she retired to her room for the remainder of the day. Before she went to sleep, she texted Karla and Chelsea to let them know that she was back home and that she would get together with them the next day for party planning.

They gathered at her house. Karla showed up first, then Chelsea within minutes afterwards. Naturally, Chelsea had a colorful comment right out of the gate. "Damn bitch, look at you! I was wondering why you ain't call nobody while you were gone. Now I see. Your ass is glowing and shit! Chief put it on you didn't he?" "Hey Chels, it's nice to see you too." Karla chimed in, "I would like to know the answer to that myself." Aiko rolled her eyes. "Let's just plan the party and talk later." "Unh uh bitch, I want to know now! Then we plan. And spare not one slutty detail." Karla slapped Chelsea a high five. "I know that's right girl." Aiko took a defeated deep breath. "Fine, okay." Karla jumped up to make some drinks and microwave popcorn. "Wait! Don't start until we have everything." "Well hurry up before she changes her mind!" Chelsea was full of excitement and could hardly keep still in her seat. Once the snacks were ready, she began painting the picture with her words leaving out the most intimate details, but giving just enough to keep the story interesting. By this time Chelsea was practically foaming at the mouth and hanging off of her every word. If only she knew how much Aiko had omitted she would probably catch an attitude. She just didn't want to share everything that happened, especially the things that she had learned. Those secret, golden nuggets of information gave her a new edge that, quite frankly, Chelsea wasn't deserved to be privy. When she finished her story, Karla and Chelsea sat in speechless awe. "Y'all can close your mouths now." "I have a question. Is he your boyfriend?" That dredged up old feelings of the Derek situation. "What does it matter Chelsea? You can't have him." "Oh shit!" Karla belted out with the intent to instigate." "I could if I wanted to, let me make that clear, but that's not why I asked. So, you need to chill." "Regardless of why you asked, that's none of your business. And, no you couldn't. You're not his type and out of his league." "And you are?" "Yes I am." "Really, then why aren't you a couple? As far as I can tell you're just a charity case hoe with a wet ass to him, Julia Roberts." Karla choked off of her soda mid sip and laugh at Chelsea's "Pretty Woman" reference. "I think you're jealous." "Of what? Maybe if he were your man, I would be, but he's not." "And that's for a reason Chelsea." "Of which you have yet to disclose. I don't' even think you know you why yourself." Chelsea had her cornered there, but she wasn't going to admit it. She had to think of something and quickly. "I'm going away to college remember? I don't want a long distance relationship." "Well shit, that's all you had to say. I don't know why you had to get all defensive." "Because that's what she does Chelsea. You should know that by now." "Yeah, whatever, let's plan this seventies shindig." She turned on the radio. "Groove Is In The Heart" by Dee Lite blasted through the speakers. Chelsea danced her way back to her seat. The party was planned within two hours. All that was left to do was to shop, which they planned to do in pieces over the next two weeks. They spent the rest of the afternoon talking and dancing.

Her eyes popped open with excitement. “It’s my birthday!” She couldn’t believe how quickly the summer had gone, especially the last two weeks. Her tattoo was a week old and healing nicely. She and Ahote spent as much time together as they could around their schedules. There were only seven days left before she would leave for college, and she wanted to make the best of them. It was going to be a bittersweet departure. There was so much to do before the party. Her family had already gone to the hall to set up the decorations. Of course Karla and Chelsea were on beauty duty. Her outfit was decade accurate and sexy. She had on a blue, paisley print, mid drift halter top that tied at the back of the neck with a wide and plunging neck line that tastefully exposed some cleavage. To go with it she wore a short, blue A-line skirt and strappy platform shoes. For accessories she had a peace sign medallion necklace, a blue and silver cuff bracelet, and large silver earrings. She wet her hair, put gel in it, let it air dry with her natural, loose curls and waves, brushed down her baby hair, and topped it off with a silver head chain. For makeup she wore shimmery blue and silver eye shadow, mascara, soft neutral pink blush, and neutral pink lipstick. She couldn’t wait for Ahote to see her. Any other day time would fly by, but it seemed to crawl, mocking her anxiousness.

Finally six PM arrived and it was party time. The DJ announced her like royalty. She hired the same DJ from her sweet sixteen party. He was on top of her taste in music. “Alright people, the guest of honor is here to celebrate her eighteenth birthday! Introducing the smart, the beautiful, the fierce, and the now grown and sexy Aiko Pierre! It’s time to parr-tayyy!” He jump started the party with Michael Jackson “Don’t Stop Til

You Get Enough." Pleased by the turnout, she scoured the guests with her eyes taking notice of who showed and what they were wearing. Everyone looked nice, though some people missed the mark on the attire by a couple of years. The decorations were just the way she had pictured. There were black light posters, lava lamp centerpieces, beaded curtains at all of the doorways, strobe light with dry ice for a smoky affect and disco ball on the dance floor, a twister tournament and Soul Train scramble board off to the side, peace sign and flower decorations hanging from the ceiling, and a coin operated photo booth in the corner. There was also a professional photographer floating around capturing the moments, and another set up with a seventies themed back drop. There was only one thing missing, Ahote. It was already an hour into the party, and he hadn't shown yet. She checked her phone umpteen times to see if she had missed his calls, but there were none. She felt herself starting to get upset. *No, this is not going to happen! Not today!* She found a private corner to hide and to get her mind together. Whispering to herself and fighting back tears, she gave herself a quick pep talk, but that was abruptly interrupted by her body being spun around, slammed against the wall, and attacked by kisses. There was no need to guess who it was. For a moment, she had forgotten that she was furious with him, but only for a moment. If it weren't for the loud music, the whole party would've heard the crack of the smack she laid on his left cheek. "You're late!" Ahote wasn't stunned at all. Instead, he was aroused. "Mmm, there's my alley cat!" He hemmed her arms above her head with one hand, shoved his tongue down her throat, and stuck his fingers up her pussy with the other hand. After he delivered her a few orgasms, he figured she was ready to listen. "I'm sorry love. I got a flat tire on the way over here. I had to wait for Triple A to change it." "You couldn't change it yourself?" "And show up even later with dirty threads? No can do. You dig foxy mama?" She chuckled at his attempt to be seventies cool. "Yeah I dig. I'm sorry for slapping you, but you could have still called." "I tried, but there was no reception. And I'm not sorry that you slapped me." He sucked the fingers that were inside of her that were still wet from her juices. "You are so nasty." "Mmm hmm, but you like it though." He pressed his body up against hers, pinning her against the wall. "You look so sexy. I could take you right here and now." "No, but you can kiss me again some more." Without another word, he granted her wish kissing her in the way that he knew would get her hot. She had to take control and stop him before they went too far. "Baby no, not now. Later, I promise. I'm missing my party." Knowing that he couldn't win this battle, he gave her a sweet peck on the nose and forehead. "Okay love." "You look hot yourself. I've got to get some pictures with you, come on." He had on a brown polyester shirt with a super fly collar unbuttoned to show his chest and gold medallion necklace, blue bell bottom jeans, brown closed toe platform shoes, a brown wide brimmed hat with a feather in it, and a big faced gold watch. Hands down, he was the fly-est, sexiest man in the room. They took photo booth and professional pictures together and separately then they headed to the buffet. After their food settled, they got on the dance floor. The first song they dance to was The Bee Gees "You Should be Dancing" followed by "Boogie Oogie Oogie" by A Taste of Honey. All of the original gangstas turned up on the dance floor when GQ's "Disco

Nights" and Chic's "Good Times" played showing the younger folks a thing or two about disco dancing. When "Disco Inferno" by The Trammps came on, the sea of mocha on the dance floor was speckled with cream as the white people started to catch the 'fever'. The John Travolta copy cats young and old did their best to outdo him and each other all in good fun. The intro to "Atomic Dog" by George Clinton started. It was time stamped in the early eighties, but it was still close enough to slide. The DJ came on the microphone. "Alright, where are all my Q dogs thirty and over at? Get on the dance floor ya'll! Bow wow!" The older Q dogs answered the call of the wild, taking their places on the dance floor with their tails wagging. They may have been older, but they were still sexy and smooth. Women howled at them like bitches in heat. After a few minutes the DJ chimed in again. "It's time for the puppies to join the pound! All Q's twenty-nine and under make some noise!" Aiko and Ahote were resting their feet at their table. All four of Karla's brothers, all Q's, headed to the dance floor. Ahote was right behind them. Before she had a chance to question him, he had already taken his place on the dance floor. The older Q's parted to the sides still keeping to their style, while the younger ones took front and center performing step routines. Ahote, being of a different flavor didn't miss a beat, and he blended in with his browner counterparts. Aiko didn't think that he could be sexier to her until then. Watching his body moving put her into a lustful trance that was rudely interrupted by Chelsea's forceful elbow nudge. She was holding a glass of Coke with a cherry. Aiko would bet her life that Chelsea showed the bartender a tittie for a splash of rum to go with it. "Girl, I didn't know Ahote was a Q!" "Neither did I until now." "And now, so does all of the other women in here. And his fine ass is single too! I can almost smell the wet panties up in here because yours ain't the only ones that are soaked over him right now. You better hope his Q dog ass doesn't pick up the scent and follow the trail in another direction." She fanned herself with the napkin she was holding and walked away satisfied that she had accomplished planting seeds of doubt and insecurity in Aiko. There was no denying that Chelsea had her troublemaking ways, but this time Aiko knew that her motive was from a good place. Though her tactic was below the belt, she lit the proverbial 'fire under her ass' to snag her man, which she planned to do later that night. Karla was standing within earshot of the conversation. She walked up to Aiko's right side. "You know that I hate to agree with that grimy bitch, but she's right." Aiko sighed resolutely. "Yeah, I know." "So what are you going to do?" "I'm going to see what's up with the relationship thing later." "What if he says no?" "Then we'll still be friends." "Will that be enough for you?" "It's going to have to be." They continued to watch in silence.

The DJ got on the microphone again. "Hey ladies, get on the floor and give these Q dogs reasons to pant! "She's A Bad Mama Jama" by Carl Carlton pulled the women young and old to the floor with magnetic force. Aiko shot over to Ahote like a bullet from a gun. If any of the women in there fancied Ahote, she was going to make sure that she made it known that her claim on him was already staked. She danced on him close and seductively, giving no thought to censor her behavior considering that her parents could be watching. After all, she was an adult now. Ahote wasn't complaining for sure. She scanned the room for jealous onlookers, taking note of whom she possibly needed to watch her back for the knife. The DJ thought it was time to change it up, but it became evident that he had a theme in mind from the sequence of the songs. “Okay people, it’s time to slow it down. This next song I’m sure some of y’all were conceived to, and after tonight, a few more. Ha ha!” “Between The Sheets” by the Isley Brothers slinked into the atmosphere. Some of the singles snuck off of the floor while the bolder ones grabbed themselves someone with which to dance. Before long, Aiko and Ahote shared the floor with other couples. Some were awkwardly paired making the best of the moment, while others were connected by their history, married or dating. Their energy was powerful, wrapping the room with an endless scroll of smooth, flowing, chocolatey silk. The DJ sensed the success of the mood he was creating. “If it ain’t broke, don’t fix it. Let’s keep it going y’all,” he said in a smooth and sexy baritone. Isley Brothers “Groove With You” played next followed by Marvin Gaye’s “Let’s Get It On.” Apparently, her parents weren’t paying her outwardly promiscuous behavior too much attention because they were too busy all over each other. Since she had just noticed that they were on the dance floor, she didn’t know how long they were there, but she was glad that they were preoccupied. Karla and Chelsea were getting their grooves on with their boyfriends too. Karla was still with Andre. The DJ wrapped up that slow dance segment with New Birth’s “Been Such A Long Time.” It was so hot from the smoldering sexual energy in the hall that the staff opened the emergency exit doors. The DJ picked up the pace with Heatwave “Boogie Nights.” Some people stayed on the floor while others scattered between the back balcony, the tables, or the open bar for drinks to cool down. Aiko and Ahote went for the latter, though ice water couldn't do anything for the smoldering heat between them at that point. Chelsea walked up behind them. "Ko girl, look who I found." Aiko turned around to see Cierra and Clay. She damn near choked on her water. Simply put, there were three men that she was currently screwing all in the same room at the same time. Kody already knew that he was a slab of meat and was okay with it. Plus, he had other women. Ahote being her new love interest was clueless, and she wanted him to remain that way. She wanted more with him. This situation could blow that up for her. As for Clay, he knew about Kody, but she wasn't sure one way or the other how he would react to another man. It wasn't as if they were even trying to be a couple, but if a man is tapping that ass, especially if it's good ass, he can get territorial. Aiko exchanged hugs with them and made introductions. "I didn't know y'all were coming." Cierra replied, "Yeah, Chelsea called me. She said that y'all were a few invitations short and since you could only order by the box, she decided to save you some money and called instead. And she told me to bring Clay." Aiko's temperature was rising again, this time with anger. "She did? That was very considerate of her," she said through furiously gripped teeth disguised as a smile. *Just when I gave Chelsea some positive credit, the bitch goes and does something else underhanded.* She wondered if Clay saw her and Ahote dancing. "So, how long have you two been here?" "About five minutes," Cierra shouted trying to cover up Clay's "long enough" mumble, but it wasn't enough. Aiko heard it. It was clear that Clay saw them and he had a problem with it. He gave Ahote a staunch stare. “Hey bro, I’m going to borrow her for minute.”Ahote grabbed her arm returning the stare. “She’s busy.” She turned to Ahote. “Look, chill. I’ll be back in five minutes.” She made sure that she and Clay were close enough where he could see them so there would be no suspicion, but far enough that he couldn’t hear their conversation. He kept his eyes on them the whole time. In her mind, he was probably trying to read their lips. “So, who is that nigga?” “Why does it matter to you? I’m not your girl.” “Are you fucking him?” “That’s none of your business Clay.” “You probably are.” “And if I am, why do you care? Ain’t that all we’re doing?” “Yeah, but that’s different.” She folded her arms “How?” “I don’t know. It just is.” “Okay, tell me something. Am I the only one that you’re fucking?” He shifted his eyes in guilt. “Mmm hmm, see that’s what I thought. Tell me something else, you don’t have a problem with me fucking Kody, but you only suspect that I’m fucking Ahote and you’re trippin’. Why?” He sucked his teeth and waved his hand dismissively. “That nigga Kody is a kid to me.” “Oh, so your problem with Ahote is that he’s a grown ass man. That’s too much competition for you, huh?” “Man, whatever. He’s got a sucka ass name anyway. I’m still going to tap that ass.” “If you keep acting up and carrying an attitude, you won’t be!” He sucked his teeth again. “Yeah, we’ll see.” “Test me and see what happens.” She started to walk away from him. “Call me when you’re ready for a real man, mama.” She rolled her eyes and continued to walk away. Ahote had a burning question of his own for her. “So, what was that all about?” Honesty was the best policy. She didn’t want him to have any reason not to trust her. “Clay is intimidated by you.” “Me, why?” “Because you have what he wants." "And what's that?" "You have my attention." "Something tells me that's not all he wants." "Well what he wants and what he can get are two different things." He wrapped his arms around her waist. "I can't say that I blame him because everything about you girl is da bomb." She laughed out loud. "I need you not to say 'da bomb' ever again. It sounds weird coming from you. Stick to what you know." "Okay. How about this? Love, you are the sexiest, most intelligent, talented, passionate, and beautiful woman I've ever met." "Now that's more like it." He kissed her making sure to check if Clay could see. Clay saw it, and flipped his middle finger at him. Ahote mocked him with a deviant smile, kissing her ears and neck, and groping and squeezing her body.

They went to their table to rest for a while. As soon as "The Hustle" by Van McCoy played, Aiko was ready to cut a rug again. Right after that, The DJ initiated the Soul Train line with Lakeside's "Fantastic Voyage." She and Ahote went down the line paired up. Some of the hall staff joined in too. Despite the small episode with Clay, she had a great time. His jealousy wasn't going to stop her show, but after three more hours, the clock did. The party ran over almost two hours past the four hour rented time. Luckily, the DJ and the staff didn't charge extra. The music was hot, the food was good, and everyone was having such a great time that they kept the party going until it died down on its own. Clay and Cierra had left about an hour before it ended. They slipped out without saying goodbye. She could understand why Clay would do that, but it wasn't like Cierra to leave without speaking. She planned to call her to find out what was up later. In the meantime, she had gifts to gather and a sexy Cherokee man to snag. She said her thank yous and goodbyes to everyone with Ahote devotedly standing next to her. Dante drove her car home so that she could ride with Ahote.

"Baby, can you turn the air up please?" "You're sweating and your pores are open. You'll catch a cold." "It's a chance that I'm willing to take. I'm hot." He did what she asked of him. "So, you never told me that you were a Q." "I didn't?" "Nope." "I thought I did. I'm sorry." "So how did that come about?" "I got a full scholarship to Freeman State University for undergrad, since I'm a minority too" "Okay, so that's how you came to Baltimore?" "Yup, and I liked it so much that I stayed for my Masters degree. Most likely I'll stay here for my PhD too. I haven't decided yet." "And here I am leaving." "That's because the best school for your field is in New York. It's worth it." "Yeah I guess, but I'll miss everyone. I'll miss you." "Love, it's only three and a half hours away. I have a private jet at my disposal, remember? Just say when, and I'll be there." "Thanks, that makes me feel better."

Once they were at the condo, they showered and made love. Pillow talk was the perfect time to bring up the relationship subject. "Ahote, how do you feel about me? About us?" "I love you. I love us." "You've never said that before." "Well I'm saying it now. I love you Aiko." "I love you too, which is why am wondering why you haven't asked me to be your girlfriend." "That's for a few reasons." "I'm listening." "Well for one, I honestly didn't think that's what you wanted. You were so guarded. And two, you're going away to college. It's not ideal for a new relationship." "Is there a three?" "Yes, and three, after what I saw tonight, you aren't ready. Clearly you have some unfinished business." "You mean Clay? He's just a friend." "He's a friend that you are sleeping with. Don't even try to deny it. I'm a man, and no man acts the way he did if he wasn't involved with a woman." She looked away trying to hide her shame. "Ahote, listen to me. I'm done with him. I want you." "You don't know what you want yet, but it's okay. You're young. You have time to figure that out, as do I." "But why can't we figure that out together, as a couple?" "Because you have your journey to take, and I have mine. What I want more than anything is for our journeys to have paths that lead us back to each other so that we can have that relationship." At that point, she was fighting back tears. "I don't want to lose you." He gently touched her arm, and the tears broke free. "You're not losing me love. I'll always be here for you." "But not in the way that I want." "But it'll be in the way that you need right now. Trust me love." She hated that she felt so vulnerable and hurt. It was an all too familiar feeling that she had hoped she wouldn't experience for very long time and especially not with Ahote. It was all her fault for letting her insecurities get the best of her. Everything she could have done differently crowded in her head until it felt it would burst. She jumped out of bed to grab her clothes. "I can't take this. I've got to go home." "Why?" "Because I'm embarrassed. I feel so stupid and rejected." "Aiko, get your ass back in bed!" "Ahote, I can't deal right now." "I said get back here, now!" She dropped her clothes and obeyed his command. He tucked the sheets around her so that it would be hard for her to escape again, and he held her closely and tightly. "What the hell is wrong with you? Why are you overreacting like that?" "I'm not overreacting." "Really, because I just told you that I love you and that I'm not going anywhere and somehow you translate that into rejection. You are so neurotic sometimes." "But you said the whole journey thing." "I just meant life experiences. I don't want to hold you back from that." "But you did reject the relationship with me." "Not forever, just right now. I want you to have the freedom to live your life as you want. I'll still be here for you whenever you need me, wherever you need me, however you need me." "I'm just afraid that we'll drift apart." "That may happen. We'll get involved in our lives and get busy, but remember that we felt each other's energies and we exchanged pieces of our spirits. We'll always be a part of each other." "Ahote, I'm scared." "Don't be. It'll all work out. I promise." He passionately kissed her while gently wiping her tears. They exchanged energies and spirits one last time before making love another round.

The next day Karla and Chelsea came over to help her open gifts and send thank you cards. She filled them in on the conversation she had with Ahote while they watched the video of the party. They could've been more neat about their work, but wrapping paper, bows, and gift bags were thrown everywhere around the den. Her gifts were mostly CDs and cards with money to help with college expenses. "I'll be back y'all. I've got to use the bathroom." As soon as she left the room, Chelsea spoke her mind. "I don't know Karla. It sounds to me that Ahote was making excuses." "How?" Well sure he wants to give her freedom. At the same time, he'll have his." "So?" "So, if he really loves her, why wait?" "Because it makes sense for right now. She's going away. And honestly, I don't think she's ready either. She's still rebuilding herself from the whole Vaughn thing.

Plus, he said he'll visit her." "Yeah, but if he can visit her as a friend, why can't he visit her as a boyfriend? He's full of shit, that's what it is! And as soon as she gets back, I'm going to tell her." "I don't think that's a good idea Chelsea." "Why not?" "Because you're part of the reason why he won't commit to her." "How?" "Because had you not invited Clay, he wouldn't have had a chance to pick up that anything else was going on. He might have committed to her if he hadn't." "If he loves her, it wouldn't matter. He would claim her. He wouldn't give a fuck about Clay," "I see your point, but you still shouldn't tell her. Let me remind you that she's half crazy." "Crazy or not, I'm telling her." "Alright, do what you want. You may have known her longer, but I know her better. When she Kirks out on your ass, don't say that I didn't warn you." Aiko returned to the room. She could sense that they were talking about her. "What's up?" "Nothing," Karla replied trying to diffuse a situation before it began. It didn't work. Chelsea had to get her concerns off of her chest. "I think that Ahote is bullshitting you. He wants you to have freedom so that he can have his. He doesn't want you, because if he did, there would be no reason good enough to stop him." At that moment time stood still. Karla watched as Aiko screamed a warrior attack battle cry and lunged at Chelsea's throat with both hands. It happened so fast, yet it was still in slow motion. It wasn't until Aiko had a good grip around her neck that Karla snapped out of it and reacted to pull her off of Chelsea. Although Chelsea deserved it, and it was a long time coming, Karla felt sorry for her. Despite the fact that she really had the best of intentions for Aiko at heart, all of the previous sneaky and underhanded actions outweighed it this time. She finally managed to pry Aiko's hands away. Chelsea coughed and choked trying to catch her breath. Karla pinned Aiko's hands behind her back to keep her from going at Chelsea again. Aiko's whole face was flushed with anger. She tried to shake Karla off so that she could finish what she started, but Karla's brothers taught her torture techniques well. Growing up with four older brothers, she was a victim of many of them when she was younger. She twisted her wrists awkwardly to cause her pain no matter which way she moved. "If you don't stop moving, I'm going to break them. Calm your ass down! Chelsea, are you alright?" Still unable to speak, she waved her hand acknowledging that she was okay. "I think you should go home now. I'll call you later to check on you. Not a word to anybody about this, or next time I won't stop her. Got it?" Chelsea nodded in agreement and exited in shame. Karla and Aiko finished the project and cleaned up together. After a while when everything had calmed, they had a good laugh at Chelsea's expense.

The time had come for Aiko to leave for college. She was all too ready to take a bite out of "The Big Apple." Her parents and godparents made sure that she had everything she needed all loaded up into two vehicles for the three and half hour drive. Ahote stopped by early to see her before she left. They stood on her front steps, he on the lower, and she two steps above so that they could be face to face. "I'm going to miss you." "I'll miss you too love. Remember everything that I taught you, and call me when you need me." "I will. I love you." "I love you too." "Goodbye Ahote." "No, it's not goodbye, just farewell, for now. Go, spread your wings and soar to new heights my beautiful Sora."

She loved how poetic he always spoke. She only hoped that it wouldn’t be the last time his beautiful, poetic words graced her ears.

CHAPTER 16—TRACK 14—THE HOOK

It had been over six months since Randall stood her up for their date that reflective night. She had broken up with him through text message, of which he never responded. That in itself was her answer. Since then, she started dating Kendryck from the part-time job that she had quit two months prior. He was tall, dark, handsome, intelligent, talented, and had a voice sexier than James Earl Jones. They got along great and had a lot in common. She admired his mind and his thought process. He opened her mind about a lot of things, yet at times she felt that he lacked the insight to understand her inner being or what made her tick. He didn't always make it comfortable for her to be vulnerable, soft, or womanly around him because he could be critical. Her quirks sometimes frustrated him and turned him off to her. Despite that, he was the kind of man that she could see herself falling in love with easily, and she cared for him more than she was willing to admit, but she restrained her feelings from going any deeper because he had a fetish for supermodel looking women. Yes she was beautiful, but she wasn't thin or tall. Eventually he would probably leave her for his ideal woman. Until then, she settled for being friends with benefits.

She had plans to meet Karla and Chelsea for lunch that day. The demands of her job kept her out of town a lot, which hindered her from spending as much time with them and her son as she would have liked. She had just gotten back from a weeklong trip and her schedule was free for the first time in a month, so she was excited to see her girls. When she arrived, she was surprised to see Cierra and Byron there as well. It had been even longer since she had last seen them. “Hey! What are you two doing here?” Byron didn’t hesitate to respond. “Bitch, if you called somebody sometimes, maybe we wouldn’t have to sneak up on your ass to see you.” Byron had a way of telling people about themselves without them getting upset with him. “I’m glad to see you too Byron.” She hugged everyone, sat down, and grabbed a menu. “I’m starving. Did you order yet?” Karla spoke for the group. “No, we waited for you.” “Cool, thanks. Let’s order.” After the food arrived, they ate and caught up on each other’s lives. When there was a moment of silence, Karla nervously cleared her throat. “Ko, have you had a chance to check your mail since you got back last night?” “No. Why?” “Well, there’s a reason the troop is gathered. We all received this a few days ago.” She slid a pastel yellow envelope with a gold sticker seal that had evidence of being already opened across the table to her. She opened it. Her furrowed brow revealed confusion and curiosity. It was a wedding invitation for her ex-husband and his new beau. It was so quiet a pin drop could be heard. Her friends were blue in the face from holding their breaths awaiting her reaction. Cierra broke the silence. "Listen, you don't have to go, but if you do, we'll all go with you. You don't have to do this alone." "Thank you, really, but I don't need to be babysat. I can handle it." Chelsea leaned over to Karla and whispered, "She's too calm. Something's not right. Do something." Chelsea never could whisper well for shit. Aiko heard every word. "Thank you for your concern Chelsea, but it's okay. I'm fine." All four sets of eyes stared at her like deer caught in headlights. The overwhelming sense of pity she felt from them was too much to bear. "Waiter, check please!" The waiter rushed over. She handed him her credit card. "Charge me for the table and bring me a carryout bag please." "Yes ma'am, right away." Everyone remained silent until the waiter returned. Aiko packed her food and put thirty dollars cash in the sleeve for the tip. "It was great seeing everybody. And please, don't worry about me. I'm fine." She put on her tan aviator sunglasses and tan belted Burberry overcoat, grabbed her purse and left. She jumped into her black on black Lincoln MKX and peeled off like lightning blasting "The Big Payback" by James Brown. In retrospect, it wasn't the best song selection to play if she wanted to hide her true feelings, but rationale had already abandoned her. They were seated at the back of the restaurant, so she didn't think that they could hear. All that she could think about was the hurt and pain that Isaiah had caused her over the years, and she grew increasingly angry. On top of that, he had the nerve to propose to that woman, willing to commit to her and play daddy to her son when he couldn't be one for his own. Lost in her thoughts, she arrived home without recollection of the trip there. Never bothering to remove her coat, she headed straight for her office where the nanny was instructed to leave all mail in a basket while she was away. She anxiously dumped the mail onto her desk pushing more important bills aside in search for the invitation. She found it, picked it up, and opened it almost expecting that the words had somehow changed. She plopped down in her Italian leather office chair exhaling rigidly as if the impact had knocked the wind out of her. Analyzing the invitation, she noticed the fancy print and delicate, expensive paper. Next, she noticed the location which was a fancy church, and for the reception, an upscale hotel in downtown Baltimore. The cost of rent was easily a five figure one. The woman he was betrothed to was a hood rat. Her parents weren't poor, but certainly nowhere near wealthy enough for that hefty expense. Isaiah being the owner of a chain of successful videogame stores, clearly was the one footing the bill. Her blood began to boil over the thought of the birthdays, Christmases, Father's days, and football games he missed with her son. He didn't bother to call, or send cards or gifts, but he had money for everything else. "That lowlife piece of shit mutha fucka!" "Mommy?" Her son's voice startled her. She turned around to see him and the nanny standing in the office doorway. She quickly wiped her tears and turned towards him again. "Hi honey! Come here." She hugged him tightly and kissed all over his fat, golden yellow cheeks. "Mommy, are you okay? Are you crying?" "No honey, I'm not crying. The cold made my eyes water, that's all. I've missed you so much." "You were only gone a week mom, but I missed you too." "Are you sure?" "Yes." "I don't think so. Come here." She tickled him until he begged for mercy, and she hugged and kissed him again. "So what are you about to do?" "Me and Maria…" "No, it's Maria and I." "Maria and I are about to have a Mario Kart tournament. Do you want to play?" "I would be glad to kick your butt in Mario Kart." "Yeah right mom. You suck at Mario kart." "I've been practicing, so get ready." She licked her tongue at him. He licked his back and ran out of the room with excitement. "Glad to see you back Ms. Pierre." "Thanks, it's good to be back home Maria. I'll be out in a minute." She turned towards the invitation again. What she saw this time turned the pastel yellow of the paper to blood red. The date for the wedding was set for June 26, the exact date that she and Isaiah were married. It was clear that he was trying to deliver the final, knockout blow to her heart. *We'll see who lands the final punch.* She jumped up and grabbed her keys. "Maria!" Maria appeared in the office doorway again. "Yes Ms. Pierre?" "I've got an errand to run. It should take about an hour. Put on some cartoons for Izzy until I get back for the tournament. I'll pay you extra." "What should I tell him?" "Tell him that I went to get snacks for us, which I'll pick up on my way back anyway." "Okay."

If it weren't for the slushy roads, she would have risked a speeding ticket to get to her destination, which was a gun shop. At that point, she had decided to kill him. Nothing and no one was going to stop her. The details of her quest had yet to be determined, but she knew the how. She picked out a nine millimeter handgun. There was a seven day waiting period for the background check to clear before she could return to retrieve it. She went back home with a bag full of snacks. Izzy remained the reigning Mario Kart champion.

Over the next few months, she practiced at the gun range. Fueled by her anger, her skills were sharpened in a short period of time. She kept the gun locked in the glove compartment of her truck. Keeping it in the house was not an option because she didn't want her son to have access to it. Not one person close to her would've suspected her plan. It was beyond even the craziest of things that they could imagine of her. After much consideration, she had finally decided to kill him on the day of his wedding. She even went as far as to case the church and reception venues to pick possible spots to pull the trigger. In the days leading up to the wedding, she put on her best behavior, but she had to do it in a calculated manner. Being too calm would send up red flags to those who knew her best, so she spewed venomous bitterness here and there in front of her friends because that was to be expected. Displaying an even mix of temperament was a safe bet in throwing people off of her trail.

The morning of the wedding, she purposely selected an all black ensemble which consisted of a short lace fit halter flare dress, black, six inch, spiked heel red bottom pumps, a wide brimmed, floppy sun hat, and pitch black coach sunglasses with a matching coach purse. As she dressed she played Etta James's "All I Could Do Was Cry." on repeat. She stood in front of the full length mirror in her bra and panties peering at herself. Her outer appearance was the same, but inside she had changed. She was a woman scorned whose repeated heart breaks released an infection that festered and morphed into a disease that had spread throughout her body down to the very bone marrow and manifested itself as the purest forms of hatred and vengeance. Once dressed, she jumped into her truck to pick up Karla. Cierra and Chelsea were catching a ride with Byron. They planned to get wasted and wanted him as the designated driver. He didn't mind. He intended to stay sober in case something went down so that he would have his wits about him to protect Aiko. She sat at the wheel for minutes before she turned over the engine thinking about select words from Etta's song that mentioned how the newly married couple was beginning their new life while she was left in the cold pining over him. The man that Aiko had invested so much of her time, energy, love, and money into had chosen another woman. She married him when he was a scrub with, as her mother would say, "No pot to piss in or a window to throw it out of." It was her whom taught him how to drive. It was her whom encouraged him to enroll in college full time while she held down the fort working and paying all of the bills. It was her whom pushed him to follow his dreams of being an entrepreneur, right by his side when the ribbon was cut at the opening of his first store. She made him the man that he had become, only for him to give the fruit of her labor to another woman. "Bullshit! It's not going to happen!" She reached into the glove compartment, grabbed the gun and ammunition, loaded it up, put it into her purse, and headed to Karla's house. Karla came out of the house talking on her cell phone to Andre. "Okay baby, she's here. I'll call you later. I love you too. Bye." "Hey Karls" "Hey Ko. How are you holding up?" "I'm okay." "You're not nervous?" "For what? It's not my wedding day." "Well, you know what I mean." "Yes I do. My answer still stands." "Okay then, let's get this over with."

On the ride over, Karla had an unsettling nag in the pit of her stomach. She couldn't read Aiko as well as she normally could. She seemed okay, but something was wrong. When they arrived, the church was already half full and buzzing with the voices of the guests. She chose the very back row of his side, sitting on the end of the bench seat closest to the aisle. Not too long after she and Karla sat down, the other three of her entourage arrived and slid past them to take their seats. They exchanged whispered hellos and scoped out the decor and other guests. Not surprisingly, the wedding colors were pastel yellow and white. The decorations were classy and beautiful. It put the shotgun wedding they had together to a shameful grave. His sister Shea spotted her, snickering and whispering to the people beside her to draw attention to Aiko's presence. It was no secret that Shea hated her and for no good reason. Aiko's guess would be that it was because Shea didn't like that she always stood her ground to her. Being a bossy, jealous, big mouth know-it- all, she was threatened by a person like Aiko who wasn't intimidated by her self-proclaimed reign of terror. Shea was a hateful, miserable bitch whose goal in life was to spread her despondency around, dragging unwittingly weaker souls under her blanket of tyranny. *Keep laughing bitch. There is a bullet with your name on it too.*

Within minutes Isaiah surfaced at his place at the front with his best friend Mark at his side as his best man. Shea must have given Isaiah a signal because he looked at her then looked straight at Aiko. Aiko remained motionless and expressionless looking back at him through her dark sunglasses. As the old saying goes "If looks could kill" he would have been dead from the hatred in her eyes, but since a deadly stare couldn't complete her mission, her nine millimeter gun was ready for the assignment. There was just a matter of when. For now, she would play it by ear and wait for an opportune moment. The tune to the wedding march began. The whole room stood up except for Aiko. Her friends stood up only to be nosy. They wanted to get a good look at Isaiah's wife-to-be in search for things to poke fun at later. Her dress was tacky and clearly off the rack. Aiko's guess was that it had cost about fifteen hundred dollars, which was expensive to someone like her who didn't know any better, and a steal for him. It was white with yellow accent trimmings, and she was carrying a yellow and white bouquet. She was nothing to write home about. Even a wedding dress couldn't make this woman look any better. She was twice as big as Aiko had ever been. To add salt to injury, Isaiah used to belittle her for her weight, and even went as far as to tell her that he wasn't attracted to her because of it. Yet there was his bride, a rollie pollie that was damn near wobbling around herself down the aisle as he glowed all over himself with love for her. It was painful enough to make her want to pull the trigger when the pastor opened the floor for rejection, but she didn't have the nerve to commit such a heinous crime in the house of the Lord. With that in mind, she concluded that she would wait for the reception. She didn't get through the rejection part without whispers and glances directed at her. Even her friends anticipated her causing a scene, but she remained calm and statuesque. If it weren't for the rise and fall of her chest, no one would believe that she was breathing. She listened as they exchanged vows and she fought back tears as he eloquently and wholeheartedly proclaimed his unwavering, undying love and commitment to her. The bride's son, who was only a few years younger than hers, was the ring bearer and happily handed them the rings. "I now pronounce you husband and wife. You may now kiss your bride." Isaiah kissed Tara the way he used to kiss her, but there was something different about it. It was more loving and powerful. She stood up and quietly slipped out before the procession. Her friends scampered behind her. They followed her to her truck. Byron caught up to her first. "Are you okay baby?" "Yeah, it was rough, but I'm okay." Her response was borderline robotic. Byron knew that she was putting on, but since she had behaved herself so far, he didn't question her any further.

When they reached the reception, Cierra and Chelsea headed straight to the open bar. Aiko scouted for their table first. It came as no surprise that she and her crew were seated together. She was relieved that the table was in the back so that she could exit easily and unnoticed when she was ready. She headed to the bar to get a drink of her own, crossing paths with Cierra and Chelsea on their way to the table. She sat at the open bar and downed two long island iced teas before she ordered another and returned to her seat. She noticed that another stage to the right of the main stage had been set up since she had last cased the room, which was large enough to seat the one hundred fifty guests expected and then some. The guests began to pour into the room with gifts in hand. Within thirty minutes, Mark announced the arrival of the bride and groom on the microphone from the main stage. "Ladies and gentlemen, may I present to you for the first time Mr. and Mrs. Isaiah Marshall!" Everyone except Aiko's table clapped and cheered. The wedding party was seated on the main stage facing the guests. The music initiated the start of the reception. She stared at them from a distance nursing her drink and responding to her friends in autopilot mode only when asked a question. Whatever music was playing she couldn't hear, in part to her fixation on them, and in part to her consciously closing her ears. She wanted no musical triggers that reminded her of their wedding. She remained still and poised only moving to refill her drink. In gut wrenching pain, she watched them interact with each other in wedded bliss, cutting the cake and feeding each other, and him removing her garter belt and throwing it into a crowd of men who only participated because of hopes of placing it on a hot bridesmaid or female guest that they could potentially take home that night. Naturally, she was nowhere near the throwing of the bouquet. Mark got on the microphone again. "Now everyone, the Marshalls will share their first dance as husband and wife." The first few notes to Maxwell's "Whenever, Wherever, Whatever" snapped her out of her trance. It was the very song that she and Isaiah fell in love to, and the song that they danced to at their wedding. Leave it to Chelsea to point it out. "Girl, ain't that the song ya'll danced to at ya'll wedding? He's a trifling bastard!" Aiko jumped up and fast walked to the ladies room. Her girls jumped up in unison to follow her, but Byron intercepted. "No, leave her alone. She needs to work through this on her own, and ya'll know it." They reluctantly sat back down. She locked herself in the handicap stall and began to wail. *How could he give her our song? How could he marry her on our day? Why is he trying to hurt me like this?* The torture in her heart was immense, and she begged God to take her soul right then and there so that the pain would cease. She buried her face into the side of her coach bag to muffle her agonizing scream. She felt the hard silhouette of her gun through the material. Something in her brain flipped on like a light switch. Her tears dried up and her heart re-hardened. She pulled out the gun and traced it with her fingers drawing from its deadly power to recharge her resolve to complete her mission. Placing it back into her purse, she exited the stall, and reapplied her makeup to cover her brief meltdown.

When she returned, the open microphone portion had begun. Those who wanted to wish the new couple well were free to do so upon the second stage that was outlined by a spotlight. She chugged another long island iced tea and ordered a tall glass of champagne. Mark was on the stage sharing stories of what he had experienced of Isaiah and Tara's love. He was a tall, lanky, hook nosed, goofy, mental cased white boy who contributed in small doses to the demise of her marriage to Isaiah. She had no problem disrespecting him off of the stage to say her piece. She charged towards the stage with her glass in her hand. Once on the stage, she bullied Mark with her body, pushing him aside and grabbing the microphone. "Aw, that was sweet, a little too long, but sweet. Let's give other people a chance Mark, shall we? Hello everyone! I'm Aiko, the first Mrs. Marshall." Isaiah looked uneasy and embarrassed, but he tried to maintain his composure. It was because his new wife had no idea that he was married before, and it showed all over her face. Aiko picked up on it and instantly used it to her advantage. "Oh, I'm sorry. Some of you didn't know that, huh? Oops." She mockingly covered her mouth with her hands like a child who had just spilled the milk. "It's okay girl. He's yours now. I'm sure he'll take care of your son like he does his own. Oh wait, he doesn't take care of our son at all."

Evidently, he had fabricated their whole history to Tara and her family because her side of the family gasped in shock. They were just as in the dark as she was, but Aiko had shed the light. Most likely he reduced her to just a baby mama and sold her on stories of being an upstanding father. Isaiah was a compulsive and habitual liar. No matter what version he told them it was an untruth, none of which would surprise Aiko. "Tara, I want you to notice how his family isn't surprised. Obviously, they already knew. None of this is new. Not only was he married before and he has a child that he doesn't take care of, but that song that you danced to was our song at our wedding. We danced to that first." By this time Tara was drenched in tears from the humiliation. She got up from her seat prepared to leave. "Wait, don't go! Sit down, there's more." Torn between her embarrassment and curiosity, Tara sat back down. "Listen, I know that this all comes as a shock to you girl, but he loves you. It's real. I can see it all over him, and this is coming from his ex-wife." As much as Byron was enjoying the show, he felt that it was time to get Aiko off of the stage. He inched his way through the crowd towards her. "I want to propose a toast." She held up her glass. "Come on everybody, hold up your glasses." The crowd, who was captivated by the moment, obeyed her like mindless drones. "To Isaiah and Tara, may you have a long and happy marriage. May the castle of fraudulence he's prepared for you hold your marriage together like crazy glue." Amused by her comment, she laughed out loud. "Oh, look at that! It rhymed! That was totally unintentional you all." She cleared her throat and continued. "May you both withstand the repugnant stench of his deceit to the end of time. As for me, I broke free and will be living life like it's golden. Cheers!" She chugged down her champagne.

Byron walked onto the stage and wrapped his arms around her waist from behind her. "Alright, that's enough. You're drunk. Come on, let's go." "No, wait! I haven't given them their wedding present yet." She wiggled herself free from Byron's clutches. "I have a very special gift for both of you that I want to give to you personally." She reached inside of her purse maliciously grinning as she felt the cold, hard steel between her fingers. Her moment of retribution had finally come. Her hand ascended towards the opening of her purse. All went silent. Shots fired.

To be continued…

Made in the USA
Middletown, DE
28 October 2023